Coff
&
Songs

BERENDSJE WESTRA

In Media Res Publishing. 2021

Text copyright © Berendsje Westra

The moral right of the author has been asserted

A CIP catalogue record for this book is available from the British Library

ISBN: 978-90-831498-1-3

Cover Design: Yana Yakubchik

'Guilt is one burden human beings can't bear alone.'
Anaïs Nin – *A Spy in the House of Love*

Chapter 1

Patsy DeMelo scarred me for life. My earliest memory of her is this one:

I am four years old and prancing up and down the pavement that runs along the endless rows of terraced houses that make up our street. Tugging a yellow toy duck behind me by a string, I keep looking over my shoulder to watch it bob its head and wag its tail as its shiny red wheels roll down the grey slabs that are darker than usual after a spell of rain.

'Is that your duck?' someone asks.

When I turn around, a tall, heavy girl and a scrawny, fair-haired boy, dressed in different school uniforms and both much older than I am, are looming over me like two ominous clouds.

'Yes,' I reply, and instantly notice the girl's fingers. They're odd. On one hand, she only has a thumb and two fingers that seem fused together; on the other hand, she only has knuckles and one long middle finger. I stare at the finger and think about the story of the witch who wanted to fatten up a boy so she could eat him. The boy had stuck a piece of chicken bone through the cage to confuse the witch and I'm wondering if the bone looked like the girl's long finger. She locks her eyes on my duck and with a nod in its direction asks, 'Where did you get it from?'

'Mummy and Daddy,' I reply.

'What for?'

'It was my birthday.'

'When?'

'Yesterday.'

The boy loosens his tie a little and says, 'But we've seen you with the duck before yesterday.'

They both look at me and I shoot another curious glance at the girl's fingers. She puts her arms behind her back. I look at her feet. She shifts them uncomfortably, as if she doesn't know where to leave them. The big black boots she's wearing have a strange shape. Maybe they have something to do with her fingers. Does she have funny toes as well?

'What's your name?' she asks me.

'Carys,' I reply.

'Do you like this duck?'

Her steely tone alarms me. 'Yes, I do,' I reply. 'Look, it can move its head.' I take a few steps forward and pull the string to demonstrate.

The girl lunges forward and scoops my duck up in her arms. She has a mean face and her eyes aren't kind. My tummy tightens. Will she give it back to me?

Without speaking, she and the boy slope off a bit further down the pavement and I trail behind them. I picture Mummy wringing a wet towel. She does that sometimes. My tummy feels like the wet towel.

They sit down on the kerb next to a storm drain that has three holes in it.

Quietly, I stand beside them as the boy carefully begins to pull my duck apart. First, he breaks off my duck's head and wings. Then its tail goes and the shiny red wheels. He passes each part that he manages to prise off to the girl and she puts it through one of the draining holes with her strange hands.

I look up and down the street for help and notice an old man walking towards us. He's wearing a woolly hat, just like Taid who lives in Wales. I don't have a towel in my tummy anymore. He will help me. Taid would too. When the old man slows down his pace to look at what we're doing, I desperately try to make eye contact with him, but he doesn't notice and continues on his way without a word.

As another red wheel disappears through a draining hole, something heavy sits down at the bottom of my heart. My duck looked so friendly with its big brown eyes and long lashes and shiny red beak. It had done nothing to deserve this.

Somehow I feel that the boy and girl aren't going to hurt me. They just wanted my duck. It gives me the courage to say a few words. 'Why are you doing that?' I ask.

'Because you're a stupid little girl,' the boy says with a calm voice, as if he's just told me that the sky is blue and the clouds are white, but not at night time.

Only the trunk of my duck is left now. The girl tries to push it through the holes, but it's too big. I stare at her hands again; they're starting to make me queasy.

'Let me try,' the boy says, grabbing my duck from her.

As I watch him, I'm feeling something I've never felt before. It's a gnawing sadness that scrapes my insides, and for a moment I picture Taid in his shed, scraping wood with a triangular tool because that's what this feeling reminds me of.

They stop trying to shove what's left of my duck into the storm drain and get up. The girl leans her face over mine and moves her big lips. 'Every time we see you with a toy,' she says, 'this is what we'll do to it.' They turn around and walk away from me, taking the trunk of my duck with them.

I turn around too and race home. Drawing sharp gulps of breath, I bang my flat palms against the glass panel in the door and yell for my mother at the top of my lungs. When she doesn't answer quickly enough, I rattle the letterbox with my fingers and begin to kick the door with my boot.

'Have you lost your mind?' she says, when she finally appears in the doorway. Bethan, my sister, is on her hip. She smiles and flaps her arms when she sees me but I'm too sad to respond.

'They broke my duck,' I wail.

'Who did?' Mum glances at the ground behind me.

'A girl and a boy,' I sniff. 'They went the other way.' I point in the direction I just came from and step inside.

Mum closes the door. 'What did they look like?'

'The girl was big and she had weird fingers.'

'Oh, that's Patsy.' Mum stares at the floor for a moment. 'Was the lad skinny with blond hair?'

I think about it and wipe my nose on my jacket. 'Yes.'

'That must have been Jason,' Mum says. She's still staring a little.

'Is that her brother?' I ask.

'No, they're friends.' Mum puts Bethan on the floor and squats before me to help me take off my jacket and red rain boots. 'But they tease the children in the neighbourhood.'

I rest my hands on her shoulders for support. 'Why?' I ask.

'I don't know,' she says. 'Some children are just like that.'

I decide then that I will never tease children because it makes them feel miserable and it's mean. I didn't get a new duck.

Chapter 2

'I've been thinking that maybe I should meet up with her. With Patsy.'

I search Patrick's face for a sign of support, but when I don't see it my gaze darts to the framed poster on the wall slightly to the right behind him. Delicate white petals sprout from crawling boughs against a background of vibrant blue hues.

Van Gogh's *Almond Blossom*, he'd told me during our first appointment, which led to a brief conversation about art. I told him my dad used to be an artist, although not for a living, and that my sister was trying to get into an art college.

Patrick does not immediately respond to my comment about Patsy, which is how he tries to get me to elaborate. It annoys me sometimes.

'So,' I say, filling in his silence. 'Do you think I should?'

Patrick crosses his legs and clasps his hands around his knees. His eyes are kind but pensive. 'That depends,' he says, in his warm Irish drawl. 'What do you hope to gain from an encounter with Patsy?'

I fidget with the hem of my denim skirt that's just above my knees, rolling it up and unrolling it, but when it catches Patrick's attention I stop.

'I don't know,' I reply. 'I haven't really thought about that. Maybe I just want to see her.'

Again, he doesn't immediately respond so I ponder his

question some more and look outside through the floor-to-ceiling window on my left. It's a drizzly morning. I'm flying to Singapore tonight; the weather is bound to be better there, but all I feel is a sense of dread at having to go. I don't like flying. I must make changes.

To get my attention back to the present moment, I focus on the golden rain tree that's in exquisite bloom on a strip of grass below me.

'I think I know why I want to go and see her.'

Patrick nods encouragingly and takes a box of toothpicks from his shirt pocket.

'I want to put myself in a position where I can confront her with everything, if I should feel the need. Maybe I'll just make small talk with her, maybe I'll yell at her… I think I'll decide that in the moment, and it would also depend on how she reacts to me of course and what she might say to me, but I suppose, the most important thing for me is having an opportunity to see her again.'

'And vent your anger if you feel you must?' Patrick says, chewing on a wooden stick.

'Yes.'

I can't help but smile at the way he's sitting there, facing me from the other side of the square glass coffee table: writing pad on his knees, his auburn hair and beard unkempt as always; a ponderous look firmly in place on his ruddy face. The orange shirt he's wearing looks good on him. Earlier I'd noticed that his trousers are too short at the hems and expose a glimpse of hairy ankles. He has hairy knuckles too. I like how he thinks nothing of gnawing on a toothpick while he's having a conversation with a client. He told me he does it because he recently quit smoking and

that he alternates between toothpicks and carrots. I'd like to be like him: older, and just unreservedly, unapologetically myself.

'Would a confrontation with Patsy bring Bethan back?' he asks me.

'No. It wouldn't.' I think for a moment. 'But I do think it would give me closure.'

'Hm.' He makes a couple of ankle circles. 'I don't know if that's true. Would Patsy have to behave a certain way, or say certain words for you to get closure?'

He's being difficult again. I need support. A mild resentment is simmering inside of me, but I try to hide it by breezily replying, 'Oh, I don't know. I haven't thought about that either.'

After a brief silence in which Patrick observes me picking my cuticles, I say, 'So, do you think I should go and see her?'

'No, I don't.' Patrick puts his elbows on the armrests, steeples his fingers and fixes me with a compassionate gaze. 'I don't think that rooting around in the past will help you move forward with your life.'

His tone is warm, almost fatherly but I'm nevertheless feeling bewildered. I really thought that looking up Patsy after all this time was a great idea and that Patrick would see that too. I need closure, don't I? How else will I get it?

Patrick glances at the clock and plucks at his beard. 'The thing is,' he says, 'you have to realise that you can't control

Patsy. You'd probably come to her with expectations she's unlikely to meet.'

He smiles at me. 'I'm sure you've fantasized about a confrontation with Patsy many a time, Carys. But what if it doesn't work out the way you envisaged? How would you feel?'

'I don't know,' I reply, staring at the floor.

Patrick gets up and walks over to his desk where he lifts up a pile of paperwork and mutters something about a misplaced diary.

I've been talking to him for two months now. Have I made progress? He has called me pro-active. And he must know by now that there's nothing inherently wrong with me. I wonder how many more sessions I'll need. He can't still think at least thirty. I'd felt really insulted when he suggested that. As if I'm some kind of madwoman, like my mother. Yes, of course, I was upset when I first came here. But I had asked my GP for a referral myself; crazy people don't do that. I just wanted someone to talk to, about Bethan and Patsy and my mother, and love. I wanted advice too. About how to rid myself of ghastly memories that had released themselves from the crevices of my mind and suddenly demanded my attention. They made me cry at work when I was talking to people—utterly inconvenient. They made me cry in bed when I wanted to sleep but lay rubbing the tears from my eyes instead. A few times, I even cried in my sleep and woke up with wet cheeks.

During my first session with Patrick I told him I felt haunted by the memories and asked him how I could suppress them again, or better still, make them evaporate from my mind altogether.

'Would you like to talk about what you remember?' he asked me. I didn't tell him everything of course, but I shared this:

> Mum puts Bethan in her high chair
> at the head of the dinner table.
> Mum holds a heaped spoonful
> of creamy porridge up to Bethan's mouth,
> coaxing and cajoling to get her to eat
> with increasing irritation in her voice.
> Bethan pushes Mum's hand away,
> again and again.
> I'm at the table too, fearful,
> holding my breath;
> my eyes are fixed on the pearl baby bracelet
> around Bethan's chubby wrist.
> I already know what's coming.
> The outbursts happen often.
> 'I can feed Bethan, Mum,' I try.
> 'Then you can eat something.'
> She snarls at me to mind my own business.
> With every blow Bethan receives,
> her little head jerks back.
> In between the blows, when her face is not
> covered by Mum's hand,
> she briefly opens her eyes.
> They are filled with shock and disbelief,

her mouth contorts with pain.
She cries hysterically.
'Close the curtains,' Mum yells at me.
'I'm going to murder a baby.
I don't need witnesses.'
Dad rushes into the living room.
They begin to fight.
He makes a little Kung Fu jump
in her direction.
I don't close the curtains.
Instead, I wrap myself up in one,
around and around I go,
until the curtain says stop.
The tightness of the fabric around my body
makes me feel safe.
I listen to "It's a Small World After All"
in my head.
It drowns out the crying and shouting.
Micky and Minnie Mouse are dancing together.
I love it here.
In my own world everything is pink,
and my life is always hunky-dory

The drizzle has turned into a proper shower and rain is pelting against the window of Patrick's office. He has found his diary and is sitting opposite me again leafing through it. I cast another glance at the golden rain tree. Its branches droop, weighed down by the downpour of water.

'When do you have time for me?' he asks.

I tell him I'm going to Singapore today and that I'll be back on Monday. 'If we don't crash that is,' I add in a wry tone. He ignores my comment so I'm serious again. 'Maybe next Tuesday at eleven?'

'Tuesday, the twenty-second of June,' he says, while he scribbles something down. My name I assume.

I want to ask him how many more sessions he thinks I'll need but I haven't got the courage. Maybe I'm afraid of what I will hear.

'You didn't bring a brolly, did you?'

I shake my head.

'Feel free to sit in the waiting room until it clears up.' Patrick smiles warmly at me and gets up from his chair. He extends his hand to me—we always end our sessions with a polite handshake. 'I'm sure your plane won't crash Carys,' he says. 'I fully expect to see you again next week.'

Chapter 3

'Is your seatbelt on there?' I glance at a young girl occupying a window seat. She's resting her arms on a tattered Dora backpack that's on her lap. Behind her, in the distance, a Virgin Atlantic is slowly taxiing towards the runway across a meadow of black tarmac. It's around four o'clock in the afternoon and the sky has finally cleared. Rays of sunlight are falling through the circular cabin windows, dancing on headrests and bouncing off the curved walls, but that doesn't make me feel better. I want to stay here, in England.

The woman beside the girl, her mother I presume, quickly lifts the bag off the girl's lap and stows it underneath the seat in front. She flashes me a broad smile and replies with a nasal twang, 'Yes, it is, we're all set.'

I stroll through the narrow aisle towards the aft galley and check the rest of my section's seatbelts, luggage and trays, nodding and smiling half-heartedly while answering questions about the inflight entertainment system, on-board tax free shopping, the fasten seatbelt signs, water bottles, baby food, turbulence, possible delays, seats that won't recline, and the weather in Singapore.

Although we haven't even taken off for Asian skies yet, my stomach is in knots and a mixture of resentment and misery is expanding inside me like a slowly inflated balloon. Tim Hardin's 'How Can We Hang On to a Dream' playing softly from the speakers above the passenger seats is not helping. I love that song but to use it for boarding music? Has it ever cheered anyone up?

It's not like I really expect the planes I work on to crash. I wouldn't be here right now if I did. No, it's more an odds kind of thing. Everyone knows that once in a while a plane will drop from the sky. I started flying at the age of twenty-three, so it's been almost seven years, and still, I wonder, before every take-off, how it's possible we even lift off. The sheer weight of these things. The people on board, all of their luggage. The tonnes of metal, the engines…

Oh, what I wouldn't give to be curled up on my sofa right now; a good book and a cup of coffee within reach. I haven't even got the time to be away from home again. I've got things to do; like going to IKEA for a kitchen table. And I really wanted to go with Flora to that talk at the SGI Centre in Richmond tonight. A Canadian Buddhist will explain how devotion to the mystic law can benefit all areas of your life. Instead, I'll be trapped inside this tube for the next thirteen hours; risking my life for strangers; offering up my peace of mind for money.

The aft galley smells like it always does: freshly brewed coffee mixed with the scent of paraffin, and I'm feeling the onset of nausea. Two pristine-looking female colleagues are standing in front of the coffee maker, chatting and sipping drinks from customised Styrofoam cups that bear our company's logo. The younger one, who has her chestnut brown hair styled in a low bun around a doughnut, is called Amy. I've forgotten the other girl's name, but I will look it up on my crew information sheet before take-off to avoid any possible awkwardness. Amy asks me if I'd like some coffee.

'Yes please,' I reply.

The girl whose name I don't remember instantly turns around and takes a cup from a metal drawer. I stare at her immaculate, French-manicured nails as she holds the cup under the spout and presses down the lever. The first thing I always do when I prepare drinks behind the service trolley is line up cartons of apple and orange juice on the sides so passengers won't see my bitten nails. I must make changes. From now on, I will grow my nails and have them painted just like hers.

Amy asks me if I want cream and sugar.

I smile. 'Just cream, please.'

These women embody what flight attendants should be like. They look the part and act the part. I'm hospitable too, but only to a certain extent. I've always felt that my colleagues are perfectly capable of getting their own coffees and not once in the years I've been flying have I offered to do the rounds. But maybe I should. The way my colleagues just took care of me, with just a small gesture, made me feel included. It wouldn't harm me to step up a little. It's odd, but lately I've been feeling like I'm at a crossroads. As though I'm heading somewhere and that the time has come to leave something behind, like a caterpillar shedding its outgrown skin so it can grow further. Yes, I'm like that, although I don't really know why I think that. It's just a feeling.

Leaning my back against the edge of the worktop, I stir

my coffee and listen to Amy and the other girl discussing their boyfriends. Amy has just been proposed to and the other girl is getting married in August. Wide-eyed, Amy laps up all her suggestions for gowns and catering.

I think of Ryan and smile. Before I met him, my only contribution to conversations about romance was: 'I left my ex, James, and I wish I hadn't, but he's with someone else now, so there's nothing I can do.'

I'm glad that's changed. Ryan and I have been on four dates, only in public places so far, but we're moving forward. He's coming to my place next week. Flora teased me when I told her that.

'So,' she said. 'Ryan's coming. Literally and figuratively.'

'Well, actually,' I replied, 'wouldn't that be literally twice?' Flora and I always like to have a bit of banter like that, although this time I told her to stop laughing, in case it jinxed what Ryan and I have. Besides, he's quite serious, like me. We'll see what happens next week. Maybe we'll do it, maybe we'll wait.

'Carys?'

I look up from my coffee cup. Pete, the senior purser, is standing before me waving the passenger list in his hand. His small blue eyes are fixed on me from under shiny etched-on eyebrows that keep evoking unwanted images of Garry Glitter.

Amy and the other girl put their cups down and start busying themselves with closing and locking all the trolleys and metal containers, while they continue their conversation.

From the disapproving way Pete looks at me I don't

think he likes me much. I already noticed it in the briefing room at the Crew Report Centre. He asks me if I'm aware of the fact there's a passenger with a prosthetic leg in my section who's sitting in an aisle seat.

I shake my head.

'Forty-four H,' Pete says impatiently. He clips a pen to his breast pocket and folds up the passenger list. 'Please ask him to move.'

'Forty-four H?' I repeat. 'But that's not an exit row.'

Pete had started for the cabin but now he turns around and eyes me coolly. 'Please tell me you're up to date with the flight safety rules.'

From the corner of my eye I see Amy and the other girl slipping out of the galley through the blue curtain on my right.

'Are you, Carys? Because if you aren't and you don't know what you're doing, you'd better tell me now, while I can still replace you with a standby.'

I try to swallow but my throat is suddenly dry. 'I passed my test,' I say meekly. 'That was only last month.'

Pete glares at me. 'Forty-four H,' he repeats, then exits the galley through the curtain on my left.

Besides being a nervous flyer and constantly homesick, there are many other aspects of my job I don't like. My sinuses feel chronically inflamed and my eyes are often watery and itchy as a result of the air-conditioner on board. There's also the boredom. Without any mental stimulation—just the tedious tasks of pouring drinks and taking meals out of ovens and shoving them into trolleys like there's no tomorrow—it's insufferable. Then there are the passengers with a bad attitude. It's especially during mealtimes that these people tend to show their true colours. I'm so tired of the crap I have to put up with after I've informed them that we're out of rice and chicken and there's only the vegetarian pasta left, which always happens at some point. Passengers have literally told me that they didn't care how I was going to do it but that I'd better turn up with some chicken for them soon. What am I supposed to do? Stop off at a mid-air supermarket? Colleagues have actually gone without food because their crew meals were given to passengers. If only people realised that we are there for their safety above anything else.

And now there's this. I'm not keen on being surrounded by strangers in a cramped fuselage all day long as it is—even my colleagues are strangers; I met them for the first time in the briefing room this morning—but now I have to go and confront someone with his fake leg.

I'm alone in the galley. Apart from someone's beauty case, the black worktops are spotless and everything's tidy. The steady humming of the APU reminds me of our imminent departure and it grates on my nerves. I take a small bottle of Neal's Yard lavender oil from my pocket, remove the cap, hold it under my nose and inhale sharply several times. I rub some oil under my nose, then pull my blouse open a little, hold the bottle upside down and sprinkle several droplets onto my cleavage. Me-time, amidst the madness. The shop employee at Neal's Yard in Richmond who calls me Lavender Girl each time I come in for oil and dried flowers drifts into my thoughts. If she were to see me now, she'd think I was the village idiot.

When I get to the passenger in question, he's leafing through the inflight magazine.

'Excuse me, sir,' I begin and slightly bend forward to level with him. I glance at his jeans-clad legs but don't notice anything unusual. It crosses my mind that maybe Pete was wrong and that I'm about to make a huge prat of myself.

His face is expressionless as he waits for me to continue. Mid-thirties maybe? His hair is dark, his skin pecan-coloured, and his eyes are grey with green specks. For a moment I wonder if I could be with someone like him and imagine him in my bed. He's got one leg (nice and hairy), a dick, and then… not another leg.

I have the attention of the elderly Indian couple next to him too, and kindly ask him if he wants to swap seats with them and take the window seat.

His glance darts from me to the couple and with a confused expression on his face he stammers in a British accent, 'Oh, but, the lady—'

He stops mid-sentence and all I can think is: I've made a complete stranger feel bad and he did nothing to deserve that.

But he seems to compose himself. He sniffs, glances at my chest area somewhat curiously, and tells me in a firm tone that the lady had asked him for the window seat and that he was happy to oblige. They exchange a look of understanding and smile at each other and the woman, who has a red bindi on her forehead, turns to me and confirms in a frail tone and with an Indian accent that she would indeed prefer the window seat. She wobbles her head as she says it.

'Yes, my wife always wants to sit by the window,' her husband adds, as if more clarity on the matter is required. He wobbles his head too.

The three of them look at me expectantly, and when I stretch my back for a moment and glance around the cabin, I notice that all the passengers within earshot are following my progress with keen interest. I'm also a little alarmed to note that in the opposite aisle a colleague is already waiting on her jump seat to arm the slide on her door. The command may come from the cockpit any moment now and after that we'll start moving.

I force a smile. 'It would be better if you took the window seat.' I find it difficult to look him in the eyes, but I do.

'Why?' he asks, defensively.

My face grows hot. Every fibre in my body tells me to just Foxtrot Oscar out of here, through the jetway, past the gate, and hop on the first tube bound for Kew Gardens. HOME!

'Well… um,' I begin. I hope that if I just start speaking the right words will come out.

'We have some rules and… if there's an emergency you need to be in a window seat.'

A puzzled expression sets on his face and I wonder if he's the type to go and lodge a complaint against me.

'Why?' he asks again.

It's a shame that being rude to passengers equates to getting the sack. It's a shame that I cannot afford to get the sack. Otherwise, I would have yelled: 'Stop asking me why for heaven's sake! Why can't you just get it? You're missing a leg, aren't you? Your life's worth less from a flight safety perspective because you could hamper the speed of evacuation for others. That's why!'

But because I like him, I would have added in a much nicer and very understanding tone: 'Look, I know you'd be a lot quicker than your geriatric neighbours in an emergency situation. They're old and fat and wear floor-length garments which they'd probably trip on during the commotion. But granted, they have four legs between them. They meet the requirements, and unfortunately, you don't.'

My internal rant has loosened my inhibitions. Staring blatantly at his legs, I say, 'In the unlikely event of an emergency the people next to you need to be able to evacuate the aircraft as quickly as possible, but you—'

Something about his demeanour makes me stop talking. I felt a shift, in his energy, and to my surprise, his speckled eyes are filled with fear. Could it be that he doesn't want the pensioners to know?

He gets up without another word and so does the couple. Strangely enough, nothing about his movement says artificial leg. Besides, now that he's standing, I notice that he's not only handsome but also quite tall. His arms, although covered by the long sleeves of a dark blue shirt, look strong and inviting. I'd be lucky to have him, I think.

I thank them profusely for their cooperation and, feeling like shit, I quickly walk back to the aft galley. Did anyone stow that beauty case? The public address system crackles into life and the captain instructs: 'Cabin Crew. Arm the slides.'

Chapter 4

It's only seven-thirty in the morning, but outside the Furama Riverfront hotel the sun's warmth already feels pleasant on my face and arms. The air is humid and thick with the fragrance of exotic flowers. Above me, bright sparkles of sunlight are scattered across a deep blue sky. This is why I'm still a flight attendant: a Saturday in Singapore. I must admit, this does beat kitchen table hunting in IKEA. And I'll have most of tomorrow here too.

I step aside to give a porter pushing a luggage cart stacked with Samsonite suitcases some more room and he and the fancy guests behind him disappear through the glass sliding doors.

Ten minutes ago, I'd decided to go to Central Mall for some shopping and breakfast in Toast Box, my usual haunt in this part of the world, but now I'm hovering between that and going to the Sri Mariamman Temple in Chinatown first.

I glance at the line of taxis some twenty feet away from me. Or somewhere different altogether? The zoo? I scold myself inwardly for wasting precious time and take resolute steps in the direction of the river. I only have a day and a half left here after all, it's not like I'm on holiday. Soon I'll be trapped inside of that smelly cabin again. Chinatown it is. It's only a twenty-minute walk and besides the temple, there's lots more to see in that area.

I follow the river for a couple of minutes, until the road veers away from it and I no longer can. I love this river. When I first came here I used it as a compass. As long as I knew where the river was, I knew where my hotel was. It helped me find my way around here, like a kindly travelling companion.

Walking in the sunshine, past flamboyant trees, food outlets and tall modern buildings, I pretend Ryan's walking beside me holding my hand. It makes me feel more contented somehow. From Chicago to Dar es Salaam, from Johannesburg to Delhi, and everywhere beyond and in between, I am always alone. It would be nice if Ryan could join me on one of my trips sometime. It would be even better if he could come to New York with me in August when I go there for my thirtieth birthday. Maybe he will. Things are going well between us. He keeps calling me and asking me on more dates. Quite a difference from guys I've dated who said things like: 'You're not looking for anything serious, are you?'

Last night I pretended Ryan was with me too. I'd slept for most of the day after we arrived here in the morning, but in the evening I went out. It was still light and warm outside and when I strolled along Marina Bay Waterfront Promenade, Ryan slipped his hand into mine. We listened to a Johnny Cash tribute band for a while, sipping fresh orange juice (me) and beer straight from the bottle (him), enjoying the music and, when it grew darker around us, Singapore's light pollution too. White, yellow, purple and blue hues poured from skyscrapers and reflected on the waters of the bay. It made it even more romantic. Ryan leaned in to kiss me several times. His lips were cool from the beer. I kissed him back. When the band played 'Ring of Fire,' I told him my dad had been a huge Cash fan and always whistled that song when he was painting.

Ryan looked deeply into my eyes. 'I really regret I'll never meet your dad,' he said.

Later, on our way back to the hotel, we bought boxes of sushi which we ate on a bench under a tree on Havelock Road, while we discussed our wedding and where we would live.

But around midnight I sent him an email from the lobby's computer because he wasn't really with me of course. It made me feel a bit stupid too. I'd had such a lovely evening but only saw half of it because of all the chatting and kissing in my head. I sat alone on that bench under the tree, shovelling sushi into my gob. I'm only trying to make myself feel better with these fantasies though. It's better than turning to alcohol, isn't it? Still, I have thought about discussing my need for fantasies with Patrick, because lately, I've even been pretending that Ryan's with me when I shop for food in Sainsbury's. It's not just abroad anymore. He'll argue with me about my dinner plans, before telling me it doesn't matter what I cook, he's sure it'll be delicious. Sometimes I even answer him out loud, and people give me funny looks; especially when I'm in my flight attendant uniform. I guess it's not normal then.

What I won't discuss with Patrick is that I've decided I will look up Patsy. I googled her in the hotel's lobby last night to try and find out where she lives and found her Facebook page. There wasn't too much information on it and the profile picture seemed quite old, but it did say she's married to a guy called Vincenzo Manozzi. She'd never struck me as the type to bag an Italian Stallion, but there you go. Maybe I'll meet him too.

♪

New Bridge Road is hot and buzzing with people and traffic. I'm feeling a little faint from the walk and wipe an arm across my forehead to prevent sunscreen and sweat from running into my eyes. A narrow shop without an awning, tucked between an electrical appliances store and a clothing outlet, catches my attention. Inside the door against a wall, an old humming fridge is loaded with plastic bottles of cool drinks. I check out the assortment and a girl at the back of the shop greets me. I take a lychee beverage and a bottle of water and walk over to her and put the items on the counter. She asks me if I need anything else. Wiping my wet hands on my hips, I glance around the shop. It's darker here, away from the door, and a strong scent of Indian incense permeates the air.

'Nag Champa,' I say, looking at the thin line of smoke that rises from a smouldering stick in a wooden holder on the counter.

'It's my favourite,' the girl says.

I smile at her. 'Mine too.'

Besides drinks, she sells hair accessories, bath products, make-up and polka dot dresses in lots of different colours. She's wearing a blue one herself. I browse for a few minutes and choose some elastic hairbands and a bandana. The girl holds up a mirror for me in the door where there's daylight, and I bend my knees to level with it. I twist my hair into a messy bun on top of my head and fasten it with a band, then tie a dark blue bandana in a knot behind my neck.

The girl gushes to me that I look great. 'Like a model,' she says, but I don't like it when people lie to me to make a sale. I don't look like a model at all. My cheeks resemble a Baboon's backside and my mascara's smudged around my eyes. I don't really want to buy her stuff anymore now but I don't know how to switch from polite and interested customer to bitch, so, I hand her ten dollars at the counter but do wait for my change.

'Is there a Toast Box around here?' I ask her, holding out my hand for the coins she retrieves from a small box embellished with sequins and beads. She gives me directions for a nearby mall and I thank her and walk further up the bustling road, taking a moment to review my thoughts about her. They were too harsh; she didn't deserve them. She was just doing her job. But I decide against going back to her with the words, 'Sorry, I forgot to tell you, you could keep the change.' That would look too stupid. Pedantic even. At least I purchased something from her.

The café isn't that busy yet and I find myself a seat near the window. The waitress brings me two pieces of toast spread thickly with Kaya coconut jam, and a cup of tea. There's a creamy layer at the bottom of the teacup which tastes like condensed milk. If Ryan were here, or Flora, we could have talked about that. About sweetening tea with condensed milk. I think I'll make them this at home, and see what they think.

After half an hour, and another order of tea and toast, I feel recharged and head for the Sri Mariamman Temple. It takes me just a few minutes to get there and before I enter, I spend some time admiring the Hindu figures on the roof.

The whole building oozes a sense of ancient spirituality. Temples, churches, graveyards and nature always give me a sense of connection to something higher. It's bliss to feel centred; I often feel anxious.

I slip off my Havaianas and place them in a rack with dozens of other flip flops and sandals, then walk barefoot through the open timber doors—feeling dwarfed by the size of them—into the hall. The sober tones of the grey, stone floor—cool under my feet—and the dozens of fat, white columns that support the temple, contrast with the colour explosion in the artworks above me.

I come to an open courtyard and watch other tourists frantically tiptoeing across it, dashing from one bit of shade to the next. It's a funny sight, but moments later I do the same, as the slabs that pave the yard are simply too hot to stand on for more than a second without burning your feet. Strolling further through the temple, I admire the paintings of goddesses on the walls, and the ceiling adorned with images of deities riding elephants and peacocks. Altars, and statues of holy figures in different shapes and sizes, painted in magnificent colour palettes, grace the main prayer hall.

But after a while my thoughts turn to my shopping list. I wanted to go to a grocery store for some jars of Kaya coconut jam and some other bits and bobs today.

Standing in front of the statue of Sri Durgai Amman, I switch on my phone to check the time. On the display it says 02:03 and I add eight hours for local time. It's just gone 10 a.m. in Singapore. My phone bleeps. I have two new messages, both from my sister Cadi, I notice. I open the oldest one first.

Mum's missing. We can't find her. She stormed out of the house this evening, told Kieran she was going to kill herself. I'm really angry with her. When will this ever end? Kieran called me and I called the police. I'm at mum's with Kieran now. They're coming to take our statement because of what she said and her history. Call me!!!

I stare at the message. That familiar sinking feeling and the prickling under my skin are already catching up with me. What the bloody hell it this time? Mum's drama follows me everywhere. I was going to have a lovely weekend, here in Singapore, but now it's ruined. Cadi's right. When will this ever end?

I read the message again and put a clammy hand on my heart. Are we here again? I want to move on from our past; look forward. But I do love Mum. I've often thought that life would've been easier if I didn't, but I do, despite everything. And now she's missing? Is she really though?

I feel like I'm spinning a bit, or that everything around me is, so I focus on my breathing. Patrick suggested I try that. Whether Mum's missing or not, when she has problems, it means there are problems for me.

Oh, hang on! There's another message of course! My thumbs work swiftly to open it. I don't know why my hands are shaking; I'm sure the message will say that they've found her and everything is fine. My day won't be ruined after all. It'll be a happy day. As planned!

…..and you know what I was thinking? Maybe it's for the best if she's dead. Then we'll finally have some peace.

That's it. That's the second message. Although I see Cadi's point, I know she doesn't mean it. She was upset when she sent this. I check my inbox for more messages but there aren't any. Is Mum really gone then? I glance at Cadi's phone number. I should call her but I don't want to. I want to be a carefree tourist; not the daughter of a fruitcake. If only I hadn't checked the time, then I wouldn't have known about this, and I could've gone about my day as normal.

I should probably go back to the hotel now and find Pete or the captain. I might have to go home today. Or do I? My thumb hovers over the green phone symbol. With Mum, it's always something, isn't it? She gets these funny moods but they don't usually last long. And yet… I'm not convinced this is harmless either.

Five years ago, Mum was hospitalized after she'd washed down seventeen pills with beer. I was there when the psychiatrist asked her why she'd only taken seventeen pills.

'I wanted to see what would happen first,' she told him.

'So, you wanted a comfortable death?' he concluded. She said she did.

On the day she discharged herself, I asked him if he thought she was ready to come home.

'Maybe for now,' he told me, 'but we are bound to see her here again.'

I always hoped she would prove him wrong and for the

past couple of years she's been much better. Less unpredictable; not as trapped inside of her own mind. Or have I missed something?

I look up from my phone straight into Sri Durgai Amman's eyes and study her pale blue face and the faint smile that plays around her glossy red lips. She has many arms but not one of them pats me on the back or hugs me, so I pretend Ryan is here. He pulls me close and wraps his arms tightly around me. I bury my face in his neck and breathe in the manly scent of his skin. It reminds me of Dad. They both have that grown-up smell that says: I'll take care of you.

I never had a chance to say goodbye to Dad. It still hurts and I can't bear the thought of losing Mum too. God, I don't want to deal with this.

My legs feel like jelly. Ryan isn't really holding me of course. For a moment I consider just sitting down on the floor, amid the handful of tourists who have gathered at my side and behind me. They're discussing Sri Durgai Amman, I think, in hushed German and Italian.

No, I won't make a spectacle of myself; I'll pull myself together. I can do this. And if there is reason to fall apart, it can wait until later.

I step away from the tourists and dial Cadi's number. It goes straight to voicemail. Of course, it's night-time in England. But would Cadi really switch off her phone under these circumstances? She asked me to call her. Does she even know I'm in Singapore? I focus on my breathing again, it makes my body feel more grounded, and begin to dissect the timeline. Cadi sent me these messages last night at around eight p.m. London time. That was four a.m. for me; I'd been fast asleep. Six hours have passed and there are no other messages. This probably means that the police really have gone to Mum's house for Kieran and Cadi's statements and that Mum is still missing. Has she actually done it this time? Is she really dead? Is that why Cadi's phone is switched off? Is she too afraid to tell me? Or is she at a morgue right now, with Kieran, identifying Mum's body?

I start walking towards the entrance doors while I call Gareth, Cadi's boyfriend. His phone is switched off too and they haven't got a landline.

I try to call Kieran. His phone is ringing and I stop walking. Will I know now? Oh, why does Mum do this to me? Kieran's voicemail kicks in and I listen to a woman telling me that the fingers I have used to dial are too fat. I don't get it. What's going on at home? Mum's phone! I'll try that. Standing before the hot courtyard and leaning my hand against a cool pillar for support, I press my mobile hard against my ear. She's really gone, I think, as I listen to the repeated ringing on her end of the line. She never goes anywhere at night, at least not that I'm aware of. Besides, Kieran lives with her. He's not answering either, which makes sense. Cadi and Gareth wouldn't leave him by himself. He's probably at their place.

I must go home. I need to be there for them.

I put my phone back in my handbag, then trot across the courtyard where new droves of tourists are hopping around barefoot to avoid burns. It's not so funny anymore.

Outside the temple I look for my flip flops. A stooped old woman with a leathery face shuffles past the entrance but when she sees me she halts and leans heavily on her cane. She lifts her head and grins at me, exposing pointy brown teeth. 'Thaaank you, goodbye,' she slurs, as if she's thanking me for visiting her home.

'Goodbye,' I mutter and run my eyes over the collection of shoes again. I don't see my Havaianas anywhere. For God's sake, did someone steal them? I only just got them in L.A.; they were expensive. I'll have to walk back barefoot now, after everything that's—oh no, there they are. They were just moved.

I slip them on and wipe my wet forehead with the palm of my hand. To my right, the old woman shuffles steadily along the busy road. Where could she be going? The market maybe? It occurs to me that I will never see her again and that maybe I should have shown her some kindness when she bothered to acknowledge my existence, but I can hardly chase after her now and say 'hello.' It might startle her. Better to accept that I wasn't very nice and hopefully I'll make a better choice next time. I turn left and start walking back towards the river and re-read Cadi's first message.

Twenty minutes later I'm back in my hotel room. I notice with some dismay that my room's been cleaned and that the double bed's been made. My pink nightgown is neatly folded and placed on one of the pillows. I usually hang a 'do not disturb' sign on the doorknobs of hotel rooms because I don't like the idea of strangers going through my personal space but this morning I forgot.

I sit down on the bed, reach for the phone on the nightstand and dial the extension number for Pete's room. As I had expected, he isn't there. Who would stay indoors after flying to a place like Singapore for free? Being able to see so much of the world is what makes up for all the shit we have to deal with in the cabin. I phone the captain but she's out too. Then I use my mobile to try and call Cadi one more time but her phone is still switched off.

I scribble a message for Pete on the hotel's notepaper in which I explain what has happened and that I need to find a colleague who's willing to stay a day longer and swap flights with me so I can fly home tonight. I will slip it under his door. My hand trembles as I write. I don't want Mum to be dead. The wall that I've built up since my childhood, one stone at a time, is beginning to crumble. But I need this wall. It shields me from her madness. I won't allow it to come down just like that. Not after everything we've been through.

Chapter 5

I've found myself a quiet spot under the stairs that lead up to the offices. Sagged into a cool leather chair next to a ficus plant in a huge terracotta pot, I'm nursing a cappuccino I bought at the crew counter, and observe the hustle and bustle at Heathrow's Crew Report Centre. Hundreds of uniformed flight attendants and pilots scurry around me like last-minute Christmas shoppers wrapped up in their own hectic worlds. Some look for briefing rooms and ironing boards, or computers to check flight schedules on. Others just look for somewhere quiet to sit, with a cup of coffee, like me.

My plane only touched down forty minutes ago and I'm feeling quite calm. I wasn't met by my supervisor at the Crew Centre when I arrived, which I took to be a good sign. Surely if Mum had died Cadi would have contacted my company? Besides, I called her again half an hour ago and her phone is still switched off but there haven't been further messages from her, nor from anyone else in my family. I could probably have stayed in Singapore. Just in case though, I've decided to stay at the Crew Centre for now. If I'm wrong, and there is bad news, then I don't want to be alone. At least here there are arms I can collapse into and people who'll rally round. At home there's no one; not even a cat.

A thin girl crosses my line of vision. She sits down behind a computer a few feet away from me; a look of concentration on her face. New floor. Yes, she told me about her new floor. We flew together somewhere. Iceland? Her boyfriend had moved in with her and was laying a new floor. She couldn't walk on it yet, he'd said, so after our flight she would stay at her parents' house. When I bumped into her sometime later and asked how she was and if she'd been happy with the floor, she told me it had been a horrible nightmare. Shortly after her boyfriend moved in with her, she'd discovered he was living with another girlfriend too.

I shift my bum in my seat because the leather upholstery is beginning to stick to my tights. The girl is checking her phone. I do think it was weird though, what she told me. Would you really not notice it if your boyfriend was living with another partner too? Surely there must have been signs? In my head, I ask the Universe to help her and send her love because she doesn't look well. Her arms and shoulders float in her jacket.

I finish my coffee, then put the empty cup on the armrest and glance at the huge round clock on the wall behind the computers. It's almost eleven a.m. I wish I could call Ryan for a chat. I miss him, but he thinks I'm still in Singapore. It actually feels like I'm not being truthful to him by coming back a day earlier than I'd said, but I can't tell him what happened. It would sound too crazy. God forbid I'll put him o—

The shrill ringtone of my phone startles me and my heart starts to throb. My fingers fumble with my jacket pocket as I try to fish it out as quickly as I can. This must be it. Yes, the display says it's Cadi. My teeth almost chatter. The amounts of stress Mum's put me through in my life…

'Is she alive?' I blurt.

But Cadi's silent and there's a strange moment in which we've established a connection but she seems absorbed by something else. I can hear Gareth's voice in the background and it sounds as if he said '*hiraeth*' although I'm not sure.

'Cadi?' I call into my phone.

'Hi Carys,' Cadi replies. She sounds calm but tired. 'Sorry I was distracted. Gareth said something. Yes, she's alive. She's alright.'

I close my eyes and let the relief flood through me. Thank God. No need for the whole Mum-is-dead-scenario. No phone calls to funeral directors, no obituary to draft up, no flicking through headstone brochures. Life can go on as normal.

'Where is she then?' I press my hand against my heart; its rhythm is almost back to normal.

'Last night,' Cadi begins, 'someone, we don't know who it was, saw Mum in her car, slumped over the steering wheel. This person, whoever it was, called the—'

'Where is she Cadi? Is she in a hospital?'

'She's in a mental hospital.'

'Oh God, not again…'

'Do you want to know what happened?'

'I do.'

'So,' Cadi continues, 'the police were called and Mum was taken to the station. Kieran and I didn't know that and we thought she was still missing. Two officers came round to speak to us, but they had only just arrived when one of them got a phone call about a woman who'd been found and who matched her description. The officers then drove us to the police station, and yes, there she was. She'd taken pills again, with beer. Same as last time.'

'Was her stomach pumped?'

'No, I asked about that too but they said it wasn't necessary, although one of the police officers did say it was bad for her health, all those pills she'd taken.'

Cadi fills me in on the rest. A police car had taken Mum to a psychiatric institution; not the same one she was in five years ago. Gareth had picked Cadi and Kieran up from the police station around ten p.m. and Kieran went with them to Hammersmith.

We don't speak for a moment or two. I'm digesting Cadi's words, its implications for myself, what to do with Kieran and Mum's cat, and Mum's mental shit that time and again drags us down into this never-ending abyss.

'Is it possible to go and see her today?' My tone is detached. The prospect of seeing Mum automatically pops a few stones back in my broken wall.

'I think so,' Cadi says.

Then I ask her why she didn't pick up her phone all day yesterday and this morning.

'Do you know what it was like for me?' I hiss. I'm not a fan of public tiffs and glance around to make sure no one hears me. 'Being in Singapore, not knowing whether there'd be another funeral or not?'

'What it was like for *you*?' Cadi pauses dramatically. 'Have you got any idea—any at all—what I've had to deal with since Friday? I had to sort out everything Carys, while you were holidaying again.'

I'm staring at the leaves of the ficus plant. I'm not going to bite back that I wasn't on holiday; that I was lonely in Singapore and miserable in the cabin, because I regret my little outburst, but I won't say sorry because she yelled at me.

'I called the police, answered all of their questions, Kieran's on our couch, I fed Mum's cat. Me and Gareth had a fight about Southport, my battery was flat and I couldn't find my charger for three days—' Reeling off her list of grievances, Cadi's voice has become tearful and I'm quietly listening to what she's saying, squeezing my empty coffee cup, not sure what to reply because I can't make it better anyway.

'And guess what,' she drones on, 'and this is the worst of all. For the second year in a row, I won't be able to pay my tuition fees for the art and design School. Once again, they've accepted my application, and once again, I haven't got the funds. Can you believe that?'

'Hello?' she says, after a few moments of silence.

'I thought we were talking about Mum.'

'Yes, we were,' Cadi snaps. 'But I've been talking and thinking about Mum NON-STOP for two days. I have my own life to live. I have dreams.'

'I know you have,' I reply. 'But I would really prefer it if we talked about that some other time, alright? How's Kieran?'

Cadi sniffs hard. It sounds like she's swallowing snot. 'He's alright,' she says. 'He's taking a bath.'

'Are you sure he's alright?'

'Yeah.' She sounds doubtful. 'He wasn't Friday and yesterday of course, but he's fine now.'

'Has he eaten anything?'

'Of course he has.'

'So, can he stay with you and Gareth?'

'No Carys, he can't. We don't have the space here, you know that.'

'Well neither have I.'

'You have that room, off your kitchen.'

'My utility room?' I mock laugh. 'I have my washing machine in there. There's no room for a bed.'

'Kieran doesn't have a bed; he has a mattress on the floor.'

The thin girl gets up and a male colleague who'd been hovering around her immediately takes up the seat. We need more computers around here. They're always taken.

'Can't we put his mattress in your bedroom?' Cadi says.

I hesitate. The idea had crossed my mind but I dismissed it. 'That's not really an option,' I say. 'I'm seeing someone and—'

'That guy from the dating site?'

'Yes, Ryan.'

'But you've only been on a couple of dates. He won't be staying the night any time soon, will he?'

There's an earnestness in Cadi's voice, a sort of innocence even, as she poses the question and it really jars on me. I happen to know that she lost her virginity at only fourteen years old, beating me to it by at least three years.

'We've been on four dates and he's coming over next week.'

'Alright,' Cadi says. 'I get the point. Moving swiftly on.'

I tell her that I'm knackered and want to go and see Mum. I fetch a pen and a scrap of paper from my carry-on suitcase and scribble down the address Cadi gives me. It's a place in Chingford, not far from where Mum lives.

'I'll call you tonight,' I promise Cadi and lower my arm to end our conversation, but then I remember something.

'Cadi. Cadi. Are you still there?'

'Yes, I'm still here.'

'The cat. Can you at least take Lulu?'

'No Carys, I can't. We're not allowed to keep pets here.'

We hang up and I stuff the note with Mum's address on it in my pocket and bin my mangled coffee cup on my way out of the Crew Centre. Lugging my suitcases behind me, I head for Terminal 5 Underground Station.

Chapter 6

I just got off the bus at Hickman Avenue and I'm walking through a pleasant drizzle to the mental health institution, trundling my suitcases behind me. The tiredness I felt at the crew centre has passed; I took power naps on the tube and on the bus. It feels good to inhale fresh air and stretch my legs. There are no other people in the street, only cars coming down the road, sloshing through roadside puddles. It was chucking it down earlier, but now slivers of sunrays tentatively peek through layers of clouds and I scan the sky for a rainbow but don't see one. When I come to a sign that says Merriam Close, I turn a shallow corner and Naseberry Court hospital, a building flanked by trees and shrubs, looms before me. I will soon see Mum now, but in what state?

In the waiting room, I'm the only visitor. The receptionist, a young bespectacled brunette behind a glass partition, briefly interrupts a phone call to point at a row of red plastic seats and informs me with a tight smile that someone will be with me shortly.

I leave my suitcases to the side of the partition and sit down on one of the chairs, slip off my shoes, rest my feet on top of them and wiggle my toes.

Opposite me there are four yellow plastic chairs. It's a small waiting room, about the size of my sitting area at home. I must get a kitchen table. I keep not getting around to it, but now that Ryan will be coming over a lot I must make it a priority. How will we stare deeply into each other's eyes over candlelit dinners when we have plates on our laps and our feet propped up on the coffee table?

The drizzle is picking up in volume again and raindrops drum against the window behind me. It feels more like autumn than spring today, although it wasn't cold outside.

The brunette is still on the phone, laughing, an unprofessional cackle. Is she taking a personal call? Unbelievable. Does she know my mum tried to kill herself? Has she seen Mum? I wonder if she likes her job and what that must feel like. She's surrounded by nutters all day and I by demanding passengers. What are the odds of her being attacked by a deranged patient? Are they higher than me crashing? At least she doesn't have to fly over oceans. I hate that the most. During my cabin training we practiced for a ditching with two safety rafts in a swimming pool. I have a picture of myself and about ten other attendants in training, hauling each other onto a raft from the water. We're all tumbled on top of each other; arms and legs flailing. We had a blast at the pool that day, but to do this in real life? We wouldn't make it. There are many like me though: flight attendants who are nervous flyers. Even pilots.

'An actual air hostess,' a female voice booms. It takes me a moment to realise that I'm wearing my uniform and that she means me.

I get up and turn to the curvy woman who comes walking up to me with an outstretched hand and a smile on her friendly face. 'I'm Maeve,' she says.

She must be in her late fifties. Short, wavy hair in an ash-blonde tone. She's motherly, at least that's how she comes across to me: taking charge and telling me it's best to leave my suitcases behind the reception desk. She briefly speaks with the brunette through the glass partition, and the brunette gets up and opens a side door and together they shove my luggage through it.

Then Maeve turns back to me. 'How are you?' she says. It's not a casual question. Her tone is serious and she gazes into my eyes as if trying to read me. Patrick sometimes looks at me like that. They're trying to come too close. I look away.

Maeve asks me if I've just come from the airport or if I'm on my way over there, and she wants to know how I'm coping.

'I'm fine,' I say, 'thank you. But how's my mother?'

'Your mother is on the first floor.' Maeve says, gesturing towards the door.

My stomach tightens. I didn't ask her where Mum was. Why doesn't she answer my question?

We walk up the steps in silence. On the first floor, opposite the stairs, there's a room with no door. A few people are sitting around a table; they've got the radio on.

'That's the kitchen,' Maeve says, when she sees me looking at them. She turns left and I follow. The floor gives off a faint whiff of eucalyptus detergent and I hear voices behind the walls coming from the rooms we pass.

At the end of the corridor, Maeve halts in front of a door. It has a vertical, rectangular viewing panel in it with striped white and grey glass, but I can't see through it because I'm half behind Maeve's broad back. She knocks on the door and I wait. She knocks again and looks through the glass panel but when there's still no answer she opens the door and pokes her head around it.

'Kathy? Someone's here for you.' Maeve pushes the door open and steps aside to let me in. 'Here she is pet,' she says.

And then I see Mum. She's lying motionless on a bed; her head turned towards a large window that's covered with mesh wiring. A single white sheet is drawn up to her chest.

I stand in the doorway and take in the scene before me. She's lying there so still. Is she really alive? Could she have died without Maeve realising it?

Edging closer to her, something's chipping at my wall— I can almost physically feel it— and Mum's voice echoes through my head: *'The walls of this house are papered with disappointment.'* She said that to me once. Something to do with Dad. I don't know why I suddenly remember this.

When I come closer to Mum's bed, I notice that she isn't asleep as I first thought, but just staring into oblivion.

'Hi Mum,' I say.

But she doesn't respond and it scares me to see her like this. Pretending I don't love her has always been the easiest way to cope with her, but it's hard to hold on to my resentment now that she's like this.

I turn around, expecting to see Maeve in the doorway. I'm hankering after a motherly smile or a nod of encouragement, but she's gone.

'Mum?' I try again.

Slowly she turns her head towards me and focusses her flat, lifeless eyes. 'Carys,' she croaks. Her lips are cracked, her mouth strangely set and her skin is grey. She really did want to die. That is clear to me now. No point in asking how she is.

I hear some voices and footsteps outside the room and glance at the door wondering if Maeve is back. Maybe she went to get a doctor? Mum looks like she needs one. But the steps and voices drift away down the corridor and we remain alone.

The wiring on the large window only lets through a dull light, and I scan the room for something to sit on. There are three other beds, all in use, I can tell from the rumpled sheets and the greeting cards on the walls. I spot a low stool in front of someone's bedside table and pull it up next to Mum. She's closed her eyes. Does she even want me here? I wish I'd brought her something. Bright flowers in a pretty vase, or her favourite chocolate bar filled with nuts and raisins, or maybe some trashy magazines that feature people in it with lots of problems—people with problems tend to cheer her up—but I didn't think of it at the airport and other shops I passed were closed.

My gaze falls on the purple and blue streaks that run down the left side of her short dark hair. A few months ago, when she'd invited us over for Easter lunch, I asked her why on earth she had her hair coloured like that.

'I wanted something that stands out,' she'd replied. 'I want to be noticed.'

When I pointed out that people would certainly notice her now, but for all the wrong reasons as this was a ridiculous look for a woman her age, she'd rebuffed me with a forthright, 'I don't care. It's my hair and I like it.'

'How's my boy?' she suddenly whispers. She's opened her eyes but avoids my gaze.

'Kieran's fine,' I say, hesitantly. 'He knows you're not dead. He's with Cadi and Gareth.'

Mum's fingers begin to squeeze and twist the top of the bedsheet as though she were a kneading kitten. 'Can he stay with them?'

'No, he can't. He's moving in with me for the time being. Probably tomorrow, if Gareth can find a trailer.' I think of Ryan; he's coming over this week. I need his arms around me. But what about Kieran?

'And Lulu?' Mum asks in a low voice.

'Yes, I'll take her in too.'

I notice some white spittle in the corners of her mouth. Little milky-white blobs. It looks weird; they're just sitting there. 'Are you thirsty?' I ask.

She furrows her brow deeply and closes her eyes. 'I'm tired,' she whispers.

'Do you want me to go?'

Her eyes still closed, she mouths a weak 'no.'

Silent minutes pass while I sit beside her. If she knew I was studying her face she wouldn't like it. It's a haggard face with a sagging jawline. A face that ages her beyond her years, but I do remember a time when there was a freshness to it, and her features weren't etched with grief. She was almost pretty then. There were periods in my childhood when she was happy and balanced and loving towards me, but her Borderline disorder and Bethan's death messed her up. Her face is a translation of our misery. And it doesn't help that she never wears sunscreen.

I take Mum's cool hand in mine and rub it with my thumb. It takes almost everything out of me to do this; I have to go beyond myself, but it's good what I'm doing because a tiny smile appears in the corners of her mouth. The blobs are still there.

Sometimes I wonder if she remembers why we went to Patsy's house that day. I hope she doesn't, but I'm not going to bring it up and find out. Did Dad remember it?

I study the limp hand with the pale nails I'm holding. The hand that groped. You betrayed me, Mum. Did I betray you? If I did, we're not even.

Everything is unfolding as it should. Someone once said that to me, but no, I don't believe that. I believe in nooses. I see one in my head sometimes, like now. And when I do, I want to stick my head through it and hang myself from the stairs. I deserve it, don't I? There's no emotion as shattering as guilt.

Mum's looking straight at me.

My heart thuds and I let go of her hand. 'Are you still using that Nivea I gave you? You have cracks on your knuckles.'

'I've used it all up,' she says hoarsely.

'I'll buy you more.'

'Thank you.'

I stay with her for another ten minutes and promise I'll be back soon.

Chapter 7

It's Saturday and I'm on the sofa eating an apple. Bethan's on her back in the wooden playpen, sucking on her knuckles and looking at a toy mirror that's wrapped around the slats. There's a strange feeling in the house; a new feeling, because Mum is different today.

After Dad left for work at the hospital this morning, she looked for the vacuum cleaner. It took her a while to find it because Dad had left it 'in a ridiculous spot,' she said, which was behind a curtain in the hallway. She'd tied Bethan to her back to stop her from crying and began to hoover; first the bedrooms and the stairs, then the tiles in the kitchen and the hall, followed by the carpet in the living room. She even cleaned the nooks of the sofa and made me get up from it.

After this, she put Bethan in her playpen and wiped the tables and chairs with a wet cloth. She dusted shelves, on top of the cabinets and even the TV. She wiped away the cobwebs in the loo because the spiders that lived there had shrivelled up and died anyway. Then she picked up Bethan again, sat down on the sofa next to me, and with a happy look on her face she gave my sister the breast.

'Can I have apple slices with cimmanum,' I asked Mum when she was done. But Mum said we were out of cinnamon and that she didn't have time to slice anything up, because she was expecting a visitor. She went to the kitchen to fetch me a whole apple.

Now Mum's flat on her bottom on the floor. Her legs are stretched before her; around a pail of water that's still letting off a little steam. The rising steam reminds me of Taid's cigar smoke. I wish he and Nain were here. I always do.

Mum leans forward and dunks a cloth that's wrapped around a bar of soap into the pail and then rubs it on a carpet stain in front of her.

'I should have cleaned it straight away,' she says, a little out of breath, 'but Mummy couldn't be bothered, could she?' I shake my head and take another bite from my apple.

'Coffee stains are difficult to get out,' she says.

I let the chunk of apple I was working on rest on my tongue and watch her wrinkled forehead. Is she still cross with me? She doesn't look upset, but I'm not sure about her voice. I try to chew more quietly in case she finds me annoying. It's weird to see her so different, so busy. She usually sits on the sofa, staring and reading.

'I'm not a homemaker,' Mum told Dad. 'I live for our children but I point blank refuse to waste my entire life on domestic chores.' But now she's cleaning anyway. I do feel sorry for Mum when she's not happy. She wants to be a midwife—that means babies—but Dad said no because the midwife school is expensive. She really tried, saying: 'We'll be poor but happy,' but he still said no.

Mum could be the Iron Lady too. Dad laughed when she said that and she got really cross.

'Don't you dare laugh at me,' she shouted. 'I could easily be in politics. I should have been. I'm intelligent.'

Mum's singing. She sings 'Knowing me, knowing you,' while she scrubs at the stain. I like her voice and I love this melody. When Mum is cheerful and calm like this, it makes everything feel sunny and bright.

'It's almost gone,' Mum says. She breathes hard. 'You won't be able to tell it's there unless you really look for it.' She looks quite happy about the cleaning and dunks the cloth with the bar of soap into the bucket once more. Dad always dunks biscuits in his tea. He says the biscuits are great dunkers.

Mum lets out a big sigh, wipes her hands on her trousers and looks around our room. Then she does something that's a little weird. She draws up her knees and leans forward and with her thumbs and forefingers, she begins to feel the edges of her toenails.

I slide off the sofa and put the apple core on the table. 'Can I play outside?' I ask.

But when she looks at me, I notice that she has her scary eyes again and I feel like I'm falling.

Mum gets up from the floor. She looks at the clock above the TV and mumbles something about brewing a pot of coffee. She lifts the pail of water from the floor and says, 'Play outside? Yes, you can.' Then she goes to the kitchen.

Before I go, I stick my hands through the slats of Bethan's playpen. She's fallen asleep and I carefully touch her soft hair and her chubby cheeks. She moves her head and opens her eyes and it looks as if she doesn't know it's me touching her, but then she smiles and grabs my finger and tries to put it in her mouth, so I let her play tug-of-war with my finger for a little bit.

'Put your jacket on,' Mum calls after me on my way to the front door. 'And do stay near the house.'

♪

We have a cobblestone garden path that Dad and Taid made together. At the end of it, I open the green fence and step onto the pavement. I have a ladybird ring on my finger and Mum told me it's on my right hand and that is the direction I take. I have bubbles in my tummy because

I'm finally going to find out what's on the other side of the secret alley. Mum and I always pass it when we go to the shops. She said that it was just a path for the people who live there and that it leads to their backyards. I was disappointed when she said that because it didn't sound very magical, but I still want to go and see it for myself. Maybe there are gnomes with red hats. They're always very nice to children.

I skip past our neighbour's house and the houses next to theirs, enjoying the sunshine, but when I see my duck's storm drain, I stop skipping and just walk.

On the side of my ladybird ring, there are six homes that look just like our own. The houses are all stuck together and when I pass the third house, I glance at a large living room window. There's often a kind lady behind it who waves at me and Mum but she's not there today. I walk on but the sound of a door opening makes me turn around.

It's the lady, stepping out of the house! She's wearing a long, yellow coat, and a large red bag hangs off one shoulder. Her back is turned to me; it looks like she's locking the door.

I quickly walk on because I don't want her to see me. What if she forbids me to go to the secret alley? I'm almost there now.

But when I come to it I'm not so sure anymore. The first part of the alley is not scary at all. It's between two front yards and it looks open and light. But the part that's between the high houses frightens me. There's no sunlight there and the alley looks narrow and dark. Maybe I should go back and forget about my plan.

Suddenly I hear my mother's voice in my head. She's telling my Auntie Mary that whatever happens, and despite everything she's already been through, she will soldier on.

I take a deep breath and run through the alley as fast as I can. When I come out on the other end it's sunny again. I stand still and look around. Green, heart-shaped leaves are growing against a tall, wooden fence on the side where my hand has no ring. I think someone's backyard is behind that fence. I take a few steps away from the alley, down the long, stone path. On the side of my ring, there are houses with backyards. Some have toys in them, and bikes and footballs and, oh! A red swing!

Opposite the gardens there is grass and a long ditch. The trees that grow on the other side of the ditch have very long branches that lean over the water and I see a picture of the trees in the water, as if it's a huge mirror. I know that this ditch also runs behind our own backyard. Dad put a fence between our garden and the ditch because he doesn't want me and Bethan to drown in it. But here there is no fence.

My gaze moves further down the path, towards the end, and to my surprise I see four children standing around a fire. I recognize Patsy straight away. The other children are boys and not as big as her. What are they doing there and why have they got a fire?

One of the children sees me and says something to Patsy. She looks up and they all watch me as I walk over to them.

It's a real fire. The flames are bright and orange and yellow, but why have they got it?

'What are you doing here?' Patsy asks.

'I wanted to see what was here,' I say, still looking at the fire.

'You're not allowed here.' It's the skinny blond boy. I remember his name is Jason.

'Oh,' I reply. And because the sound of his voice worries me, I turn around and start walking back to the alley.

'Wait!' one of the boys calls out behind me. 'Let's throw her in the fire.'

'Yes!' Patsy says.

I stop.

Patsy walks over to me and reaches for me with her horrible hand. 'We're going to throw you in the fire,' she says.

I blink my eyes. What is she doing? How can she have such bad thoughts in her head?

'You can't throw me in the fire,' I say.

Patsy wraps her one long middle finger around my arm. 'Yes, we can.'

I walk along with her because I'm frightened and I don't know what else to do.

We stop before the fire and I start to cry.

'Aw, what's wrong?' Patsy lowers herself before me and touches my hair.

'You're going to throw me in the fire,' I cry.

'You don't want to be thrown in the fire?'

I shake my head and through my tears I look at her, and at the boys who are watching us.

'Alright,' Patsy says, 'we won't throw you in the fire.'

'Patsy!' one of the boys says. 'We will.'

'Shush.' Patsy's still leaning on one knee and she looks into my eyes. 'I will not throw you in the fire,' she says, 'if you tell me you love me.'

I stare at her big face; her fat lips, and think about these words. They are wrong; I don't love her at all. And Nain always says that children shouldn't tell fibs.

I press my lips together as tightly as I can, so no words can escape my mouth.

'Do you love me?' Patsy says.

I look past her at the fire. My legs feel so wobbly; like runny eggs with soldiers, but I shake my head.

'Alright then.' She jumps up and takes me by the arm. My heart jumps too and I start to cry again.

'Let me do it,' one of the boys says. He's hopping on his feet and his smile is very mean.

Jason steps closer. 'No, I wanna do it. Patsy, can I do it?' He glances at my hand. 'What have you got there?' he says.

I look at my hand but I don't know what he means.

'Show me,' Jason says. He grabs my hand while Patsy's still squeezing my arm with her scary finger.

Jason pulls at my ladybird ring and Patsy doesn't say anything; I think she's waiting for him. Jason holds my ring on his flat hand and shows it to the other two boys. When Jason puts the ring in his pocket, I know I won't get it back, just like my duck.

Patsy lowers herself before me again. 'I will not throw you in the fire, if you tell me you love me.'

My tears feel warm on my skin and I let out a wail; for my dadi, my duck and myself. I think of Bethan and wail louder. Even for Mum.

Patsy lifts me up but I hold my body rigid like a plank and she puts me down again. 'Just say you love me,' she says, squeezing my shoulders with her scary hands. 'The other children have told me as well.'

Through my tears, I look at the three boys. They all nod and say 'yes,' but I don't speak.

Suddenly, Patsy turns me around, towards the fire. Her hands are under my armpits and she lifts me up and holds me in front of the flames. The heat stings my face and eyes.

'No!' I scream. 'No!' Will someone hear me? A grown-up from the houses? But what if they are as bad as the children? Maybe they want to kill me too. I want to go home. I want to be with Mummy and Daddy.

'Tell me!' Patsy shouts.

'Alright,' I cry.

Patsy puts me down and we step away from the fire. She kneels before me and places one hand on my back. 'Really?'

she says. Her breath smells of bubble gum and there are little lights in her eyes.

'I love you,' I whimper.

'Do you really?' Patsy's fat lips have the shape of a heart, like the leaves on the fence, and she keeps them apart, and her cheeks are a bit pink, like apples.

I nod.

'Say it one more time.'

'I love you.' I almost whisper the words but it's not so difficult to say anymore.

Patsy hugs me tightly. 'Aw, that's so sweet.' She wipes my tears away with her scary finger and I feel like I'm a doll you can play with whenever you want.

Patsy's kisses are wet and horrible and she plants them all over my face.

'I wanna kill her,' one of the boys says.

'Shut up, or I'll throw you in the fire,' she warns him. It makes me feel safer.

'Can I go now?' I ask.

Patsy lets me go from her arms. 'Yes, you may go now. Are you going home?'

'Yes,' I reply.

'What if she tells her parents?' Jason says.

'Are you going to tell your parents?' Patsy asks.

I shake my head.

'Are you not going to tell your mother?' one of the boys asks. They're all standing before me.

'No, I won't say anything.'

'Good,' Patsy says. 'Because if you do, we'll throw you in

the fire after all, alright?'

'Alright,' I reply, and then I start running.

'Carys!' one of the boys calls out to me.

I stop and turn around, feeling very heavy. I thought it was over but now I'm not sure.

Patsy asks the boy something, and they talk together, and I wait.

'No, it's alright,' Patsy says. 'You can go now.'

I run for the alley as fast as I can. When I come out of it, on my own street, I keep running and don't slow down.

Chapter 8

Mum told me off for constantly banging my hands on the front door when I need to be let into the house. She said she'd leave the backdoor open for me during the day and that I should use that. This is what I'm thinking of when I rush past the red tulips that grow against our green fence in the front yard. Without slowing down, I run past our neighbours' home on the corner—their curtains are still closed—and take the path that goes around their house. Their backyard is wild but the curtains are open on this side. I rush past the pear tree they let us pick from in summer, to our backyard where I fumble with the latch on the fence before pushing it open. Could Patsy get me here? I keep running, past Dad's shed and his rabbit hutches, until finally, I'm safe; I'm in the kitchen now, where it always smells of vegetable soup, apart from Sunday afternoons when Dad makes fresh custard.

I close the door with a bang and leave my boots on the doormat. The tiles feel cool underneath my socked feet as I move past the wooden cabinets with the speckled countertop and the green stove that was a present from Nain and Taid. I open my mouth and take a big breath before I step into the living room. Mum will be furious when she hears about Patsy and the fire. But I close my mouth when I notice she's not there.

Surprised, I look around the room. The playpen is empty

too, apart from some of Bethan's toys and a bib. On the floor, beside the sofa, there's a red bag with a packet of paper handkerchiefs poking out from a side pocket. I stand before the dining table and listen to the silence. It's a strange silence.

My gaze falls on a plate with biscuits on the coffee table, and I walk over. They are my favourite ones! With sugar and cimmanum! I take one and bite it in half, and chew while I glance at the back window. Patsy won't come in here; she wouldn't dare. I think my legs know that too. They've stopped shaking.

I take another biscuit. Everything on the table is so pretty. Like the blue china cups and biscuit plate with the pink roses on them. Mum only uses them for special occasions. It is strange that the cups are still filled with coffee. I look at the door. Where is she?

I finish my biscuit and begin stirring one of the coffee cups. The cup feels warm against my palms when I carefully lift it from the saucer and bend my head over it. It smells awful. Slowly, I dip the tip of my tongue into the brown fluid. Yuck! How bitter it tastes! I tug at Nain's crocheted doily to move the sugar bowl that's on it towards me and put two heaped teaspoons of sugar in the cup. Only a little better. The bitterness is still there. I'm surprised Mum is so keen on this.

I place the cup back on the saucer, but when I let go of it my thumb catches in the ear and the cup tumbles to the floor. It's not broken but there's a big dark stain on the carpet. Shocked, I stare at it. Oh no, what will she do? Will she smile at me and say: 'It's alright, love,' and pat me on the head? Or will she shout at me: 'Look what you've done!' and smack me on the head?

I don't know which one it is and now the wet towel in my tummy is back. Mum only just cleaned the other stain I made. That was my fault too. I had helped Dadi with bringing her coffee, but it went wrong. He gave me the cup on a saucer and I walked to the living room with it. I took very small steps and so did Dadi; I felt the warmth of his body behind me.

But then the coffee sploshed over the rim of the cup, and there was a hot puddle of coffee on the saucer and my thumbs were in it. Dadi didn't know that my thumbs were hurting in the hot puddle and that I almost couldn't balance the saucer anymore. And Mum was on the sofa, reading, and I still feel sorry for her because she thought she was getting coffee, and she was nice to me. She smiled at me, and said: 'is that for me?' And I said: 'yes, it is.'

But the hot coffee suddenly dripped on my wrist. I saw Dad's hands shooting out beside me. He wanted to help me but the cup tumbled off the saucer, and it broke, and there was a big coffee spill on the carpet.

'My favourite cup!' Mum yelled, and she threw a magazine against the window that landed on a cactus with purple flowers.

'Don't worry,' Dadi said. 'I'll get you another coffee and I'll clean it.' But this made it worse.

'No, just leave it there,' Mum shouted. 'It'll be a reminder for us all, of how I can never get a moment of peace in this household.'

The household is me, because on her way out of the room, she slapped my shoulder and it hurt.

Dad didn't move; he didn't say anything, so I fled to the garden and climbed up the neighbours' pear tree.

Later, Mum said: 'I'm really sorry, please forgive me, Carys. I love you.'

But her sorries don't mean anything anymore. Nothing ever changes.

♪

I'm glad the cup's not broken and quickly put it back on the table. Some coffee has splattered on my clothes as well. I press my foot into the carpet. The stain feels cold and wet and when I step off it my yellow sock is brown around the toes.

Now what? I want to flee but I'm afraid to leave the house. If Patsy and Jason are still there, they may throw me in the fire after all. Maybe Mum will be nice to me. Where is she anyway? And where's Bethan? I decide to go upstairs.

On the landing, the door of my parents' bedroom is open a little. Strange sounds are coming from it. Is someone crying? I don't think Dadi's home. He's usually at work this time of the day.

I want to be sure Bethan's alright, so I go to her room first and quietly open the door. It's a bit dark in the room because the curtains are closed and I hear her breathing before I see her in the cot. I tiptoe over and kneel before the slats.

She's asleep but the sheet and blanket almost reach her chin and I think of something Mum told Dad. Mum is sometimes scared she'll walk into Bethan's room and find her dead in her cot. *Cot death* was the word she used, like the neighbours' baby. But Dad said that the neighbours' girl was younger than Bethan and that it wouldn't happen to us. I did feel better when Dad said that.

I stick my hand through the slats and touch Bethan's hair. She smells so nice, like baby soap and banana sweets. I pull the blanket away from her chin so she can breathe better.

She moves her head but she's still sleeping. I can't lean over the cot to kiss her, like my parents do, but when Mam wakes her for her milk, I will cuddle her and play with her.

I slip out of the room, and take one more look at my sister in the cot before I close the door.

On the landing, I remember that I was looking for my mother because of the coffee spill. The sounds are still coming from the bedroom. I push against the door to open it wider and see Mum lying on her back on the bed with her knees drawn up. Her huge bare breasts are hanging to the sides of her body. Her eyes are closed and her mouth is wide open. She's got a funny look on her face. There's also another woman on the bed. She isn't wearing any clothes either. The skin on her bottom reminds me of sand on the beach; a nice colour, and it looks as though she's got a line of pebbles on the middle of her back. Her head is between my mother's legs and it's moving up and down. She makes a sound that reminds me of a growling dog. But not an angry dog; just a dog that wants to play.

I walk over to the side of the bed and stop next to the woman. They don't even notice me, but then the woman looks up with a tired look in her eyes, and says: 'Oh God! Kathy?'

Her breasts are much smaller than my mother's and her buttons aren't so red.

'Carys!' Mum sits upright and puts her hands on her breasts, like she doesn't want me to see them, even though I see them every day.

'Rotten child. You know you're not supposed to come in here.'

I let out a wail.

'Yes, cry all you like.'

Mum tries to come off the bed but I think she finds it difficult to do; she makes small movements with her bottom. She still has one hand on her breasts and puts the other on the beard between her legs. If I had to come off the bed like that, I would find it difficult too.

'You're gonna get stick for this, I can tell you that much,' she says.

At the foot of the bed, the woman is quickly putting on her clothes.

My head feels hot, like it did in the alley. If only Dad were here. I wail again, hoping she'll feel sorry for me.

'Hush,' Mum says. 'You'll wake up Bethan.'

'It's alright Kathy,' the woman says. 'It's not her fault.'

Mum takes her clothes from the floor and puts them on too.

'I only wanted to tell you I dropped a cup and now the

carpet's dirty,' I say through my tears, but Mum is doing the buttons on her blouse and doesn't make a reply.

'Wait outside pet,' the woman tells me. 'We'll be right there.'

On the landing I think about the pear tree. Patsy and Jason won't find me there; shall I go outside and hide in it?

I hear Mum's voice behind the door. 'She's only four years old. She won't remember this. She's not even aware of what she saw.'

The other woman says something too, but I can't hear it.

They come out of the bedroom. 'It's alright love,' Mum says. 'We were only in bed because we were a little tired. It's okay. Are you alright?'

I do think it's weird, what she's saying, but Mum isn't angry anymore and now I've got sunshine in my heart.

The woman smiles at me and I take a better look at her face. I think I've seen her before. Isn't she the lady who always waves at us?

Chapter 9

'You're not a big talker, huh?' Gareth glances at me but I pretend I don't notice. I'm in the passenger seat of his old Nisan that stinks of cigarette smoke. We're on our way to Chingford to pick up Kieran. He's moving in with me today.

'I'm not in a talkative mood at the moment,' I reply curtly. 'That's a different thing.'

'Ah,' Gareth says, sighing dramatically, 'the Monday Blues.'

I raise an eyebrow at him but he's got his eyes on the road ahead. 'It's not that,' I reply. 'I've just got a lot on my plate at the moment, that's all, and besides, I'm still jetlagged.'

Gareth makes a strange whistling sound. I have no idea what it's supposed to convey and don't ask.

We drive along the M25 for a while, listening to the radio, not speaking much to each other, and my thoughts are with Ryan. He sent me a text message at eight o'clock this morning. It said: *Welcome back babe. I hope you had a great weekend in Singapore. Shall I come over on Friday? I can stay 'till Sunday!*

I bite a nail and look up at the grey heads and wrinkled faces of some elderly women travelling in a large charter bus we overtake. I'll have Kieran on my date this weekend. What will I do? *Take care, babe, I'll ring you tonight. X!* That's how Ryan ended his text. I can't wait to speak to him tonight and hear his voice again. Only, Kieran will be there. I can hardly tell him to go and keep the washing machine company because I'd like to talk to Ryan in private. He doesn't deserve that. I'll have to tell Ryan to call me back on my mobile, and retreat to my bedroom; sit on my bed, as if I'm a tenant in my own home.

'Isn't this great,' Gareth says. 'A sunny Monday afternoon and we're not stuck in an office somewhere. Nothing beats the freedom that comes with being your own boss.' He reaches for the radio and turns the Beatles' 'Penny Lane' down a notch. 'It's like I always tell Cadi: 'I wouldn't have it any other way.''

'It's definitely a luxury that you never need anyone's permission for a day off,' I reply. 'Especially on such short notice.' I glance at the shoulder tear in his faded blue denim jacket. He's been wearing that thing for years while Cadi works in a clothes shop and gets good discounts. 'I don't know how I would have done this without you.'

I smile at him, but he keeps his eyes on the road, which is just as well as he's steering with only one hand.

'I did the rat race thing,' Gareth continues, 'but starting for myself is by far the best career move I've made.'

'You mean your beanie hat business?'

Gareth glances at me. 'Of course that's what I mean. It's going very well.'

My question must have come out more surprised than I'd intended it to because he sounds a little testy.

Gareth checks his blind spot, indicates right, and manoeuvres around a green and white Waitrose truck. 'Did Cadi tell you I'm going to start my own line?'

'No, she didn't.'

'Yeah, I'm going to sell them online, through my own website.' The skin around Gareth's left eye crinkles. 'It's under construction at the moment but it should be up and running before the end of summer.'

Unsure of what to say, I stare at the license plate of a Polish car driving ahead of us. How Gareth can put all his hopes and dreams on a beanie hat business is truly beyond me. Cadi works five days a week; sometimes six during busy periods. Maybe, if Gareth would man up and find himself a proper job, Cadi could save some money, cut back on hours and go for that art degree. Still, Gareth's being so helpful with moving Kieran. He was on the phone all yesterday evening, calling people he knows from the Camden Lock scene for a trailer. I don't share his enthusiasm for his business endeavours, but don't I owe him a little support?

'Well, it certainly sounds promising,' I say, after a brief silence.

Gareth flashes me a smile. 'It does, doesn't it? Online, I'll reach a lot more potential customers than I do now with my stall in Camden.'

After a while, we turn onto the B160 and I notice a sign for Highams Park, which is where Kieran goes to school. I realise with a pang of regret that it's going to be a terrible commute for him from my home in the mornings. But then, it's almost July. He'll probably break up for summer in three or four weeks or so.

We slow down for a traffic light and Gareth rolls down the top of his window a couple of inches. 'Do you know how to roll a cigarette?' he asks. 'There's some tobacco and

Rizla in the glove box.'

'I don't,' I reply, glancing at the closed compartment.

'You don't?' Gareth gawks at me. 'Cadi does.' He rolls the window back up. 'Bummer. I'm dying for a ciggie.'

'Do you mean a spliff?'

The radio presenter enthusiastically jabbers on about something in the background while Gareth gives me a penetrating stare. 'That was a nasty stroke,' he says.

'Was it? Why?' I study his face. He seems to have a vaguely amused smile around his lips, but I'm not sure. 'I didn't mean it like that,' I say.

'No, I know,' Gareth says. 'I was only joking. Anyways, I meant a regular cigarette.'

'Do you still sell it?'

The light jumps to green and Gareth revs up the engine and moves the gear lever twice. 'You're quite upfront, aren't you?'

'Am I?' I reply. I don't see what the problem is with asking a few questions. We're practically family.

'Yes, you are,' Gareth says. 'Did Cadi tell you about that?'

A car in front of us distracts me. It has a yellow 'Baby on Board' sign on its rear window with a drawing of a baby drinking from a bottle. I want my own baby. I'm sick and tired of always buying gifts for other people's babies. I want Ryan's baby. I want to stick my own 'Baby on Board' sign on Ryan's car.

'Yes she did,' I say. 'She didn't mention your line of beanie hats but she did tell me about the weed.' I giggle but I don't think he finds it funny. 'So,' I say. 'Do you still sell it?'

'I have a little dabble, occasionally.' Gareth slides his hands to the top of the steering wheel and stretches his arms. 'Why do you ask?'

'I was just thinking that if your website takes off and you'll sell thousands of beanie hats, world-wide, and models will wear them in Vogue Magazine, you wouldn't need to anymore.'

Gareth is silent and I'm wondering if I've pissed him off. The Verve is singing 'The Drugs Don't Work' and I consider pointing out the irony but think the better of it. He clearly prefers not to talk about his side venture.

We're driving through Larkshall Road now, past well-kept houses with low walls and fences that mark boundaries, and patches of grass on the sidewalks. We're almost there, and the sense of unease I've felt ever since we set off from my home is turning into proper dread. It's just the idea of having to be in her house again, which is now the scene of someone who left it in an almost psychotic state, I imagine, believing that life had too little value to go on living it.

We pull up before her house. 'Does your mum still have that big cat cage?' Gareth asks. I tell him I have no idea. Gareth turns the radio down to silent, twists his body and peers behind him at the enclosed trailer that he tries to back up neatly alongside the kerb.

Kieran must have seen us through the window because he opens the front door and watches us, leaning against the doorpost, with Lulu clutched in his arms.

'It looks like he's still in his pyjamas,' I say, glancing at my brother.

'Is he?' Gareth's mouth is half-open and he doesn't take his eyes off the trailer.

'I hope he went to school today. That's why I said we'd be here at four.'

Gareth switches off the engine and the car shudders to a halt. 'In one go,' he says, turning to me with a proud smile on his face. 'I didn't even jack-knife it! I'm really getting better at this.'

'That's great,' I say dryly. 'Well done.'

We get out of the car, cross the pavement, and walk up the cobblestone garden path that leads to Mum's house. The last time I was here, which was for Easter, she'd told me to leave. I'd taken down the Christmas tinsel and the fairy lights that still lined her bay window, thinking I was doing her a favour, but it had really angered her. 'What do you care,' she'd said, scowling at me while meowing cats crawled around her feet. 'This is my home and if I want Christmas decorations all year round then that's what I'll have. You're always so critical of me. You don't like my hair. You don't like my house. Just go away if you hate it here so much.'

So, having spent less than an hour in each other's company that's what I did. Cadi and Kieran begged me to stay, but I wouldn't listen and Foxtrot-Oscared out of there with my head held high, but outside, I slammed the door shut behind me as hard as I could, hoping to break the glass panel, and then I shouted 'Happy Easter' through the letterbox. I'd felt like a fourteen-year-old then. Not my best moment.

♪

'Alright matey?' Gareth offers Kieran the knuckles of his closed fist and my brother bumps it with his, his face breaking into a grin.

'Why are you in your pyjamas Kieran?' I ask, glancing at his burgundy checked bottoms. I step past him into the hallway and the overwhelming, sour stench of cat faeces immediately makes my eyes water. When I turn to face Kieran, I catch Gareth flinching.

'I took a nap,' Kieran says. Lulu presses her pink nose against his chin. 'I got up really early this morning in Hammersmith.'

I don't think Gareth is listening to a word we're saying. He's staring at the brown splatters of cat diarrhea that cover the bottom of the stairs and the white skirting boards along the hallway and I've never felt so embarrassed in my life. I just hope he won't blab about this to his family in Wales. What Gareth doesn't know is that whenever he and Cadi visit Mum, she goes over here a day in advance to scrub and tidy and to spritz air freshener on everything— even on the cats Mum used to have— to make her house at least a tad presentable. Obviously, when Cadi was here on Friday, she had other things on her mind.

I shut the front door behind me which jolts Gareth out of his trance and we look at Kieran. 'Did you go to school today?' I ask him.

Kieran is no longer grinning; the expression on his face looks almost pained. 'I couldn't go, I had to pack my things, didn't I?' He presses Lulu closer to his chest.

'But you promised. That's why I said we'd be here at four. See? This is why you can't be by yourself. You said you wouldn't bunk off, but you did.'

Gareth turns around and walks through the hall and Kieran follows him.

'Kieran?' I march after them.

In the living room Kieran plonks down on the sofa with a sulky expression on his face and Lulu nestles herself in a ball on his groin.

I'm about to nag him some more about school and pyjamas, but close my mouth when I notice the state of Mum's living room. As I feared, it's like getting a tour of her brain. The cat cage, a large piece of floor-to-ceiling chicken wire that Mum had put up to cordon off a section of the room, is still there even though the cats are gone. Dozens of scraps of paper, documents, letters, bills and reminders are scattered across the sofa, coffee table, and floor. The Christmas decorations around her window are back in place. In front of it, a plastic cat carrier and a large bag of cat litter, carelessly torn open at the top, sit on top of the dining table. On the floor next to the table, a withered poinsettia is lying limply in a broken red pot: its roots exposed and soil spilled all over the carpet.

But worst of all, I find the cat faeces— here too, they're splattered on the skirting boards and walls— and the urine-soaked carpet that's growing mould in the corners. You just don't get used to having a mother like this. How could she let this happen to our family home? Bethan lived here for the few years we had her. Don't the memories of her and Dad make this house sacred? I think so. Why has all the therapy Mum's had never done anything for her? It's helping me, so why not her?

Gareth has picked up a newspaper from the floor and is sitting next to Kieran who's still looking moody. 'Have you packed everything we need for Lulu?' I ask him. I don't understand why he seems so upset. We're here to make things better for him.

'No, I haven't,' Kieran says. 'I've packed most of my own things but everything's still upstairs. Lulu's bowls are in the kitchen. Can't I just stay here?'

Gareth and I share a look and I walk towards the door.

'No, you can't,' I say.

♪

In the kitchen, my shoulders drop. More chaos. The sink is filled with unwashed dishes and cutlery and the dishwater is so putrid, it's growing thriving specks of mould. More dishes, stacked on top of each other and caked in perished food crusts, are balanced on the speckled kitchen top next to a litter tray that Mum's clearly been using as a bin. It's filled to the brim with used teabags, empty soup cans—mostly Cream of Mushroom I notice—and mouldy leftover ketchup spaghetti: Kieran's favourite food.

I open a few cupboard doors and when I find a pack of cat food I stick it under my arm. Lulu's plastic food bowls are on the grimy tiles under the radiator and I pick them up. There's still water in one of them, but I think better of tipping it into the sink. The cactus on the windowsill will do just fine. It's growing small pink flowers; that must be why Mum bought it. The plant's sprouting new life, while

Mum, who is so much more valuable than a bloody cactus, was ready to end hers.

My eyes brim up, and through the window, I glance at Dad's shed in the back garden. The grey roof tiles glint in the sun, and I stare at the empty space where his rabbit hutches used to be. Something moves behind my eyes, and suddenly, I see him. He twists open one of the wooden door latches, takes a small, orange bunny from a hutch, and places it in Bethan's arms. She beams at him and pets the rabbit's head with her hand.

The two of them are there, for just a few moments, before the image fades, like a ripple on water. I'm glad this memory's come back to me. I'm grateful I still have Dad and Bethan in my heart. I just wish, I had better memories of Mum. Maybe, if I take my wall down, we could create them; now that we still have time.

I turn my attention back to the grimy plates in the sink and the litter tray-turned-bin on the worktop. If I want to create positive memories with Mum, I'll have to get past all this, and not judge her. Can I though? I do miss her. It feels wrong to be in her house without her. Had this been a regular day, she would have made me a cup of coffee and offered me a biscuit.

'Which one do you fancy?' she would've said, holding out two packets.

At least I know that I do love her. Not a bad place to start from, I suppose.

The police officers who were here on Friday drift into my mind. What did they make of Mum's home? Did they ask Kieran where his father was? Did they ask him how old he was, and if he knew where his mother kept her hoover and the washing up liquid?

I take one last look at the mess. This is not going to fly when Kieran lives with me. At my place he will get chores, and I'll ground him if he doesn't do them.

♫

Back in the living room, I put Lulu's food and bowls on the dining table beside the litterbag and cat carrier. Kieran's still on the sofa, talking with Gareth who's standing in front of the cat cage.

'This wouldn't be hard to take down, you know,' Gareth says, eyeing the cage from top to bottom. He puts his fingers through the mesh and squeezes the wire. 'The ceiling would need a fresh lick of paint.' Gareth tilts his head back and peers at it, then lets his fingers slip from the cage and glances around the living room. 'So do the walls of course, but just one weekend of DIY could make a huge difference here.'

'We're keeping the cage,' Kieran says, scratching an ankle and Lulu's head simultaneously. 'Mum's getting the cats back. She's on the phone about it every day.'

'You're joking, aren't you?'

Kieran scowls at me. 'You don't know how upset she was when they took them away. She said the RSPCA was out to destroy her and that they succeeded.'

He draws up his knees and cuddles Lulu—her paws are

on his shoulders—and adds in a sad tone: 'Mum was going to send them a cake to congratulate them but it was too expensive.'

I glance at Gareth, who's still near the cat cage, hoping to share another look of solidarity and unity between us, but he's busy with his phone.

'They're bastards,' Kieran goes on. 'I wasn't even here. If I had been here, if I hadn't been at school that day, we would still have them.'

When Kieran is upset, he takes after our father the most. He'll set his lips in the same straight, determined line while his pale brown eyes come alive like bolts of thunder. I have a sudden flash of Dad in his casket. That's when all this cat-madness started. I blame Dad. If he had allowed Mum just one cat, she might not have abducted Lulu, whom she found skulking in the car park of the Welsh funeral home where he was laid out. Lulu didn't even look like a stray. And who knows, maybe then, Mum wouldn't have taken in the other fifteen cats either. I actually think that she did this to get back at him. Dad was too strict with her. He always said no to everything. That's why Mum said the walls of this house were papered with disappointment. I remember now.

Gareth scoops some paperwork off the floor before his feet and puts it in a neat pile on the coffee table. 'The RSPCA do a lot of good work, Kieran,' he says, sitting down beside him again. But when he sees Kieran's disappointed expression, he changes the topic and says, 'No chance of a cup of coffee around here, I take it?'

Kieran gives him a funny look but doesn't reply.

I pick up some handwritten letters from a wicker chair and sit down too. 'Gareth's right, Kieran,' I say. 'The RSPCA aren't bastards. I actually make a donation to them every fourth of October. They were only looking out for the cats' welfare; that's what they're there for. Sixteen cats in a terraced home is way too many. I know she only wanted to help them but some needed veterinary care and if you can't afford that, well, then you shouldn't have pets.'

Kieran suddenly eyes me suspiciously.

'No,' I say in a stern tone, 'I already told you. I'm glad they stepped in, but it wasn't me. I didn't call them.'

Gareth says something to Kieran and I study the handwritten letters in my hands. They're letters of complaint Mum wrote to the RSPCA. She drafted several versions. The sentences are incoherent and her handwriting is almost illegible, which tells me she spit the words out when she wrote them. They've really hurt her, but then, she's so easily hurt.

'I do feel for Mum,' I continue, 'but you shouldn't have to live like this.'

'It's not always this bad,' Kieran replies.

I glare at him. It's all really beginning to piss me off now. Am I the only one who gives a toss?

'Yes-it-is,' I say. 'It is always this bad. You're growing up in a pigsty.'

'Don't talk about my house like that.' Kieran's eyebrows shoot up and his gaze flits around the room, as if he's taking it in for the first time. I'm a little surprised by his reaction. He looks so lost and confused all of a sudden. Like a wet, featherless chick, clinging desperately on to a nest its parents left a long time ago. I feel for Kieran too, but he needs to know the truth.

'Maybe, you've grown used to living like this,' I say, and remembering something I discussed with Patrick, I add: 'maybe you've become desensitised to it.'

Gareth's regarding me with a sceptical look, as if he's trying to make me shut my gob with his eyes, but I don't care. He's got nothing to do with this.

'You might think this is normal, but believe me, it isn't. This whole house reflects Mum's craziness. She's in that nuthouse for a reason.'

'Don't talk about Mum like that!' Kieran sits bold upright 'Why are you always such a bitch?'

In the silence that follows, Kieran doesn't look away. He lets me stare into his tear-filled eyes and at his quivering chin. Not often have I heard Kieran raise his voice. Certainly never at me. He always looked up to me. Or so I thought.

Lulu's disappeared. She jumped off Kieran's lap when he yelled and scampered into the hallway, probably in search of a quiet bedroom. Gareth slouches in the corner of the sofa, an elbow on the armrest; his chin cupped in the palm of his hand.

I sit limply in my chair. I've done this all wrong. A bitch? Yes, I am a bitch. That's why Daddy shouted. That's why Mummy left. And that's why Bethan is dead….

My head's beginning to spin, and then the room spins. Sharp sunlight hurts my eyes. The ice is black and slippery under my feet. We shouldn't be here. I want to go home.

Come on Bethan, let's go back. Bethan! Oh no. No! Patsy help me. Patsy. No!

My face is hot; my eyes ache. God, give me a noose. I deserve it. Can I still move?

I must come out of this.

Look around the room. Patrick's soothing voice whispers in my ears. *What do you see?*

But I can't look up; they'll see my tears. The letters. The letters on my lap.

I keep my head down and pretend I'm reading Mum's letters. The RSPCA are bastards. No, they're not. I move a finger over the word *why?* I'm not on the ice now. It was a long time ago.

'Let's go upstairs and get your stuff,' Gareth says. 'I need to have the trailer back by eight. When you've calmed down you are going to apologize to your sister; you hear me mate?'

I half look up, through a curtain of hair, and catch Kieran looking into Gareth's eyes and nodding vaguely.

'Come on then,' Gareth says, patting Kieran on the leg. 'Let's crack on with it.' When Gareth walks past me, I make sure my head's down. These letters are so interesting. He hovers near me for a moment, then follows Kieran into the hallway.

Chapter 10

I'm sitting on the foot of Mum's bed and take deliberate breaths. Just had some cold water in the bathroom. Dabbed some on my face too. Picked a spot on my chin. I'm almost back to normal. It feels like I am.

This room is fairly tidy. Traffic noise filters in through the awning windows that are both ajar. A soft breeze makes the green-checked curtains that Nain once made flutter softly. It's a little nippy in here, but at least it smells fresh.

Mum still has the green velvet Victorian chair. It's stacked on top of our old coffee table in the corner near the window. She meant to sell the table for a tenner when she got a new one but never got round to it. She'd found the chair in a pawn shop and meant to have it reupholstered but she never got round to that either. Meanwhile, she thinks nothing of letting them sit there like that for years on end.

I survey the room. She has a lot of Dad's paintings here. Around forty, I estimate, and there might be more in the attic. Some are on canvas but he used a lot of wood panels too because they were cheaper. The paintings vary in size and they're propped higgledy-piggledy against the pistachio walls. Dad put so much time and effort into his dream of becoming a successful artist.

I get up from the bed and move to the window. A cool draft brushes my face.

In the street, a couple of cyclists on racing bikes whizz past tailgating cars, and my thoughts automatically turn to Ryan because he's into cycling too. He told me he has a BMX bike. An uncomfortable niggle flutters through my belly. The last time I saw him, which was the Saturday before my trip to Singapore, there was this moment. He suddenly went all moody on me, and I didn't understand what caused it. When I asked him what was wrong, and probed him a bit, he told me he didn't mean to offend me, but he was missing his Saturday structure.

On Saturday mornings, he said, he always practises for bicycle races with his team, from nine a.m. to ten-thirty. With a proud smile on his face, he told me he'd been with the same team for five years and that they have an indoor as well as an outdoor track. At eleven o'clock, Ryan went on, he and his team give bike training to teenagers from underprivileged backgrounds, encouraging them to be active and all that, which is for another hour and a half. And after that, Ryan said, he goes home, picks up his dog, and together they go down to the dog training centre where they spend the rest of the afternoon. It bothered him, he told me with a look of discontentment plastered on his face, that he couldn't do any of it because he'd come to London to see me.

I froze up when he said that. I wanted to ask him why he'd signed himself up on a dating site. And point out that if he wanted a girlfriend, he'd have to invest time in getting to know her. That sometimes in life, you have to make choices and accept that you can't have it all. But I didn't say anything in case I made it worse.

The rest of our Saturday was wonderful though. We French-kissed a lot, and traipsed around Camden, holding hands. I introduced him to Gareth who was at work in his stall. They seemed to get on and chatted for ages, about being self-employed and the Inland Revenue. I just hope Ryan will get used to making the odd sacrifice—he probably will—and then it won't matter to him anymore because he's getting my love in return.

♪

Gareth and Kieran are talking on the landing. It sounds like they're trying to get Kieran's mattress down the stairs. Leaning my back against the windowsill, I listen to Gareth giving Kieran instructions. I'm still feeling a bit funny about the way Kieran just yelled at me and what he called me, and embarrassed that Gareth had to hear it.

My gaze falls on Dad's final work resting against the coffee table and I kneel before it to study it better. It's an oil on canvas of Brecon Cathedral. Unfinished. Dad has let an idyllic path, flanked by tall trees, spring from the bottom right corner. The Cathedral is shown from a side angle and the path meanders towards it, enticingly, as if Dad wants to encourage passers-by to pay it a visit.

He painted Brecon Cathedral often and sold quite a few of them too. His stock phrase 'I'm a Brecon boy,' still echoes through my head now and again. He was a very proud Cymro. At every family gathering, he'd get on his hobby horse and start a discussion about Saunders Lewis. I still see him in my mind: perched on someone's sofa, elbows on his knees, his fingers wrapped around some dainty plate, while raving about Lewis's *Tynged yr Iaith* lecture and guzzling slices of Bara Brith. He offered my cousins a fiver if they could pronounce the place name:

Llanfairpwllgwyngyllgogerychwyrndrobwyll-llandysiliogogogoch in one go (and they could!). Still, at home he was very serious about what it meant to be Welsh. Dark thunderbolts danced in his eyes whenever he spoke about the English who had beaten children for speaking Cymraeg amongst themselves in schoolyards. Dad always spoke Welsh to us, but we mostly answered him in English, especially as we got older. Recalling this now, I feel a stab of regret because I know it hurt him.

I pick up the painting and move back to the window to take a better look. It lacks light, and there's almost a gothic feel to the cathedral because of that. Dad used to dot light into his works by using a small brush and pastel tones, but sadly, for this one, it wasn't to be. I'm taking it home with me though. I'm sure Mum barely looks at it; she probably won't mind. And who knows, maybe Cadi can finish it for him. Dad would like the idea of that, I think, but finished or not, this painting will be honoured with a prominent spot in my living room.

I leave it on the bed for a moment and open the middle drawer of Mum's bedside table. I'm not sure if she needs more underwear, there might be a laundry facility at the institute, but I can't keep coming back here if she does. I dig up four pairs of L-sized knickers and link my forearm through the leg holes because I haven't got a bag.

Mum's duvet is almost draping over the carpet on my side of the bed so I rearrange it a little. The Marks & Spencer cover, with swirling russet and ochre leaves, was my present to her when she turned forty-eight. It cost me sixty pounds and I regret not keeping it myself; it would look better in my own bedroom. Maybe I should just take it home with me. I don't think Mum would mind; she doesn't really care about pretty things, not like me anyway.

What's that? Frowning, I step closer to the head of Mum's bed. When I straightened the duvet, it pulled away from one of the pillows and now something's poking out. Surely, it's not... I stare hard at the long, pink, bullet-shaped device. Yup. My mother's got a vibrator. And she not just has one, she must have recently used it. What else is it doing on her bed?

I shift my feet, needing a moment to come to terms with this new bit of information, then reach for the duvet and draw it back over the device. I have the same, even in the same colour, but it's hidden in a box under my bed. What if I unexpectedly end up in a hospital again? I'd be mortified if someone found it whilst going through my bedroom in search of clean undies.

Kieran's laugh pierces the wall behind the coffee table and the pawn shop-chair. His bedroom, which used to be mine as a child, is also at the front of the house. I'm not sure what time it is but it must be nearing five o'clock. I promised Gareth pizza and tiramisu for dessert, but if he needs to have the trailer back by eight, we'd better get a move on.

♫

Gareth's sitting at Kieran's pine desk in a khaki tank top; his jacket's slung over the back of the chair. The desk holds a small fish tank that's filled with twigs and leaves.

'Look at this,' Gareth says when he sees me standing in the doorway.

Kieran ignores me but at least he's dressed, wearing a dark blue shirt and red, skinny jeans that make the black sneakers on his feet look disproportionally large.

Standing beside Gareth, he watches a stick insect crawling down Gareth's bare arm.

I step closer and take another look at the fish tank. It's teeming with beasties. Some are brown and really do resemble twigs while others are smaller and a pale green. Looks like my brother's got a new hobby. A hobby he probably expects me to make room for in my home.

'They're quite fast, aren't they?' Gareth says. He tries to pick the insect up from the back of his hand, but its spindly legs cling to his skin. Gareth tugs at it a little harder, then places it on his shoulder. 'Why has it got red legs?'

Kieran shifts his feet. 'I'm not sure, but they don't usually live that long after their legs turn red. Oi, come here you! It's going down your back.' Kieran peels the bug off Gareth, then lifts up a corner of the netting that covers the tank and puts the insect back on a leaf.

'You're bringing these things over to mine, aren't you?' A vision of Lulu chasing escapees and bringing down my flower pots in the process flashes before my eyes.

'Yes, of course,' Kieran says. He sounds surprised I'm even asking, and when our eyes meet, he quickly looks away. I guess he's still feeling a bit funny about it too.

'Are you all packed here then?' I ask, scanning the room. Lulu's on the windowsill, watching the world go by through the voile curtain and there's a bare spot in the corner on the floor where Kieran's mattress used to be. The Tupac poster he tacked on the wall when he was fourteen is gone and I wonder if he got rid of it or packed it.

'Just Lulu and my sticks,' Kieran says.

'And,' Gareth adds, 'we were wondering if you have room for Kieran's desk at your place.' His gaze lingers on the knickers that are dangling from my arm and Kieran's looking at them too. 'We won't be able to fit it in your laundry room, from what I've heard,' Gareth says, 'but maybe you have a spare corner somewhere? It's not that big.'

I can't help smiling. I love how Gareth's got Kieran's back. My brother doesn't have much else. But even so, this is where I draw the line. There's only one spot left in my home for a table, which is against the right wall in my open kitchen area, and I'm reserving that space for a dining table and four chairs so I can have my candle-lit dinners with Ryan. I can just picture myself sitting there with him, and, in time, with his parents too when I invite them over for lunch or dinner.

'Well actually,' I say, 'I was wondering if we could take Mum's dining table and her chairs. They will fit in the trailer, won't they?'

'You can't just take Mum's furniture,' Kieran says, crossing his arms. 'She's coming back.'

'I know that,' I say. 'And when she does, I'll hire transport to get it back here.' I glance at Gareth but he shifts his gaze to the tank on the desk. 'I'm not stealing it. And you'll have more room to do your homework.'

'Kieran drops his arms and puts his thumbs through the belt loops of his jeans. 'As long as you bring it all back.'

I look at my brother, a little exasperated. The older he gets the more he's like Dad. Difficult.

'It'll fit,' Gareth says. *No problemo.*' He scratches the back of his head, and adds: 'Opportunist.'

I stare at him. Am I? Is that how I come across? Gareth tends to crack jokes with a straight face, so I never really know what the deal is with him.

Kieran picks up the tank from his desk and Gareth gets up. 'Do you want me to carry that,' he says, but Kieran's already walking past me towards the door. Gareth puts his jacket on and follows him to the landing.

'Have you brought enough clothes and everything you need for school?' I call out to Kieran.

'Check,' he calls back. I hear them sniggering while they thump down the stairs. Are they taking the piss? I know I can come across a little controlling sometimes but I'm only trying to make things run smoothly for my brother.

I'm about to walk through the bedroom door, but stop and look up at the three-dimensional corner above it; the point where two walls meet the ceiling. I've never forgotten what happened to me here, one evening, when I was seven years old:

Something had been very close to my eyes, as if someone was holding a hand before my face. I didn't know who it was, but it annoyed me, so I turned around to get away from it. But, after I'd turned myself around, I became aware of a semi-dark room. There were contours of furniture: a chest of drawers and a bed. And the angle from which I was viewing this, made me realise I wasn't standing on the floor. I was in a high position, against the ceiling above the door, and I understood then that the 'annoying thing' before my eyes had not been someone's hand but the corner behind me, where two walls met.

Everything looked so strangely familiar though. The long white chest of drawers; I had one just like it in my own room. The green curtains above the bed let light through, like mine always did. But what was that? There was Mr Owl, holding a book between his wings, the two beaver brothers and Miss Stork! I had those curtains in my own room too! Aunty Mary had given them to me and she'd told me the names of the animals.

Then it hit me. This was my room. I looked at the bed again and now I noticed the dark shape of someone lying under the covers. So, if this is my room, I thought, then that is my bed. But, if that is my bed… then I'm the person lying in it.

Unsettled. That's how it made me feel. Not frightened, but definitely unsettled. Maybe that's why my body woke up, and I was in it again. I lay awake for some time, after this experience, trying to wrap my mind around what had just happened.

Later, when I was older, I came to see the experience as a gift. This incident, together with my accident in Sweden, became a source of deep comfort in the many moments during my life in which I grieved for Bethan and Dad. We can leave our bodies, and when we do, we're still alive. Although I don't know what life is like in that state. During my near-death experience in Sweden, which happened when a horse threw me, I saw a glimpse of the other side, but even then that didn't become clear to me. All I know—from these experiences—is that we are energy forms and that we go somewhere. It's enough for me to be convinced I'll see my loved ones again one day.

♫

Downstairs, I scour the kitchen for a plastic bag for Mum's undies and take it to the car along with Dad's painting, then look for Kieran and Gareth in the living room. They're sitting opposite each other at the dinner table; the cat carrier between them.

'I'll be honest with you, bro,' Gareth says, rolling a sheet with tobacco between his thumbs and middle fingers. 'We're really scraping at the moment. But once I have this all up and running we'll be able to save some serious money.' Kieran nods at him. He seems almost enthralled. He used to look at me like that, when he was younger, but I think Gareth's taken my place. It's good for Kieran to have a male role model in his life. I just wish he had one who didn't do drugs.

'Shall we go then?' I say.

Gareth seals the rizla with the tip of his tongue. 'We've got news.'

'I'm going with them to Southport this weekend!' Kieran slams his hands down on the table.

I haven't seen my brother this excited in a very long time, but that doesn't mean I'm particularly happy with their announcement.

'Won't Cadi mind?' I say.

'No, she doesn't.' Kieran's put a knee on his chair and he's leaning forward on the table. 'We already texted her and she said it's fine. They're picking me up from school on Friday.'

Gareth sticks his ciggie behind his ear. 'It would be a nice break for him. He's had a stressful weekend.'

I'm thinking for a moment. I can't believe I've been thrown a lifeline. I can have my weekend with Ryan alone. But, I'm responsible for Kieran now. I realise they didn't just ask me for my permission, but I don't think he should go.

'Are you going to that festival again?' I ask Gareth.

'No, that's in August,' he says. 'We're going there too, but this weekend it's just clubbing.'

'I don't want Kieran to take ecstasy pills.'

Kieran rolls his eyes and kisses his teeth, but I don't care that I'm embarrassing him. 'I'm serious Kieran,' I say. 'It's dangerous. You'll get thirsty and not know how much water to drink—'

'Carys,' Gareth says. 'What do you take me for? I promise you I'll look out for your brother. Come on, he's my brother too. He won't take anything, if that makes you feel better, and we'll drop him off at your place again Sunday evening.'

'Are you staying at a hotel?' I ask.

Kieran sits down on his bum again and cups his chin in his hands, as if he's resigned himself to being discussed by the adults.

'No, we're staying with a cousin of mine,' Gareth says. 'We stayed with him last year too.' He sniggers. 'Like we could afford a hotel.'

'But you are going to school on Monday, right?' I'm talking to Kieran but I'm still looking at Gareth.

'No worries,' Gareth says. 'He won't bunk off. Not again.' He casts Kieran a mock-stern glance.

'Alright then,' I say. I'm still not happy but what can I do? I'm not his mother and he is seventeen. And of course, I do have Ryan to consider. 'I guess he can go. As long as you don't drink and drive.'

Gareth slumps his shoulders and closes his eyes in a dramatic gesture, but Kieran smiles at me.

'Are we done here then?' I say.

'Just your table,' Gareth says, getting up.

Kieran grabs the cat carrier. 'And Lulu of course.' He disappears to the hall and thumps up the stairs moments later, in search of his pet.

I step back to make room for Gareth. He tries to lift the table by himself, but when I offer my help, he tells me to just do the chairs.

♪

It's a quarter past seven by the time Kieran and I thank Gareth for his help and he sets off for Camden. Standing on the pavement, before my landlady's house in Kew, we wave him goodbye and watch the empty trailer he's returning rumble down the road towards the roundabout, until it disappears from view and joins the muted hum of distant traffic.

Kieran turns around but waits when he sees me making a visor with my hand against the glare of the evening sun. Four white streaks cut across the pale blue sky above us, in multiple directions and at different altitudes. The only good thing about this whole situation, I think, listening to the fading drone of the engines, is that I've been given special leave from work and won't have to fly for another ten days. One of the many things I sorted out this morning. I also spoke to Patrick. When I called his office to move my Tuesday appointment to Friday, he'd called me back for a chat. That was nice of him.

I slip my hands into my jean pockets and we walk around the red-brick end of terrace where I'm renting the first floor plus attic from Mrs Meads, the elderly lady who lives below me.

'It was quite a day,' I say, as we saunter through the garden at the back of the house.

'It was quite a weekend,' Kieran replies. I notice him looking at the stained-glass owl on Mrs Meads' rear door. It's perched on a tree branch in front of a full moon. Next to the door is Mrs Meads' kitchen window. Behind it, on a rusty chain, hangs a large panel of a still- life fruit bowl, crafted with thousands of pieces of coloured glass. Her home is filled with glass art, especially downstairs. It's like she lives in her own museum exhibition.

At the far end of the house, a winding metal staircase

leads to my front door, and when we enter my narrow beadboard-wallpapered hallway, Lulu greets us with querulous meows.

Kieran quickly scoops her up. Already, it feels as if the energy in my home has changed. Not necessarily for the worse, but it does feel different now.

The living room still smells sour. A potpourri of pizza cheese melted over mushrooms, greasy pepperoni and onions. Kieran slouches on the sofa with Lulu on his lap and I decide that this is the perfect moment to treat my brother to a mini-lecture on lavender tea and all its glorious benefits for body and mind. But after just a few sentences, a blank look comes over his face and he cuts me off mid-sentence: 'I'll have Tetley, please. One sugar.'

I tell him I haven't got sugar, but in the kitchen it occurs to me that I have got icing sugar and I ask him if he'd like that. He says he doesn't.

'As it's sugar it'll probably taste the same,' I say. 'Do you want me to stir some through your tea?'

Kieran leans his head back against the sofa and closes his eyes. 'No, that's alright, thanks,' he says. 'Just some milk, please.'

'I only have soy. Is that alright?'

Kieran keeps his eyes closed. 'I guess.'

The empty boxes of the pizzas we devoured still litter the kitchen top. Kieran had initially put his fish tank there, next to the kettle and toaster, but I told him to take the sticks to his room and suggested leaving them on the washing machine. 'There's too little space here,' I said, and to further prove my point of needing every bit of working space available, I took out my drying rack and put it on the right, against the windowsill, under the herb pots.

Mum's dining table is covered with my Habitat plates and dessert bowls and I think Lulu may have helped herself to my pizza crusts. I glance at Kieran. He's still resting with his eyes closed. I was going to give him some domestic chores, but I guess it can wait.

I put two mugs of tea on the coffee table, step over Kieran's outstretched legs and sit down beside him.

He opens his eyes. 'I dozed off there for a moment,' he says, rubbing a finger over the fluff that's sprouting above his top lip. He does that a lot, I noticed today. He puts Lulu in between us and reaches for his mug. 'It's hot,' I say, and after that we slurp tea and don't talk for a while. The evening's last rays of sunshine create a warm glow in the kitchen but don't extend to where we are sitting. I consider switching on the lights of the Venetian chandelier that hangs above the coffee table, but then remember that only one of the six light bulbs is actually working and don't bother.

After a few minutes the silence between us is beginning to get on my tits. Kieran's either staring into his tea or straight ahead of him, blinking his thick lashes sporadically, acting as if I'm not here. I've put a teaspoon of icing sugar in his mug but he doesn't even comment on its subtle sweetness (I sipped from it myself; I've made him a really nice cuppa). Does he even feel comfortable around me? I've always loved him to bits because he's my little brother, but we were never that close. He was always closer to Cadi. Maybe the age difference between us is too big.

I ruffle his hair with my hand. 'How are you matey?' I say, trying to mimic Gareth's voice.

He makes a dodging movement with his head. 'Don't'.

'I wish I could give you a better room.'

Kieran's eyelashes point south again. 'No worries. It'll do. It won't be for long anyway.'

'That's true,' I say. 'It won't be for long.'

Kieran sits up with a start, spilling drops of tea on his hand. 'Do you have any idea how long it will be for?' Lulu, jolted from her nap, glances at him cautiously.

'Not a clue,' I reply.

Kieran wipes his hand on his jeans, slumps back and we're silent again, absorbed in our own thoughts, until my landline rings. It's on a side table in between the sofa and the window and I lean over, against the armrest, to see if there's a number on the display. As I expected, it's Ryan. I move back to the middle of the sofa.

Kieran looks at me. 'Aren't you going to get that?'

I shake my head.

'But maybe it's the hospital. Maybe it's Mum.' His voice is a good octave higher.

'It's someone I'm seeing,' I reply. 'He's just phoning for a chat, but I'm not really in the mood to talk right now.'

'Neither am I,' Kieran says.

The answering machine kicks in and Kieran and I listen to Ryan's voice.

'Hey babe… it's me. I hope you're alright and you had a good trip. I just checked the news… no planes have come down. Just kidding. Um... you're probably asleep, you must be very jetlagged. So, yeah, as I said, I can come over this weekend. Friday evening, if that's alright with you. I wouldn't have to leave until Sunday. So, um, yeah, let me know. I'll probably speak to you tomorrow. Bye.'

Oh, no. He's gone. I so wanted to speak to him. I want us to move forward. But what could I have said?

'Hi Ryan. I'm not in bed, actually. My brother's just moved in with me, and I came back from Singapore yesterday.'

'Why?'

'I don't know, I just did. Que sera sera, eh?'

'Was that your boyfriend?' Kieran asks.

'Sort of.'

'It's just as well I'm in Southport this weekend,' Kieran says. 'You don't need me around when you're with him.'

From the corner of my eyes I see Kieran sipping tea and I'm thinking of what to say. I need to be quick. Something to let him know he's wrong. What though? My silence takes too long and in the end I say nothing and Kieran and I just sit awkwardly beside each other.

'Mum always wakes me in the morning.' Kieran leans forward and puts his mug on the table. 'I have to get up at six tomorrow. It takes a lot longer to get to school now.'

'I'll wake you up.'

He gets up from the sofa, his body half-turned to me, and moves a hand through his fringe. 'Can I brush my teeth in the kitchen or do you want me to use the bathroom?'

I smile at him. 'You can do that here, whatever you prefer.'

He moves towards the kitchen, but stops mid-way and

stares at Dad's painting of Brecon Cathedral on the wall beside the hall door. When Kieran and Gareth were taking stuff from the car earlier, I'd removed a poster-sized picture of a splendid Santa Monica sunset to make room for Dad's art but he hadn't noticed yet.

'Wasn't that painting in Mum's bedroom?' Kieran asks, sounding confused.

'It was. I was going to ask Cadi to finish it actually.'

'But Mum wants it back. I know she does.'

'I'll give it back then, Kieran. No worries.'

He nods and moves past Dad's piano and a fully stocked bookcase. The door to the laundry room opens and closes and my heart almost aches at the sound. I'm worried that something inside of Kieran's been damaged. He's lived with a mental patient for years, and now he sleeps in a utility room at his sister's house.

Lulu climbs onto my lap and nuzzles her wet nose against my hand.

Oh Dad, I think. Why did you die? You were supposed to take care of us. My eyes seek out the framed picture of a rainbow on the mantelpiece and I feel a jolt of guilt. 'I know it's not your fault,' I mutter. 'You didn't go on purpose.'

Chapter 11

Patrick's got a crotch bulge. I've never noticed it before, but then, I've never seen him wearing jeans before. He's sitting across from me, knees touching, flat hands resting on his thighs. A dust-speckled shaft of sunlight brightens the silver bits in his hair. Before him, on the glass table, is his clipboard with notepad and three scraped carrots on a saucer. There's a cup of coffee for me—and a box with tissues.

'Was this completely unexpected?' he asks. His eyes flit to the window, as if he's pondering his own question.

I shift in my chair and glance at Van Gogh's blossoming branches over his shoulder.

I now understand what Cadi meant when she told me she was sick and tired of talking about Mum. She's all I've talked about this week too.

'Yes and no,' I say. 'She's done this before, of course. Five years ago. And her psychiatrist at the time did say they were bound to see her there again…' I pause to think about how to finish this sentence. The crotch bulge is quite big. It's distracting me.

Patrick glances at me and crosses his legs.

'We thought she was doing better,' I continue. 'She seemed to have her life back on track. Only then the RSPCA took her cats.'

'She had cats?' Patrick picks up the clipboard.

'Yes. Sixteen. She still has one, but that one's with me now.

The neighbours complained about the smell a couple of times. My brother told me that, so I think they were behind it. Anyway, a few of the cats needed treatment… she says she took them to a vet, but, I don't know… apparently, she has to go to court.'

Patrick makes ankle circles and writes. I feel like I have to let out a big sigh, but I try to hold it in, in case Patrick thinks I'm bored or tired. My breathing's getting worse though.

It feels as if big fat Patsy's sitting on my back, and my chest hurts when I inhale. I close my eyes and place a hand on my stomach. I can sense Patrick's eyes on me while I breathe in through my nose and out through my mouth.

'I hear you saying how stressful all this is for you,' Patrick says, when I open my eyes.

I meet his remark with silence.

The carrots glint in a beam of light that breaks through the large window; the shiny glass of the coffee table reflects a strip of white ceiling. My breathing's getting better.

Patrick flicks through his notepad and seems to be reading his own comments. He raises his eyebrows. 'How would—'

'I'd rather not talk about my mother.'

'You don't think we should address what your mother did and explore your feelings about it?'

'Not really. No.'

'Hm.' Patrick nods pensively.

'We already talked about it when you called me on Monday,' I say. 'And I've also talked about it with my best friend Flora, my supervisor from work and my sister, Cadi. Everything's always about Mum, and talking about it doesn't help anyway; it doesn't change anything. I need to think about what she's done, and come to terms with it, and then I can talk about it again, but not now.'

'Carys, if you're not ready for this then we won't talk about it.'

Patrick writes something down, then pauses and plucks at his beard. He holds the notepad flat on his legs. The crotch bulge rises over it, like a mountain over a lake.

I fantasize about Patrick sometimes. In one of my fantasies, his beard tickles the inside of my thighs while his tongue works its magic down there. I can't say I particularly fancy him. I'm just curious. Curious what it would feel like to have him on top of me. And inside of me.

Patrick puts the notepad on the glass table. The teeth of his zipper pull taut across the curve of his crotch when he sits back. My belly button twitches. Maybe he's got a big fat cock. Or enormous ba—

Patrick's staring sharply at me.

I stiffen in my seat and stare back, feeling my pupils dilate.

Oh, God. He can't know what I was thinking, can he? Or, did he pick it up somehow? My heart flutters. Nah, surely not? That's impossible.

Outside in the street, someone shouts. The room is quiet.
Oh, stop looking at me like that!

Patrick shifts in his seat. 'I'm setting up a family constellation group,' he says, still holding my gaze. 'Do you know what that is?'

I shake my head and try to listen to him with an expression of utter interest on my face. Anything to get past this dreadful moment.

'So, it's in a group setting?' I ask when he's explained it. 'I'm not sure about that.'

'I think it could really benefit you,' Patrick says. 'And not just you. Kieran as well.'

I stare at the glossy varnish on my bitten nails. I don't want to go to this family thing but I find it difficult to tell him that because he's so nice. How would strangers pretending to be my family members ever help me? It sounds like a complete waste of time. Maybe I'll tell him I'm abroad on the day.

'I sense some resentment,' Patrick says.

'Well, yeah... I just don't think it's for me.'

'Why is that?'

'What if there are people in the group who know me? I'd be mortified.'

Patrick gets up and returns with a different notepad which he took from a drawer in his desk. 'Let's see,' he says, sitting down. 'I have someone named Mitchell. He's over forty. Do you think you might know him?'

I shake my head.

'A girl called Mandy?'

'No. I don't know anyone called Mandy.'

'Someone called Rose.'

I almost give a start. 'Rose?'

'Not your mother's Rose. This Rose is much, much younger.'

'I don't know,' I say. 'I just don't think group therapy is for me. I don't like to be surrounded by strangers.'

'It's not always about what's comfortable and what's not,'

Patrick says. 'But you don't have to decide now; I still have some places left. If you could let me know by the end of next week?'

I tell him I will.

He gets up and walks to a large metal filing cabinet against the wall to my right; there's a hollow clang as he opens and closes a sliding door.

I take this moment to drink my coffee. Patrick's window is gleaming in the sun and I notice he's stuck three white bird silhouette stickers on it. No more snapping of little feathered necks against this office.

The golden rain tree is still in bloom. From here its flowers resemble bunches of yellow grapes. Maybe Ryan and I will have a little cottage one day, with a sprawling garden, somewhere in the countryside. I'll definitely plant a golden rain tree then, and some fruit trees and—

'Right.' Patrick sits across from me again, holding a carton box on his lap. 'I have something here.' He rummages through the box and takes out several Playmobil figures which he lays out on the table before me: adults and children, males and females.

'I used to have those,' I gush. 'I had horses and chickens and sheep. I pretended the figures were me and my family and that we were living on a big farm in Wales.'

Patrick smiles but doesn't reply, still going through the box. 'I used to have a toddler figure,' he mutters under his breath, 'but maybe Carol took it... Oh, wait, here it is.' He places a toddler in a lime green dress on the table with the rest of the figures and puts the box on the floor next to his feet.

I stare at the toddler figure and pick her up. 'Is this Bethan?' I ask, surprised.

'She could be,' Patrick says. 'If it feels right.'

'For some reason, it does,' I say. 'But I don't know why.'

I study the toddler in my hand. It's a toy, and yet it's not. Could it be the colour of her hair and the dress? In one of the pictures I have of Bethan she's wearing a dress in a similar shade of green. Is it that?

'You may place Bethan on the table before you,' Patrick says, 'and what I'd like you to do now, is take a look at the other figures and choose one of them to represent yourself.'

It feels a little silly to me but I do as I'm told. Glancing at the figures, I waver between a female adult and a child, both with brown hair and red dresses, then go for the female adult— I am almost thirty after all—and stand her on her feet.

'Now, I would like you to look at the figures again,' Patrick says, plucking at his beard, 'and pick one that represents your mother.'

I study the figures in front of me and pick one with black hair and a green jacket.

Patrick leans forward in his chair to take a better look. 'That's a male figure.'

'I know.'

A smile moves across his lips. 'Why does this figure represent your mother?'

'Because this one's not wearing a dress. It's just more like her than the other figures.'

Patrick writes while I try to decide who should represent Kieran and Cadi. I'm beginning to enjoy this little game. I pick a boy with blue trousers and a red jacket, move an arm, and let him hold hands with the figure I picked for myself. 'This is Kieran,' I say.

'You're holding Kieran's hand,' Patrick observes.

'Yes, I have to help him.'

'Why does Kieran need help?'

'Our parents have abandoned him. And now I'm going away next Friday. I have to go to Toronto for three days and I'll abandon him too.' My eyes tear up as I talk because I see him in my head: all alone in my home, picking at the burnt toast he's made himself for dinner.

'What emotion does this bring up for you?' Patrick asks. His own eyes gleam too, but probably because of reflecting sunlight.

'I feel sorry for my brother. And I worry about him. But I'll help him become more independent. I'm going to teach him how to cook. Or at least show him how the microwave works. My mother doesn't have a microwave. And I'll give him money for groceries, so he can buy his own food when I'm flying.'

'You're a caring sister.' Patrick pauses, then says: 'I, too, think that seventeen-year-old boys need looking after, and you're providing him with his basic needs. Should it turn out however that this current arrangement is not working, for whatever reason,'—Patrick casually waves a hand—'there may be other ways to support him as he's under eighteen. I could help you with that, so do keep me in the loop, alright?'

'I will, thank you,' I say, and Patrick writes. I turn my attention back to the table. Which figure should I pick for Cadi? Definitely a child. The one in the red dress or the yellow? I go with the latter and stand her up on her feet. 'Meet Cadi,' I say, upbeat.

'You've picked another child,' Patrick observes. 'Not an adult figure.'

'No, I'm the adult in the family. They always call me when they have problems. Although it's not as bad as it used to be. I tell them *no* a lot more now and sometimes I just hang up the phone if it gets too much.'

Patrick leans his elbows on the armrests and makes a roof with his fingers. I thought he would give me some feedback on my comment but he seems preoccupied with the toys on the table. After a short silence he says: 'Cadi's wearing a yellow dress… I'm just wondering…why didn't you pick the child with the red dress for Cadi?'

'Because, the girl in the yellow dress is kinder,' I blurt. 'She looks sweeter.'

'Why do you think that?'

I glance at both figures.

'Their faces are the same,' Patrick says. 'Their hair, too.'

I keep my gaze on the figures on the table. I suddenly don't like the game anymore. It's stupid.

'Your figure is wearing a red dress,' Patrick goes on. 'Is she not kind and sweet?'

I open my mouth, but nothing wants to come out. I search my mind for the best possible answer to Patrick's ridiculous question, when suddenly it feels as if a dam breaks open in my brain and everything I've tried to contain floods out.

'No,' I say, my voice shaking. 'She's a horrible cow.'

Patrick shifts in his chair. 'What makes you say that?'

I stare at my thumbs and shrug my shoulders. 'Because… she does everything wrong.'

'Can you name a few examples of what it is she's doing wrong?'

I think of where to start and swallow some saliva that still tastes of coffee. 'She's not pretty enough. Her job makes her nervous but she doesn't know how to change it…' My voice trails off because I wish it wasn't so wobbly. Patrick's watching me. I feel safe here with him, so I go on. 'She only has one friend, and she's quite judgemental and too upfront. And she let her sister drown.'

'She let her sister drown.' Patrick allows a silence. 'Is that really what happened, Carys?'

I look at the figures on the table and seek out the child with the red dress. She's lying there alone, apart from the family I chose.

Patrick watches me, as I lean forward and stand her up on her feet, next to my empty coffee cup and saucer. 'This is me,' I say flatly. 'The child-me. That's why I didn't pick her for Cadi.'

'Do you think you're being fair on that little girl in the red dress, Carys, when you accuse her of letting her sister drown?'

I sit back and tuck a strand of hair behind my ear. 'Fair? I don't know. I'm just very angry with her, about what she did.'

'What did she do that's making you so angry?'

'She upset her mum. On purpose.'

'She upset her mother?'

'Yes, and if she hadn't done that, Bethan would still be here today.'

Patrick leans one elbow on the armrest. 'Did she know what would happen, when she upset her mother?'

I shake my head and feel my eyes brimming up. 'No, not at all. She had no idea of it. If she had known, she wouldn't have said anything that morning; she would've stayed in bed.'

Tears trickle down my face and Patrick plucks two tissues from the box on the table and gives them to me.

'Such small decisions,' I say. 'How can they have such an enormous impact? Nothing can be taken back.'

I dab my face with the tissues and sniff. 'It was the first step in Murphy's Law.'

Patrick holds my gaze and nods.

'That's what they always tell us at work. Avoid Murphy's Law by breaking a chain of mistakes. Intervene in time.'

I sniff and wipe my fingertips over my face. 'But Patsy… what she did…'

Tears drip down the sides of my nose, catching on my nostrils. It tickles and I blow into the tissues.

Patrick hands me more and I dab my wet eyes. The tissues are streaked with mascara smudges.

'When I brief passengers who sit next to an emergency exit, I always have to ask them if they are afraid of flying,' I say, after a pause. 'That's because some people who panic freeze up, and when that happens, they might not open an emergency exit when they should.'

The tips of my wet lashes graze the skin above my eyes as I glance at Patrick. 'I sometimes wonder if Patsy belongs in that category. She was eleven years old. She could easily have pulled Bethan out. But maybe she didn't, because she panicked.'

I sniff and look down at the scrunched-up tissues in my hands. 'Only.. that still wouldn't really explain it, because... even if she did panic, she could have let me try to save Bethan, but she did the opposite of that. She did act, but it was the wrong action.'

Silence. Patrick's computer is not humming today, and the window doesn't creak. I just hear cars driving down the road.

My forehead throbs and I gaze at Patrick. I wish he were an oracle. I want answers. I want everything clarified. I want to feel at peace.

Patrick opens his mouth and there's a noise coming from his throat that sounds as if he's clearing phlegm. 'Excuse me,' he says. 'It's difficult to grasp what happened in that moment, Carys. I think it's quite possible that Patsy's actions were driven by panic, but then, I wasn't there. What I do know is that you were all children. You were six. Patsy was eleven and...'

Patrick's voice is growing distant, as if he's floating away from me. A bright light hurts my eyes; the ice is so cold, so slippery. We shouldn't be here. I want to go home. *Bethan! Let's go back. Where is she Patsy? Oh no. No! Patsy help me. Patsy. No!*

'….part of your story, and I think that would help you...'

The boughs. The boughs on the poster. I see them behind Patrick's shoulder. He's looking at me, but I'm looking at the boughs. White petals on crawling boughs. Van Gogh painted that. Dad's cathedral was like an anchor. White petals and the blue is so vibrant.

'Are you alright Carys?' Patrick's beard moves when he talks. His cheeks are ruddy.

'I'm tired,' I softly reply. 'I'm very tired.'

'I hear what you're saying. This is draining; we've done a lot of work today.'

Patrick glances at the clock on the wall above the filing cabinet. 'Next time you're here, we'll look at some rituals that could help you with—'

'I want her to say she's sorry. That's all I want. I need to see her.'

I pick Bethan up from the table, bend her legs at the middle and sit her up in the palm of my hand. Her hair is brown; her complexion peachy and her smile full of innocence.

I wanted to help you, I tell her in my head. *But she stopped me. Do you know that? No one believes me, because no one else was there.*

I'm feeling dizzy. I'm not breathing right, but I don't let my sister out of my sight. *She'll say sorry to you Bethan. I'll make sure she will. And I can't wait for the day when I'll see you again.*

Everything's unfolding as it should. Surprised, I listen to the voice in my head. It's a male voice; one I've heard before. A long time ago. Almost thirty years.

I shake my head. 'No,' I reply. 'I don't believe that. Not at all. It's not true.'

'Are you alright, Carys? Can I get you some water?'

I glance at Patrick. 'No, thank you.'

He looks at me in a way I've not seen before. The frown between his brows is deep.

'Are you sure?'

I tell him I'm fine and smile, but I can see that his eyes don't trust me.

'We did a lot of work today,' he says again and starts putting the figures back in the box next to his feet. Bethan is the last to go.

He gets up and walks to his desk where he flicks through a large diary. 'When do you have time for me?'

'Next Thursday.' I lean to the side of my chair and drop my scrunched-up tissues in my handbag. I don't see a bin anywhere. I can hardly leave this ball of snot and tears on the table. 'I'm flying again next Friday.'

We shake hands and Patrick sees me to the door where I fish my jacket off a wooden coat stand. A scruffy boy, maybe Kieran's age, with clumps of hair missing from his head, jumps up from the sofa in the waiting room the moment he sees Patrick. I wonder what they discuss together.

'Will you think about my project and call me?' Patrick says, before I leave.

I tell him I will. I won't though.

Chapter 12

Lulu greets me at the living room door an hour later. Patrick's office is just a ten-minute walk from my home but I went to Sainsbury's on Lower Richmond Road for some shopping first.

She brushes her body up against my ankles on my way to the kitchen where I plonk two paper bags with groceries down on Mum's dining chairs. I'd left the radio on for Lulu, but now I turn it off and open the kitchen window that overlooks the back garden. It's a sunny day, but windy. A breeze sways the herb plants I keep in terracotta pots on the windowsill and I catch a pleasant whiff of basil. The leaves of the alder and poplar trees rustle, and the wind chime I strung up on a branch tinkles faintly.

Mrs Meads suggested getting more chimes and in different sizes for different harmonies but I haven't got round to it yet. She's still sitting on the wooden garden bench taking a break from weeding. She just asked me if I was coming back from the airport, as if she can't distinguish two paper bags from two suitcases. I cut the conversation short by saying that I wasn't, whilst briskly walking on and wishing her a good weekend over my shoulder. I'm just not in the mood for small talk right now.

Trevor, Mrs Meads' black Pug is roaming through the garden. He craps everywhere. Last year, on a warm spring day, Cadi and I thought it would be nice to have a picnic on a blanket in front of the pansies and tulips, but the wind kept blowing whiffs of Trevor's poo up our noses as we were about to gorge on bread spread with brie and mushroom pate. When Cadi cracked a joke about the pate and the poo that was it for me. I packed up and we went back inside.

I take a glass from a cupboard, fill it with water and pour it over the herb plants. My bare arm looks pale where sunlight hits it. Hopefully, the weather will be nice this weekend, like today. Ryan wants to go to Kew Gardens. I spoke to him last night and he said he only knows the gardens from brochures. He wants to take me to lunch there and go for a walk. He said he has to leave around twelve on Sunday because he's got a few things to sort out, but that works out brilliantly for me. Kieran's coming back in the evening, so for now their paths won't cross and I don't have to explain what's going on to Ryan.

I glance at the Sarah Kay clock on the wall next to the fridge. It's almost four o'clock. Kieran should be on his way to Southport by now, with Cadi and Gareth. I have about two hours left before Ryan gets here. He said he'd drive over to my place after he finished a job at five. I quickly put my shopping away in the fridge and cupboards, then look around and go through a mental list of what needs to be done before he arrives. What's important? Hiding stuff. Everything related to what Mum did and the consequences for me. Starting with the sympathy cards on the giant flower bouquets in glass vases Annette, my supervisor, sent me. Important clues to my dysfunctional family that I should hide at once.

One of the bouquets adorns Mum's dining table. Luscious lilies, peonies, and dahlias are set off by fresh ferns and silver eucalyptus leaves. My company really splashed out to show me they care; they had the florist sprinkle in some white and pink roses too. I reach for the little card that's tangled around the stem of a peony with a thin green wire and remove it. This bouquet arrived three days ago, on Tuesday, but on Wednesday an identical bouquet in an identical glass vase arrived with the same card and handwritten message: *A little something for the shock,* signed by Annette. I placed that one on the coffee table. It had made me chuckle though. The flowers perfectly reflect the typical miscommunications in my company.

Annette called me on Monday. I detected a little scepticism in her tone at first, when she asked me what the emergency had been that made me swap flights with a colleague and come back from Singapore a day early. But when I explained to her what happened she was very understanding.

'I really sympathise with you Carys,' she said, and then she became rather personal, telling me about her brother who had committed suicide when he was forty-two, and that she still struggled with it, saying that it was something 'you never get over but learn to live with.'

I almost wanted to repeat that Mum had made an attempt but wasn't actually dead, but thought better of it. It would have spoiled the moment. Before we hung up, Annette told me she would ask Scheduling to take out my next Chicago flight, giving me a total of eleven days' leave. Hopefully enough to sort myself out, she said, but my throat tightens when I realise that five days have already passed. Before I know it, I'll be swiping my passport at the Crew Centre again, leaving my life and home behind, serving strangers, working with strangers; praying we'll live.

I stick both of Annette's cards in a kitchen drawer; who knows, I might show them to my children one day when I tell them all about nutty Nan.

Right, next: Kieran. I must hide all evidence of the fact he's living in my laundry room. I pick up his shoes from the hallway and his red Adidas jacket that's slung over the rocking chair and put them in his room. His stick insects are on top of the washing machine, next to my laundry detergents, and Tupac's smiling at me from the wall beside it. The edges of Kieran's duvet drape over the lino and his schoolbooks and clothes lie in a heap on the floor next to the laundry basket that doesn't have a lid. The room has no window. It smells faintly damp in here, but mostly of lavender fabric softener. Kieran complained about that the other day. He said the scent of lavender reminded him of old biddies. I told him I'd get a different fabric softener as soon as I finished this bottle. He doesn't deserve the crappy hand of cards he's been dealt, but he's better off here than at Mum's house. I'll try to help him as much as I can in life, and for now, I hope he's having a good time in Southport.

I move on to the next item on my mental list: my bookcase. It's just off the kitchen, against the outside wall of the laundry room, next to my father's piano. Knowing Ryan, he'll head straight for my books because he's an avid reader, like myself. We've discussed several of Paulo Coelho's novels on our dates. I scan the spines for any titles I don't want him to see, but it doesn't take long before my eyes are drawn to a purple silk scarf that's wrapped around a pack of tarot cards, tucked between four books of which the tops have an even line and the bottom of a shelf. Patrick's got tarot cards too, but he doesn't consult them about every little thing—his words. I think he meant that I shouldn't either.

The question is: is my relationship with Ryan a little thing? I reach for the pack of cards because the answer is: no, it isn't. Besides, something isn't sitting well with me and I'd like some answers. I had actually wanted to ask Patrick for his advice on it today, but our session happened to go in a different direction when he took out that Playmobil set.

The thing is, during the months Ryan and I were emailing each other, he seemed rather reluctant to meet me. We were sending each other these lively, personal emails, two or three times a week, but not once did he suggest meeting up in real life. I didn't really understand it. He wanted a real girlfriend, didn't he, not a virtual one? So, I waited and waited for him to suggest it, and in the end I broached the topic myself. But between the lines of his reply, I sensed that he wasn't too keen on the idea. He said something about meeting when the time was right and not wanting to rush into anything. It was only when I wrote: *If you don't want to see me it's fine by me, but you should know that I am not sitting around waiting for anyone* that he picked a date and drove from Godalming to London to see me. But that was almost five months after he sent me his first email.

Standing before Mum's dinner table, I push the vase with Annette's flowers to the wall and unpack the cards, shuffle them, and spread them out in three half-moon rows. I'm going for a full spread using the major and minor arcana. Patrick suggested I chuck the cards or give them to a charity shop because they make me feel nervous. Like now; I'm too tense to even sit down, but I know it's my own fault. I keep asking questions I'm not prepared to receive any answer too. I can't help it though. Once I feel the cards pulling at me, I can't resist the force. I'm definitely not getting rid of them.

Lulu jumps on the table and sits down on top of the cards. I lift her up and put her on the floor, then close my eyes for a moment and try to evoke a sense of detachment. *How will my relationship with Ryan develop over the next three months?* I ask in my head. My right hand hovers over the cards and I wait until I feel the familiar warm tingling under my palm. When I feel this above a particular card, I select it. One by one, I place four cards upside down before me, then turn them over with a trembling hand. Scanning them, my heart drops.

The first two cards are great: the Lovers and the Star. But the last two cards are respectively the Moon and the Devil. I sit down on a chair and stare at the horned beast guarding the chained-up lovers. It just has to work out with Ryan. Since I left James, there hasn't been any other guy who's made me feel this hopeful of a future together. I want to be with someone who loves me. I thought Ryan would.

I glance at the table and grab a random card from the

spread. But when I turn it around, my breath catches in my throat: it's the bloody Tower. I'm done with this. Stupid cards! I stare at the three half-moon rows for a moment, then get up and begin putting them back in the box. Anyway, I think, nothing's set in stone. These cards don't decide my life.

I suddenly remember Patrick praising my ability to comfort myself, or something like that, so I think of more positive things to think. Everything is susceptible to change and I will prove the cards wrong. In fact, I might even bin them after all, but not right now. People always say that you shouldn't make important decisions when you're feeling upset, don't they? Like when I left James, just a few months after Dad died. Big mistake.

I wrap the silk scarf around the deck and put it back in its spot on top of the books. I shouldn't have done this. The self-comfort mechanism isn't working today and now I'm anxious about seeing Ryan and not knowing how wide to open my heart. When I'm feeling like this my behaviour is different from what it would have been if I hadn't consulted the cards, which somehow ends up fulfilling the cards' prophecies. Well, this was the conclusion I arrived at after discussing it with Patrick. Or something like that.

I reach for another pack of cards on a different shelf. My angel cards. They're bound to make me feel better. I don't bother sitting down and spreading them out on the table. I stand before the bookcase, shuffle the deck, ask the same question about Ryan in my head, and peel out a card. I've drawn the one that says 'Signs.'

This isn't helping me at all! There are much better cards in the pack. Disappointed, I put the deck back on the shelf. I walk to the kettle and flick it on, but then remember I still have to change my clothes and tidy my bedroom. I sprint up the stairs and decide I'll pretend this didn't just happen. I can do that. I do it all the time.

Chapter 13

'Who wrote FUCK KNOWS on here?'

I look up from my Jamie Oliver lasagne recipe. Ryan's standing in front of the bookcase, holding up Erica Jong's *What Do Women Want?*

James's comment, which he'd scrawled below the title with a permanent marker after I left him, almost reads like a subtitle.

I tuck a strand of hair behind my ear. 'Oh. My ex did that.'

Ryan turns the book over in his hands and reads the back and I glance at the spines on the shelves. I've shoved my tarot cards, Dr Phil's *Love Smart* and a Kamasutra book I once bought in India under Kieran's mattress at the very last minute, but is there anything else I should have hidden?

'Your ex,' Ryan says, slotting the book back in its place. 'Is that the guy you lived with for four years?'

I'm somewhat dismayed to note that Ryan's using the piano as a side table and put his glass of wine on it. Dad wouldn't be pleased.

'Yes,' I say, opening the cutlery drawer. 'That's the one.'

'Do you still speak to him?'

We share a glance. 'No, I've not spoken to him in years.'

'When did you split up again?'

'Five years ago.'

'So, it wasn't an amicable break up?'

James's hurt face swims before my eyes and his bitter

voice rings in my ears. '*You're kicking me to the kerb. Thanks for ruining my life.*'

I put a wooden spoon on the worktop. 'No, it wasn't.'

Ryan reaches for his wine and takes a sip. 'It's probably best to leave your skeletons where they are.'

'Yeah, probably,' I say and I smile at him because he said it in a funny tone, but he doesn't notice. He's moved his hand behind his back and lightly touches the edge of his phone which is sticking out from his pocket. James used to tell me that I think too much. Right now, I'm thinking that maybe Ryan's thinking about someone. A woman? What woman? And only because I saw him touching his phone after he mentioned skeletons. Maybe James was right. He was right sometimes. I did kick him to the kerb.

'Have you ever lived with a girl?' I ask.

Ryan turns towards me. 'No. Never.'

'Are you still in touch with any exes?'

'No.' He looks at his glass and swirls his wine. 'At least not with anyone I've not drawn a line under.'

♪

The evening sun casts a warm glow on my herb plants and I close the window because of the mosquitoes. Lulu is dozing on the windowsill between basil and sage. When I showed Ryan into my living room an hour ago, she'd immediately sidled up to him and brushed her body against his legs.

'I didn't know you had a cat,' he said.

I told him that I was looking after her for someone; that she was a temporary guest. He didn't pet her. I don't know why that stood out to me, but it did.

'Can I have some more of this?' Ryan's beside me, lifting a bottle of Chianti from the worktop. 'Of course,' I say and he tops up both our glasses. My stomach twists pleasantly at the scent of something sandalwoody emanating from his skin. Some stray chest hairs poke out from the collar of his shirt.

Ryan swallows and flattens his lips. 'Are you going to serenade me after dinner?' he says, nodding at the piano. 'Do you play any Bach?'

'I don't play at all.'

I take a packet of cheddar cheese from the fridge. 'That piano belonged to my dad. My sister inherited it but she hasn't got the space for it, so I'm keeping it for her here.'

I grab a pair of scissors from the drawer under the worktop and cut the packet of cheese open. An image of Mum wheeling the piano away from its corner to make room for her cat cage flashes though my mind. The real reason it had to go.

Ryan leans his backside against one of the kitchen cabinets and gazes at the piano as if it were a beautiful, exotic woman.

'Steinway and Sons. It must have been expensive.'

'Yes, but it's very old,' I reply.

'Didn't you want it?'

'No. My sister's the only one in our family who plays it. She's really, really good.'

'Is that your sister who works at H&M?'

I pop a sliver of cheese in my mouth. 'Yes. I only have one sister.' Bethan's little face floats before my eyes the moment

I say it. *I know you're there*, I tell her in my head.

'Oh right,' Ryan says. 'And you have a brother.'

I think of Kieran's mattress on the floor in front of my washing machine. I hope he's having a good time with Cadi and Gareth. I hope he's not taking pills.

'I meant to ask you...' Ryan puts his glass on the worktop and walks around the dining table to the painting I hung on the wall next to the hallway door. 'Is this your dad's work?'

'It is. It's the last painting he worked on. It's not finished.'

'It looks finished to me. It's very good.'

I blow a strand of hair from my face. 'Thank you. It's Brecon Cathedral. We used to go to Wales almost every Christmas to see my parents' families.' Well, Dad's family really, I think.

'Did he sell his paintings?'

'He did. He sold them at Bayswater Road on Sundays. He couldn't live off it though.'

'Most artists can't,' Ryan says.

He turns to me and I'm glad the kitchen table is between us. This conversation is starting to make me feel a bit wobbly.

'Was your father ill?'

I avert my face. Our wine glasses have attracted a tiny fruit fly and I wave at it with my hand. It bolts towards the window. I don't really want to talk about Dad. Isn't it better to keeps things a little light? But Ryan waits, not unlike Patrick, so I begin.

'No, my dad had an accident. He was an ambulance driver and one morning he was on his way to an emergency. But a lorry overtook him and clipped his ambulance. He crashed through a barrier on the motorway. A female nurse who was with him died too.'

Ryan looks at the floor. 'Was this on the news?'

'Yes, it was. It happened five years ago though.'

'I think I remember it.'

We're silent for a few moments, then Ryan says: 'So, in the space of one year, you lost your dad and you split up with your boyfriend. Was that the order in which it happened?'

'Yes, it was,' I say, and think: *And then Mum tried to kill herself, sort of, was taken to a mental hospital, told us she'd always been a lesbian but with Dad dead she was finally free to be herself, and expected me to sort out the mess she'd left behind.*

'That must have been tough.'

I nod. 'Yes, it was.'

Ryan changes the topic. 'Are we eating here?' He glances at the candles and plates I've set out on the kitchen table.

'Yes, I thought we could sit here and chat,' I say.

'We can chat all night,' Ryan says, winking at me, 'but I brought that French DVD I told you about. I thought we could watch that while we eat.'

He lunges for his black satchel that's hanging from the back of a dining chair.

I watch him and smile. He said he'd bring a French DVD and he did: he's dependable. And not only that. He's also taking steps in cementing our bond. We've talked about wanting to learn French a few times, and about what it would be like to own an idyllic holiday cottage in the Dordogne, and now he's showering our French dreams with attention. Hopefully, it'll make them come true.

I take the DVD he hands me and study the quirky, black-haired girl smiling at me from the cover. I love her name: *Amélie*. If Ryan and I ever have a girl we could call her that.

'What's it about again?' I ask.

The wine glass envelopes Ryan's narrow nose while he takes a gulp of wine. 'Read the back,' he says.

I turn the DVD over but then he says: 'It's about a girl who falls in love with a guy but she doesn't want to reveal herself to him. She leaves him clues and she's being all mysterious, but in the end, he finds her.'

'Does he fall in love with her too?'

Ryan stares into the middle distance. 'Can't remember actually. I haven't seen it for a while.'

I suggest watching the film without subtitles to see how we get on.

Ryan likes the idea. He scoops up our glasses and puts them on the coffee table. The vase with Annette's flowers goes on the floor beside it. 'We don't need the candles, do we?' he says. 'It's not even dark.'

I shove a red ceramic dish bursting with cheddar cheese into the oven. 'I guess we don't.'

'Why did you frame this picture of a rainbow?' Ryan's moved to the yellow brick wall above the fireplace; his head is bent towards the picture on the mantelpiece.

I put my oven gloves on the kitchen top and walk over to him. 'I just liked it,' I say.

Ryan regards me curiously. 'You just liked it? No, there's got to be another reason.'

'That's really the reason,' I lie. 'I just liked it.'

Ryan takes the picture in his hands and inspects it from

up close. 'Did you take it?'

'Someone else did.'

He gives me a penetrating stare. 'Your ex?'

'No, not him. A journalist gave this to me.'

'No offence,' Ryan says, still looking at the picture, 'but I've seen better pictures of rainbows. This one's really grainy.'

'It was taken on a cloudy day.'

Ryan turns to me. 'I don't think it was. Or why was there a rainbow? And good photographers know how to take pictures on cloudy days anyway. It's all about shutter speed and apertures and IS—' He glances at me but I look away.

'Never mind,' he says, putting the picture back. His fingers fold around my upper arms and he pulls me close. 'If you like rainbows so much, then I promise you I'll get you a better picture. With brighter colours.' He bows his head and leans his body into me and I melt into him. His tongue tastes of wine: dry and wet and the earthy smell of his skin makes my knees weak. Ryan closes his mouth and pulls away to look into my eyes. 'Framed,' he says, before putting his lips back on mine.

The barking of what sounds like a pack of vicious dogs startles us both. Ryan lets go of me, takes his phone from his back pocket and presses a button.

'Hello,' he says. A girl on the other end of the line instantly starts to chatter away. She sounds young and chirpy. I wish I could hear what she's saying; I can't glean it from Ryan's answers. I stare at my dad's rainbow while Ryan speaks to her.

'That would probably be best,' he says. 'Really? Right.

Well, I'll have a word with him. No, I can't. Yes, that's right. Yes, you do that. I've gotta go now. Speak to you tomorrow.'

He puts his phone back in his pocket. 'That was Leah,' he says. 'My best friend. You don't mind me saying that, do you?'

I'm not sure what to reply so I don't answer. Why didn't he mention he's here with me?

'Look,' Ryan says. He takes his phone back out and scrolls through it. 'This is her.' He shows me a picture of a girl sitting on the armrest of a sofa, evidently watching Coronation Street: a close up of Ken Barlow is plastered across the screen. Next to the TV is a leafy plant in a white pot; the cabinet below it holds a collection of CDs and DVDs. There's a cream shag-pile carpet on the floor and on the right of the picture I can just make out a pair of blue jeans in a crumpled heap on an armchair.

'Is this at your place?'

'No, this is at hers.'

'How old is she?'

Ryan drops his arm and the picture is gone. 'She's twenty-three.'

'So is my sister,' I say.

'She's very intelligent,' Ryan goes on. 'She joined Mensa when she was twelve.'

'Mensa? What's that?'

Ryan knits his eyebrows together and says in a lecturing tone: 'it's an organisation you may join when you belong to the top two per cent of Britain's population and have an IQ score of at least 132. Leah's IQ is 140.'

I think for a moment. I remember something Ryan emailed me when we'd bantered a bit about what we were looking for in a life partner. He'd written: *I'm attracted to intelligence.*

'If she's your best friend,' I say, 'and she's a girl, wouldn't it make sense to date her?'

'God no.' A look of disgust crosses Ryan's face. 'I'm not attracted to her at all! She's not pretty and too fat and all she ever wears are tracksuit bottoms and sweaters. Even in summer.'

'Can I see the picture again?'

Ryan gives me his phone and I take another look at Leah. Before, I focused on her surroundings because I wanted to know where the picture was taken and if this was Ryan's home and if there were any clues of him and Leah being an item. Now I focus on the girl. She's wearing grey jogging bottoms and black socks. A navy jumper is pulled over her thighs and her hair is mousy and cut into a bob around the ears. I agree with Ryan that she's not much to look at, but neither am I, so I don't comment on that.

'She's not fat.'

Ryan sticks the phone back in his pocket. 'She's definitely chunky.' He still has a disdainful look on his face. The way he speaks about her surprises me. He called her his best friend. It has killed the niggle of doubt I was feeling though. Who would talk about their own girlfriend like that?

'You told me you didn't like it when a girl only picks at salad leaves,' I say.

Ryan snorts. 'Did I?' His eyes roll back while he thinks.

'Yes, you did. When we had pasta and spinach balls at

Carluccio's on our first date.'

'Well, I also don't like it when a girl orders three different burgers at McDonald's because she can't make a choice or when she orders a whole pizza and has it for a starter.'

'She does that?'

'She has on occasion.'

'Maybe she's depressed.'

Ryan looks a bit puzzled. 'She has suffered with depression actually. But so what? Does stuffing your face with grub make it better?'

'Yes, it does.'

'It's self-abuse. Have some control!'

When I don't reply, he takes my hands and winks at me. His winks are becoming annoying— I'm not a child.

'You women and your food, eh?' he says.

Chapter 14

My bedroom curtain blocks most of the daylight. I've been awake for a while, lying in semi-darkness; feeling the warmth of Ryan's skin against mine; listening to the sound of the rain clattering against the window and drumming on the roof tiles.

Ryan stirs too. 'What time is it?' he says groggily.

'Around nine, I think. It feels like nine.'

He stifles a yawn, then rests his chin against the top of my shoulder and slings an arm across my bare breasts. 'It's raining.'

'It is.'

'We've had such a shoddy spring.' Ryan's breath feels warm against my neck. 'I hope summer won't be like this.'

'It's summer already,' I say, snuggling closer to him. 'It's been summer for six days. But if it doesn't clear up, we could still go to Kew Gardens for lunch this afternoon. We'd just have to do the flower gazing some other time.'

Ryan doesn't reply, so I run my finger over his smooth jawline and ask: 'Have you got any holiday plans?'

'Canada, maybe.'

'Whereabouts?'

Ryan pulls his arm off my breasts and turns on his back. 'I can stay with a friend of mine in Quebec. I stayed with him before, for ten days, but I want to go back and see more of the country.'

'I'm flying to Toronto next Friday.'

I feel Ryan glancing at me. 'You are?'

After a short silence he says: 'You were in Singapore for four days, you come home and have eleven days off, and then you fly to Canada. Is your company recruiting?'

'No, normally it's not like that,' I say. 'I took an extra week off to sort some things out.' If he asks what needed sorting out, I think, I'll tell him I wanted to do some DIY.

But Ryan's silent, then says: 'anyway, I really hope I can go. My dog needs to pass two more rounds of tests. If she passes those, I can sell her to the police and buy a plane ticket.' He yawns and adds: 'It all depends on that. I can stay with my friend for free but I still need money for food and travelling of course.'

'Won't you miss your dog when she's gone?'

Ryan turns on his side so we're face to face. 'I missed the first dog I sold. But now, every time I get a puppy, I know it's just for a few years and I don't let myself get too attached.'

'I couldn't do it.'

Ryan pulls me closer, squashing my breasts against his chest, which hurts a little.

'I know you couldn't. That's why I like you.' He plants a kiss on the top of my nose.

As he doesn't ask me about my plans for summer, I decide to mention them myself.

'I'm thinking of going to New York for my birthday.'

'Are you?'

His chest hairs tickle between my fingers and his heart

steadily pulsates against my hand. I'm waiting for him to ask me who I'm going with, and for his suggestion to come with me.

'Do you get a discount when you travel?'

'I do. When you get a standby ticket you basically just pay taxes.'

'Hm. When's your birthday again?'

'The ninth of August.'

Ryan shifts his body and stretches his arms behind him. 'Mine's September sixteenth.'

♪

Downstairs, still in my pink sleepshirt, I put the TV on and feed Lulu. Ryan said he was going to hit the shower. I take eggs from the fridge and whip them up in a bowl. Raindrops trickle down the kitchen window but it's clearing up quickly now with sunlight breaking through the clouds. This bodes well for our afternoon in Kew Gardens.

I rest my hand on the worktop, tilt my head back and close my eyes. Spring rays penetrate the kitchen window and caress my face. I vaguely listen to the upbeat voice of a BBC Breakfast presenter in the background. An Al Qaeda leader in Afghanistan has been killed in an American strike. I come out of my Zen moment and open my eyes.

Outside below me, a door closes with a thud and I see Trevor stomping into the garden, sniffing, and lifting up a leg against a fern tree. Mrs Meads lets him out by himself several times a day, often unsupervised but so far he's never wandered off into the street. I told Ryan about the two of them on our first date and said that if I ever got a dog it would have to be a pug because they're so adorable with those bulging eyes and tongues poking out. Had I known what my casual comment would unleash, I would've shut up.

'Their eyes bulge because they don't fit in their heads,' Ryan had snarled at me. 'Pugs have actually toppled over into their water trays and drowned.'

'Have they?' I said.

'Yes, they have. These dogs can hardly breathe.' He pointed a finger at me. 'If you get a pug, you'll support reckless breeding. It's criminal. It should be made a criminal offence.'

He looked so angry as he spoke. I actually thought it was the end of our date. A tone had been set from which we couldn't recover. All those months of emailing back and forth for nothing. But it wasn't like that, thank God, because Ryan suddenly moved on from our discussion as if nothing had happened. As if it was completely natural to have a go at someone you didn't even know that well, in a packed restaurant. But it sort of made me like him more. We could fight and move on—together. James and I never argued about anything and I moved on without him. I did think it was ridiculous though, when a few minutes later, Ryan stabbed a spinach ball with his fork, held it upright as if he'd just picked a fluffy dandelion, and told me he uses electric shocks on his dog whenever it's disobedient.

♫

'What are we having?' Ryan presses his chin on my shoulder and wraps his arms around my waist. A few drops of water land on the front of my shirt.

'Eggs, vegetarian sausages—if you want them—baguettes and fresh orange juice.'

'Sounds great. I'm starving.' He gives me a peck on the side of my head. 'Can I just ask: why did you become a vegetarian?'

I stare at the four pale sausages sizzling in fat on a low flame. 'Because, I felt sorry for the animals.'

'You mean the way they are treated?'

'Yes.'

'You could buy organic.'

'Not really. It's too expensive.'

Ryan loosens his embrace. 'Fair point.'

He moves to the piano and sits down on the stool. He opens the lid and tentatively begins to play the first chords of 'Für Elise.'

'You play?' I say, surprised. 'I didn't know that.'

'There's a lot you don't know about me yet,' he says, winking at me.' Then he starts again but this time he plays the full song and I'm almost enthralled by the melody.

'You can play that off the top of your head?' I gush when he's done. 'That was beautiful! I play the guitar a little.'

Ryan's eyes search the front room. 'Have you got one here?'

'No, I gave it to my brother Kieran for his birthday but he swapped it for a Warcraft game.' I roll my eyes and Ryan smiles. 'Shame,' he says. 'We could've had a musical soirée.'

He closes the lid, then gets up and watches me slice more oranges. 'Do I have to help you with anything?'

'I'm almost done.' I glance at the frying pan on the hob. 'You can turn off the heat if you want, the eggs are done.'

Ryan turns a knob and I look at him sideways. He seems different suddenly; hesitant, as if something's changed.

Our eyes lock.

'Hey um, I'm not going to Kew Gardens anymore. I can stay for another hour or so but then I'm heading back to Godalming.'

'What?' I drop the knife on the chopping board. 'You're going home? I thought you were staying until tomorrow. We were going to have lunch together. That's what you said.'

I'm not even bothering to hide my disappointment. I can hear it in my voice and feel it in the tightness of my face, but I don't care. I am who I am, and right now I'm very, very disappointed.

'Calm down woman.' A light shifts in his brown eyes. 'I know I said that but I've thought about it and I really want to train my dog today. The centre closes at four on Saturdays, so I could still go there for a couple of hours. I don't have to leave right now. As I said, I can stay for another hour or so.'

'Well, we'd better hurry up with our breakfast then.' I start putting coffee, orange juice, the eggs and sausages and bread and butter out on the dining table, then sit down with my back to the living room. Lulu jumps on my lap and starts purring.

Ryan sits down across from me and reaches for his mug.

Behind him, in the frame of the kitchen window, a bird soars freely through a blue sky.

'Have you got the hump now?'

'Of course I have. We made plans.'

'I'm sorry babe.' Ryan half gets up and leans his body over the table, puckering his lips.

I automatically lean in to meet him, steadying Lulu with one hand. His lips are warm from the coffee.

'It's nothing to do with you,' he says, buttering a piece of baguette. 'You're absolutely lovely. I just really want to do this, you know. If my dog passes the tests, I can go to Canada this summer. When you mentioned Toronto, you all of a sudden reignited my dream, and it's almost July already; I really want to go.'

He bites into his baguette and I stir my coffee.

'Shall I come with you to Godalming?'

The look on Ryan's face tells me he didn't see this coming.

'I could watch the dog training,' I say. 'Or, if you don't want me to, I could just walk around the town. I'd like that, I've never been to Godalming.'

A grimace has crept across Ryan's face and his Adam's apple moves as he swallows. 'No babe, not today. We'll do that some other time, okay?' He takes another bite and chews, still frowning.

Breakfast with Ryan isn't exactly how I'd envisaged it when we woke up together an hour ago. A sense of emptiness swirls through me at the thought.

'Why not?' I say. 'You won't need to drive me back here; I can take a train, tonight, or Sunday maybe.'

'Because,' he says, locking eyes with me, 'I want some time by myself.'

I lower my gaze. 'Oh.'

'It's not you Carys. I really like you.'

I'm silent and stare at my plate.

Ryan sighs loudly. 'Alright then, if you must know… I live with my parents. There. That's why I don't want you to come. Are you happy now?'

I am surprised by this. I never asked Ryan about his living situation; just assumed that at his age he would have his own pad, like me.

'You do?' I say.

'Yes, and I find it really embarrassing that I still live at home but I do it for my dog. They've got a big garden. I did have my own flat, but my dog still lived with my parents, so I was travelling to their place all the time. In the end, I just moved back home.'

'But I don't mind that you live with your parents, I really don't.'

He glares at me. 'Well I do mind. I really do. If I bring you home, my parents will want to have dinner with us. They'll ask me lots of questions about you when you've gone. I just don't want that.'

♪

After breakfast Ryan starts to pack his satchel. I give him the *Amélie* DVD but he tells me I can keep it.

'I left the towel I used on top of the laundry basket,' he says.

I nod.

He moves to my bookcases and shows me *Veronica Decides to Die*.

'Can I borrow this?'

'Sure,' I say. 'So, when will I see you again?'

'That's a song.' He walks over to the sofa, scoops his shoes up from the floor where he kicked them off last night and sits down.

Is he avoiding my question? Does he even want to see me again? Maybe I slept with him too soon. I'm glad he's taking that book; he'll have to see me again now. Although, I suppose he could send it.

'I'm not sure I can come over next weekend.' Ryan leans forward, pulls the heel of his shoe back with his index finger and slides in his foot.

'I'm not here next weekend,' I say. 'I'm in Toronto from Friday till Sunday.'

'Oh, right.' Ryan glances at me. 'I forgot. I was gonna say that I was supposed to go to the dog races in Brighton with my best mate Ian, on Friday and Saturday, only—'

'I thought Leah was your best friend.'

'Leah's my female best friend.' He smiles a little. Because he's thinking of her now? Who is this Leah, really?

'Anyway,' Ryan continues, 'Ian called me a few days ago and told me he's not going anymore. You wanna know why?'

'Yes?'

Ryan pulls a face. 'He and his girlfriend want a baby and apparently Emma's ovulating around the weekend and she forbids him to go. Can you believe that?'

I look at the floor. I just don't know what to say to that, but I have a sudden image in my head of my own baby: Amélie. She's floating away from me on a dark cloud in a poo-filled nappy. She needs me to be her mother. And then I have a thought. Several thoughts, in fact. Passengers who yell at me when I'm out of chicken. Passengers who snarl at me when they discover their seats don't recline. The angry looks I'm shot when a flight is delayed—usually for safety reasons, but they only care about arriving on time. I see myself sitting on metal containers, in freezing galleys during night shifts. Faces of homosexual colleagues flit by, confiding to me they call in sick when they are scheduled to fly to certain destinations, terrified of being publicly hanged. Colleagues with kids who call in sick to be there for their children's birthday parties, or to be home for Christmas. It's my turn now. Nothing will stand in the way of my happiness. Not my miserable job. It's not worth it.

'I could come with you.'

Ryan looks up at me from the sofa. 'But you're going to Canada on Friday.' A mistrusting expression sets on his face. 'Aren't you?'

'It's on my roster, yes. But I can extend my leave. It's not a problem.' I think of Annette. I can prove I'm seeing a therapist if I have to. I really am too unstable to fly right now.

'I don't want you to get into trouble at work.'

'I won't, it's not a problem. I'll call Scheduling to sort it out.'

'Alright.' Ryan stares at me. 'I guess I'll go with you then.'

Chapter 15

'What a knob. Ditch him.'

Flora is an opinionated woman. I called her the minute Ryan sped off towards the roundabout up the road. I watched him leave from the window but he didn't even wave at me.

'He's not a knob.' I draw my legs up under myself and lean my elbow on the armrest of the sofa. 'He just wants to train his dog today. That's important to him. He's impulsive, yes, but that doesn't mean he doesn't like me. He always calls me when he says he will; he drove up here from Godalming to see me and he's taking me to Brighton next week.'

'Did you bonk?'

'Of course we did.' I stare at the pink curtain that partially covers the window. An image of Ryan's nude body on mine flashes through my mind. 'I can still feel him between my legs.'

'Oooh,' Flora groans.

'Are we having phone sex now?'

Flora snorts loudly but then turns serious. 'I know you really like this bloke, Car. He's probably very handsome, but I wouldn't give his words too much weight. He says he's taking you to Brighton but he also said he was taking you out to lunch in Kew Gardens today and that he would stay until Sunday. How well do you even know him?' I listen to Flora's utterly unpleasant words while I watch

Lulu's soft flank rising up and down. She's curled up in a ball on the other end of the sofa. Oh, to be a cat; not a worry in the world; not the fear of loss pulling at your heartstrings and making you feel all cold inside.

'If you ask me, he sounds rather self-centred,' Flora jabbers on, although she suddenly sounds oddly strained. 'To just abandon the plans you'd made for this weekend, without any consideration for you. You're playing second fiddle to a dog. Have you thought of that?'

'No, I haven't,' I reply, 'because I know he's training his dog for the police and he needs money for a ticket to Canada. His dog only needs to pass two more rounds of tests and after that, he'll be able to sell it. So I'm really playing second fiddle to Canada, and that I can understand.'

'He sells dogs? I thought he worked in IT.'

'He does, but he also trains dogs for the police. That's what he really wants to do.'

In the background, a female voice with a Liverpudlian drawl asks Flora if she's still comfortable.

'Where are you?'

'I'm near Marylebone Road.'

'Oh my God. Are you telling me you've got a tube stuck up your arse while we're having this conversation?'

'That's exactly what I'm telling you. And my poo is very healthy, isn't it, Louise?'

Louise makes some affirmative sounds and then Flora says in a teasing tone, 'How about meeting me for coffee and a brownie in Kew Gardens later? 'I can be there in an hour and a half. I'll take you out to lunch. Sod that Ryan bloke.'

♪

After Flora and I hang up, I run upstairs. Pieces of my uniform are still scattered across the floor, discarded where Ryan ripped them off me: my heels and skirt near the door; my blouse, bra and tights in a heap near my bed. He could have picked it all up, I think, pulling my sleepshirt over my head and throwing it on the pillow. He was the last person in here this morning and he wanted me to wear it in the first place. I didn't really see the point in it. Why change into a different set of clothes when the expectation is you're going to get naked together? What a hassle. But he kept banging on about it. He was dead happy when I finally caved.

I pick up the pieces of my uniform and drape them over the metal frame at the end of my bed. I wish I hadn't caved. I played *flight attendant deals with unruly passenger* with a guy who prefers to have lunch with his dog. Flora was right.

In the bathroom, Ryan's towel is neatly folded on top of the laundry basket. I place my hand on it; it's still damp. *Calm down, woman*, he told me. My cheeks flush at the thought. I should've played it cool. From now on, I'll try and be more relaxed about us and give him the time he needs to develop his feelings for me. Next time I speak to him, I'll be all calm and collected.

I step into the shower cubicle and seconds later warm water streams over my face and body. It pissed me off what Flora said; she's one to talk.

I take a dollop of coconut shampoo and work it into my scalp. Ridiculous! *How can you say all this to me?* In my head,

I'm having a go at her over coffee in Kew Gardens.

You're the one who's having it away with a married colleague. His poor children. You are so afraid of being alone Flora. You hadn't even ended your relationship with Ollie and already started another. Do you remember, when you told me you found not having a bloke embarrassing because of what people might think? Completely barking mad if you ask me. At least I'm not like that!

I swallow some water and try to remember when she'd said that. Was it eight years ago? I think it was. Not fair to dredge that up. I don't agree with how she ended things with Ollie, she knows that, but she is my best friend. We've been friends since the age of six. We piss each other off and we are different in many ways, but we also have a lot of fun together, and we know each other through and through. If I don't accept Flora— warts and all—then we simply can't be friends. I can't even imaging not having her in my life. And it's not like I'm perfect.

I step out of the shower onto the bath mat and take a dry towel from the cabinet under the sink. I'm looking forward to seeing her this afternoon; there's lots I want to discuss. Like my plan to ask Ryan to come to New York with me for my thirtieth birthday.

I rub the coarse towel across my back then grab another towel from the cabinet and wrap it around my hair. And, I'm going to look up Patsy. I googled her husband and discovered they live in Hackney. I'm going there next week— unannounced of course— or maybe the week after that. I hope Flora will be more supportive about my quest for closure than Patrick's been so far, but even if she isn't, I am going. I just want to look Patsy in the eyes, speak my mind, demand answers and leave.

I still feel, quite strongly, that I'm at the crossroads of my life, but I also feel that I'm taking important steps, and that I'm moving forward and that good things are waiting for me.

♪

A blue sky stretches over Kew Gardens as Flora and I walk towards the Orangery. Roses, reds, whites and pinks, still wet, are playfully assembled in borders and the grass field glistens with moisture.

Flora stops to smell the flowers of a jasmine plant that's climbing up a birch tree.

Watching her inhale the scent, her eyes closed, I remember I was supposed to be here with Ryan, but given the choice now I wouldn't change a thing. His sudden exodus doesn't hurt me anymore. Not this minute, anyway.

Flora wipes the tip of her nose with a finger and links her arm through mine.

'Is your bum not sore?' I ask her.

'Nah,' she says. 'They use a small speculum, but now that we're on the subject of nether regions, I really have to pee.'

The restaurant is housed in a grand white-walled building with a view over the gardens. Hovering near the bar, while Flora nips to the loo, I take in the atmosphere. The place is alive with blended conversations, lounge music and sizzling food. Ryan would have liked it here. His loss though, the idiot; I hope he's having fun with his dog.

A waitress starts foaming up milk with a steam wand by the espresso machine and I study its gleaming stainless steel. If only we had coffee machines like that on board. I might actually reconsider looking for another job.

A handsome male customer approaches the till and says something to a young spotty waiter. I study the man while he takes a bank card from his wallet and pays a bill. He's wearing a business suit on a Saturday. I wonder what he does for a living. He thanks the waiter, then walks to a table near the wall where he joins a woman who's got her back to me. Her hair's stunning. Waist-length and deep black. Annette's got hair like that. Oh, but wait—

I back away from the bar to take a better look. I don't believe it—it is her! Crap. Don't fancy making small talk if she sees me. Speaking on the phone when I need some time off work is one thing, but as for *tête-à-têtes*, my annual performance evaluations with her are more than enough.

I slink back to the bar and shuffle sideways a few steps to get further away from them. Poor Annette though. She's sitting there, so casually, enjoying lunch on her day off with that gorgeous man, while I've decided to make her work for her money again by calling in sick on Friday.

The waitress is pouring cappuccino froth on four cups of coffee that she grouped together on a tray and I glance in the direction of the loos. What's keeping Flora? I'm dying for a coffee. I knew having colonic irrigation couldn't be good.

Annette's getting up! The gorgeous man takes a mint

from a white saucer on the table and pops it into his mouth. She takes a silk emerald shawl from the back of her chair and wraps it around her bare shoulders. They cross the restaurant towards the exit. I should have thanked her for the flowers. Would've been nice if I'd done that.

'Sorry I took so long.' Flora slips her phone into her handbag.

'Were you taking a dump?'

'No, I wasn't. I had a missed call from Edward and I wanted to call him back.'

'In there?'

'Yes. I just needed to have a quick word with him, in private.' Flora glances at an empty table near the window and I picture myself on my bed chatting with Ryan while Kieran watches telly downstairs and I completely understand where she's coming from. Sometimes in life, all you want is a bit of privacy.

'Shall we sit there?' Flora points at the table. 'Anyway,' she says, 'I was talking to Ed about the ultimatum I've given him. His wife is using their kids as pawns now and he says it makes it harder to leave. But that's exactly why she's doing it! God, I hate her.'

'She probably isn't too keen on you either.'

Flora gives me a resigned smile.

I'm about to follow her to the table when a flustered woman, wildly scanning her surroundings, rushes past us to the bar.

'Excuse me,' she says to the young spotty waiter who's tapping at some squares on the till's touchscreen. 'Do you know if a man in a business suit and a woman with very long, dark hair have been in here?'

He thinks for a moment and shakes his head. 'No, I don't recall a woman with long, dark hair. Not in my section.'

'Oh, but I do,' I say.

The woman, the waiter and Flora stare at me.

'They were over there.' I point to the table against the wall. 'They only just left.'

'Have they?' The woman eyes me as if she doubts my intelligence. 'Did she have very long, black hair?'

'Yes,' I say. 'Down to the waist.'

The woman's face hardens. 'All fake,' she sneers. 'She thinks she's Pocahontas, but she's not.' A hysterical cackle escapes her mouth.

I stare at her. Why is she talking about Annette like this? What a weird woman.

'Do you know, by any chance, if they paid by credit card?' she asks me.

I shrug my shoulders. 'Not a clue.'

Flora and I share a glance and the waiter turns to the till. 'If they were sitting at table three…' he says, opening a drawer. 'I think this might be theirs.' He takes out a small paper slip and shows it to the woman. She rips it from his hand and studies it carefully. Flora and I lean in a little closer for a peek too. It's got a signature on it in blue ink.

'Yes, that's him.' The woman purses her lips, inhales hard through her nose, then gives the slip back to the waiter. 'Thank you.' She curtly nods at me and without another word she stomps off towards the door.

The waiter has barely shut the till drawer when the

waitress who made the cappuccinos marches up to him. 'You weren't supposed to do that,' she hisses, grabbing him by the elbow.

'I wasn't?' he stutters.

The waitress pulls him behind the bar. Beside the coffee maker, out of full view, she has a proper go at him.

Flora and I look at each other. 'That was weird,' I say.

'Mm,' she says.

We cross the restaurant, but just before we've reached the window table, someone's shoulder bumps hard against mine. For a moment, it actually feels as if I'm being shoved. Deliberate? What's that sour odour all of a sudden?

Confused, I look up, straight into the face of a scruffy guy with a Chicago White Sox cap on his head. He locks his eyes on my mouth.

'Snitch,' he hisses and then he paces it to the door, where a few customers step out of his way.

Flora's mouth drops open. 'Did he just call you snitch?'

'I think so,' I say, feeling a little wobbly from this sudden onslaught.

'What an idiot,' Flora fumes.

Through the arched windows I see the White Sox guy walking down the broad garden path on spindly bowlegs. Had he been watching me all along? What a strange thought. I hadn't noticed him at all. And why did he call me snitch? I thought I was being helpful.

'We should've gone somewhere else,' Flora says. 'All these lowlifes here are ruining our lunch.'

'Annette's not a lowlife.'

'Who's Annette?'

'My supervisor from work. The woman at table three, who that lady called Pocahontas.'

Flora bites her lip and I know she does it to stop herself from laughing.

'Is that the supervisor who sent you two flower bouquets in one week?'

'Yes, her. I thought the man she was with was her boyfriend or husband.'

'They're probably having an affair,' Flora says.

'You think? Well, you would know.'

It was just a joke but Flora blinks her eyes and says: 'Cheers Carys.'

♪

Around five p.m., I saunter through the garden behind the house with my shopping bags.

Mrs Meads has a visitor, I notice when I glance at her kitchen window. Looks like her son, Paul, but they don't see me and moments later the steps of the metal staircase clang under my feet.

The day didn't start off too well but my afternoon with Flora has completely recharged me. She's the only person in the world I can totally be myself with and share whatever's on my mind. She said she thinks Ryan will call me on Thursday to cancel our trip to Brighton. I told her I don't think he will do that, and said that I don't believe Edward will leave his wife. She pointed out that Ed's wife was, in fact, his girlfriend and that she was glad he never married her. I told her that after sixteen years and three kids she was definitely his wife but Flora didn't agree with me and said she was sure Ed *would* leave his girlfriend, because, A (Flora raised her thumb): he promised her he would and, B (she held up her index finger): because he kept telling her how good they were together.

I told Flora her two fingers were destroying his children's lives but she didn't agree with that either. 'Kids are resilient,' she said. 'They will bounce back. My parents got divorced when I was twelve and I'm fine.'

In the end, we grew sick and tired of talking about men, agreed to stop criticizing each other's choices, and went to Richmond for some shopping and more coffee.

Sticking the key in the lock of my front door, my thoughts turn to the evening in by myself: I'll take a long, hot aromatherapy bath first, then slip into the cosy pyjamas I've just bought, pour myself a glass of red wine and stick *Amélie* back in the DVD player. Hopefully, Kieran saved me some of the cheddar cheese puffs.

I step into the hall and, instantly, my gaze is drawn to the skull on the back of Kieran's black jacket that's on a coat hanger above my suitcases. I'm sure that wasn't here when I left. Kieran took it to Southport with him. Didn't he?

I push the door to the living room open. Kieran's in the kitchen, scrubbing at something in the sink. Has he really not heard me come in or is he in one of those moods again? He's squirting with a bottle of washing up liquid and turns on the tap. He's cleaning his fish tank, I notice, walking up to him.

'You're back already?'

Kieran turns around. His emo hair flops over his face and the yellow sponge pad he's holding drips water onto the floor.

'I am.' He pushes the chrome lever back to turn off the tap. 'Gareth wanted to go home. The trip wasn't fun at all.'

I watch him peering at a spot on the tank and wonder, with mild tiredness, what on earth happened this time.

'First, they take my cats,' he says, scrubbing at the spot, his shoulders moving with effort, 'then Mum tries to kill herself and now my weekend in Southport's been ruined.'

He stops scrubbing and glances at me; his eyes have moistened up a bit. 'I was really looking forward to tonight. We didn't do anything yesterday because Gareth was knackered from driving. All we did was unpack and order pizza and discuss what we were going to do today, but we didn't do any of it.'

'Was Gareth ill?' I pull up a kitchen chair and put my shopping bags on it. My gaze moves to Lulu, who's dozing in her favourite spot on the windowsill between basil and sage, and to another fish tank that's on the worktop below her. The glass of the tank is grimy; covered in brown stains and limescale. For a fleeting moment, I resent Kieran for bringing the thing into my kitchen.

As if reading my thoughts, he says: 'The only thing I liked about our trip is that Kenny gave me this new fish tank. My sticks will have a lot more room now.'

'That fish tank is not new.'

'Of course it's not, but I got it for free and it's bigger than my own. Kenny used to keep his lizard in it, but it died.'

I've got no idea who Kenny is and don't ask.

'Was Gareth ill?' I ask again. I sit down at the kitchen table and watch Kieran work. 'He didn't take anything, did he?'

Kieran lets hot water clatter into the tank. He picks the tank up and swirls it around to rinse off the soap suds. 'No,' he says through a rising gush of steam. 'Gareth and Cadi had a huge fight this morning. That's why Gareth wanted to go home.'

'That's it?' I say, surprised. 'It was Cadi who wanted to go home, wasn't it? Sounds more like her.'

'No. Gareth did.'

'What were they fighting about then?'

'I don't know.'

'But you were there.'

'No, I wasn't.' Kieran puts the tank down in the sink, presses the tap's lever back with his fingers, and looks at me. 'I go to the corner shop with Kenny. We come back twenty minutes later and all of a sudden Gareth's gone batshit mental and Cadi's crying into a cushion on the sofa. When Gareth saw me, he just said "pack your bag mate, we're going home." It was really embarrassing. We were guests there.'

'Cadi was crying?' I say, sitting up straight. 'Why? And who's Kenny?'

'Kenny is—'

'Sorry. May I just interrupt you there?' I get up and walk over to the left side of the worktop. I've only just noticed that two of my saucepans and a skillet are covered with tights and I hope this is not what I think it is. I peer through the stretched fabric. Dozens of stick insects are languishing on twigs and leaves.

'Seriously? You've put your insects in my kitchenware? That's disgusting Kieran. I cook in these pans.'

Kieran knits his brows together. 'I didn't have anywhere else to put them. Mum never minds. I always use our pans when I clean the tank; where else can I keep them?'

'Not in my pans. I put food in there. I want them back in my cupboard when you're done, Kieran. Scrubbed down and dried off. I'm not Mum.'

'I know,' he replies, sullen-faced.

I flick the kettle on and sit down again.

Kieran pulls the green tea towel off the door handle near his crotch, presses the fish tank against his chest and starts drying it with brisk strokes.

'Was Cadi alright by the time you drove home?'

'No, not really. They didn't speak a word to each other in the car and she didn't want to sit next to Gareth anymore. I wouldn't, if he'd called *me* a slapper.'

'What?'

Kieran turns to me. 'Gareth called Cadi a slapper. I really like him but that was totally out of order.'

I frown. 'Are you sure that's what he said?'

'One hundred per cent. I was in the hallway and that's when I heard it. Kenny heard it too. Gareth said: "I can't be with a slapper."'

I stare at Kieran for a few seconds. 'Did you ask him why

he said that?'

'No, of course not. It's none of my business, is it?'

I lean my chin on the palm of my hand and gaze out of the kitchen window. The sky is milky-blue. Lulu's still dozing on the windowsill. 'I'm really disappointed in Gareth,' I say quietly. 'You do think they're still getting married, don't you?'

'I hope so.' Kieran puts the clean tank next to my pans with his stick insects. 'I was really looking forward to their wedding.' He lifts up the tights on one side of the skillet and quickly begins to transfer the sticks to the cleaned tank.

'I know it's hard to believe,' I say, 'but you don't think Cadi cheated on him, do you?'

'Nah, I don't think so.' Kieran covers the tank with another pair of nylon tights and turns to me. A wet patch darkens the front of his shirt. 'I hope she didn't,' he says, 'but I don't know that for certain.' He glances towards the living room. 'I thought you were with Ryan today?'

I automatically look behind me too. 'Yes, but he left. He had things to do.'

Kieran gives me a quizzical stare but says nothing and moves back to his clean fish tank.

'Oh, no!' His shout is raw.

I'm at Kieran's side with one big step and immediately see why he's panicking. Inside the tank, the sticks are frantically running around on the bottom and on the partitions. They seem to be scalding their feet. The glass must be too hot for them.

'Please help me!' Despair rings through Kieran's voice.

He rips the tights from the tank and with a swing of his

arm chucks them on the floor behind us. The stick insects rush to the top, making a break for freedom, crawling over the edge of the tank, but a few lie still. Maybe it's too late for them, although I'm not an expert.

'This has never happened to me before,' Kieran cries.

He plucks the slower sticks off the tank as fast as he can and releases them on the worktop from where they scurry down the cabinets, up the walls and into the sink.

'Help me,' Kieran pleads again, but I don't know how. I haven't got the courage to pick one up; they may as well have been spiders.

Somewhere in the distance, the echo of a child's voice is ringing in my ears. *Help me. Patsy help me.* Bethan's slipped into the hole. She's up to her armpits in black water, her hands are flat on the ice. She looks into my eyes but she knows I'm not going to help her. Her eyes glaze over. *Patsy, no! Help me.* For God's sake, help *me.*

Chapter 16

There is before and there is after. These are the last moments that belong to before:

'It's a male, trying to fuck the female.' Mum pensively studies the big, green duck with a curl in its tail.

The duck is being naughty. It keeps trying to use one of the smaller brown ones as a climbing frame. That must be what Mum means. I feel sorry for the brown duck. It's quaking loudly and trying to escape. I was just feeding the ducks pieces of bread. And they were happy with my bread; everything was fine until that big, green one arrived. I kick my leg at it. Not to hit it but to make it go away.

'Leave it, Carys,' Mum says.

But I think we should help the brown ducks. They all look nervous.

I glance at Mum on the wooden bench. She's still moving the buggy back and forth with her foot even though Bethan's already asleep.

I move closer to the ducks and kick at the green one again.

'Don't do that, Carys,' Mum says, but this time it works! The green duck quacks too and stops trying to climb on top of the brown one that now quickly waddles off.

'I saved it!' I beam at Mum.

Mum scrabbles around in the sling bag that's hanging from the buggy's handles and hands me a carton of apple juice.

'Bethan's still asleep,' she says, glancing under the hood. 'You can drink that while we walk. We're going to see Rose now.'

'Who's Rose?' I ask.

'You know Rose,' Mum says. 'You've seen her before. She's a very nice lady.'

I hold my carton in one hand and help Mum with pushing the buggy while we walk back to our street. A leek and the green bits on a bunch of carrots are sticking out from the bag. Mum is going to make vegetable soup for dinner.

The street we live in is very long, and our house is at the end of it. When we pass the alley with the fire, I grab my mother's hand. We walk past a few more houses until we come to the house with the lady behind the window who always waves at us. Mum stops in front of it and opens the fence. I'm surprised we're going here. Bethan wails; she's waking up, and Mum pushes her up the garden path.

I'd say that this is where after started:

'Right,' Mum says when we get to the door. She combs her hair with her fingers. 'Do I look alright?'

I glance at her. She looks the same as always. Mum rings the doorbell and the woman who was naked in our house opens the door. She's also the woman who always waves at us behind the window.

'My favourite person,' she says. Mum looks happy and shy. Together, they lift the buggy with Bethan in it over the threshold and I step inside too.

'Hello Carys,' the woman says. 'How are you, sweetheart?'

'Fine,' I say softly, which is a fib. I want to go home.

I follow Mum and the woman into the living room. It's the same living room we have, but this one's brighter with more daylight and the wallpaper is prettier. The TV is on and a big girl is slouching in an armchair, watching *SuperTed*. Oh, but that is… I look again. No. It can't be. It's Patsy. Why is she in this house?

'Look who's here, Pat,' the woman says to her. 'It's Carys.'

Patsy glances at me. 'Hi,' she says, then her eyes flit back to the TV.

'Carys has come to play with you,' the woman says, but her voice sounds a little embarrassed.

Patsy makes a strange sound with her nose. Mum takes the baby beaker with juice from her bag and gives it to Bethan because she's wailing again.

'Does Bethan like *SuperTed*?' the woman asks Mum, and she turns to me. 'Why don't you go upstairs and play with Patsy? She's got lots of toys you can play with.'

And then it hits me. This woman is Patsy's mother. That's why Patsy is here. I'm in Patsy's house. For a few moments I don't breathe, and my knees almost buckle. Everything is so heavy. Taid's tool is scraping at my heart. Mummy's wringing a wet towel with her hands. I am the towel.

♪

Maeve's walking up the stairs with a phone pressed to her ear, but she half turns when she hears me coming through the door and points at the waiting room. I already know I'll find Mum in there because it's where she told me to meet her when I called earlier.

She's on one of the plastic seats, reading a newspaper. The brunette's not behind the partition. The only person I see in the office is Mum's psychiatrist, Dr Seymour, a kind man; he introduced himself to me last week and we had an interesting conversation.

Mum looks up from the paper with a blank face. She doesn't greet me; nothing about her tells me she's glad to see me. She gets up and leaves the paper on the seat. 'My room's upstairs,' she says and I follow her across the auburn floor tiles towards the staircase.

Mum tilts her head sideways while I trudge behind her up the stairs. 'You told me you'd be back in a couple of days.'

'I've been very tired. There was a lot to sort out. Work, Kieran. Your cat.'

My legs feel heavy. I'm not in the mood to be here. Only came because I thought I should, but I've changed my mind about that. I miss Ryan. We should've enjoyed a lazy Sunday morning together. But no... his dog. It's another five days before our trip to Brighton.

'Cadi and Kieran haven't been to see me yet,' Mum says. Hurt tinges the accusing tone. Her hands slide up the banister, the skin on her arms, soft and pasty, hangs like an upside-down parachute. She's wearing a short-sleeved white blouse and old jeans. She looks poor, but I know she'd still buy her clothes from charity shops if she won the lottery. Being frugal is her hobby.

'Cadi's angry with you.' I say.

Mum meets my comment with silence.

'And I think Kieran finds it too much to see you in here. It was quite a shock to him, what you did.'

Mum tilts her head to the side again. 'You can tell Kieran I'm fine. He doesn't need to worry about me. He's welcome to visit me.'

At the top of the stairs Mum turns right.

'Are you in a different room?' I stop and scan the left side of the corridor where a week ago I'd followed Maeve.

'Shh.' Mum glances at the kitchen and I do too. Just like last week, there are people gathered around a table, dunking biscuits into mugs and having a bit of banter with the nurses. A familiar tune drifts from the room. Vicky Brown's 'Look for Me in Rainbows.' I stop to listen, but Mum shuffles on. We played this song during Dad's funeral service.

A man at the table looks me straight in the eyes. He's scruffy, unshaven, and something about him reminds me of the guy who called me snitch. I take a few big steps to catch up with Mum.

'Why did you want me to be quiet when we passed that room?'

'Shh,' she says again and opens a door. Mum's in a single room now, so I guess it's an improvement— the pungent sweat odour aside, the other room was airier.

A narrow bed fills up the left corner and there's a small

wooden table with a chair in front of the window that's framed by beige curtains and covered with wire mesh, like in the other room. The lino on the floor is beige too and the walls are bare and white.

'Why were you moved here?' I ask.

Mum folds up a large sleeping shirt and sits down on the bed. 'A woman in the other room called me filthy dyke.'

I gasp. 'Seriously? That's horrendous. Are you even safe here?'

'She's been reprimanded,' Mum says flatly. 'But I told them I wanted a different room.' She glances at the carrier bag I'm holding. 'Did you bring me something?'

'Yes, I did.'

Mum takes the bag from me and I sit down beside her on the foot of the bed. 'Are you sure you're safe here? Can she get to you at night?'

'No, she can't, they lock the doors.' Mum examines the contents of the bag.

'Aren't you scared?' Again, I think of the guy who called me snitch.

'Scared?' Mum chortles. 'As if.'

'Why did you tell me to be quiet when we passed that room?'

'Because I think she was in there. I just don't want to see her.'

I begin to bite my nails and Mum takes a small tin from the bag.

'That's tea from Iran,' I say. 'Loose tea. There's a strainer too. I bought it from a souk.'

'A souk?'

'A market.'

With a cautious expression, Mum studies the floral print tin from all angles. 'Isn't there poison in it?'

I close my eyes, breathe, and open them again. 'There are tea leaves in it. And dried figs and peaches, and rose petals. But if you don't want it, I'll take it back.'

Mum glances at me. 'I'll keep it.

She gets up and puts the tin on the table, then takes the rest of the items out of the bag and places those on the table too: the tea strainer, hand cream, a new toothbrush and toothpaste; the undies from her drawer, coconut shampoo and shower gel, *Take a Break* and *That's Life*, a new pen for the crosswords and a chocolate bar with raisins and nuts.

'So, this woman, who called you a name, did you say anything to her?'

Mum pulls up the wooden chair, sits down sideways with crossed legs, and looks at me squarely. 'I said, "Dyke? Yes. Filthy? No. I shower every day."' But after this, she stares anxiously at the floor.

Poor Mum. It's always something. Why can't she have a normal life? But she did handle the situation well, I think. She stuck up for herself and remained calm. It's not true what she said of course, about showering every day. She doesn't even shower once a week. I can smell her armpits from here and her hair with the purple and blue streaks on the left is shiny from built-up grease, but that's not the point.

'Did someone file a complaint?' I ask.

'It's been dealt with.'

She doesn't want to talk about it, that's obvious, but I just can't let this go. I'm surprised at the level of loyalty I'm feeling for her. It's like the woman who said it insulted me personally.

'But why did she say that to you?' I ask. 'Did you have an argument?'

'I didn't do anything.' Mum glares at me. Her small eyes are so light; more amber than brown, and sometimes there's a sheen in them that's almost evil. My dreams were haunted by those eyes when I was a child and they still make me uncomfortable now.

'Why do you always think it's my fault?' Mum snarls. 'She just said it. End of story.'

'I didn't think it was your fault. I was just wondering what happened. Why would she—'

'I told you what happened.'

We're silent. In the distance, the shrill siren of an ambulance blares. I think of Dad and his rainbow. One day, we'll all be fine.

'Shall I make us a cup of tea?' I say.

Mum says she doesn't want anything. She stretches her short legs before her. 'Kieran can stay with you permanently, can't he?'

'No, he can't. He's staying with me until you come back.'

'I don't know when I'm coming back.'

Mum gets up and takes a book from the table, then sits down beside me on the bed and starts dangling her legs. It looks ridiculous.

I toy with the idea of broaching the topic of her bathing habits but don't because it'll probably piss her off again.

'Why did you try to kill yourself?' I ask instead.

Her legs stop dangling and she looks down at the book in her hands. In a child-like voice she says: 'I wanted them to have something to think about.'

'Who's them?'

She shoots me an irritable glance. 'The RSPCA of course. Who else?'

'But they don't even know you're in here. They don't know what happened. Do they?'

'They think they can just destroy lives and that it doesn't have consequences,' Mum huffs. 'I'll show them it does.'

'So, we're going through all this shit because you're angry about your cats?'

'No,' she bristles. 'This is about character assassination. I'm a good person. I took those cats in out of the goodness of my heart, but they've twisted everything. They're lying. I did take care of them properly. They're using my good deeds against me.'

She moves her hands and I glance at the book. *Law School for Dummies*. I begin to bite my nails again.

'When I go to court, I'll—'

'You're going to court?'

'Yes, they want to sue me. But don't tell Kieran, he doesn't know this.'

I stare at Mum in shock.

'As if I'm a criminal,' she says, dejected. 'I was only trying to help. Animal cruelty my foot.'

'I thought they'd just taken your cats,' I say. 'I didn't know they were suing you.' I picture Mum on a prison bench behind iron bars. Is that where she'll end up? I'm scared now. It would be the end of her.

'Well they are,' she says. 'But my vet's helping me. John knows how I tried to get help for those cats. Hundreds of pounds I've spent. He will vouch for me. And my cats were very fond of me as well. They must miss me a lot. It breaks my heart when I think of that.'

I'm feeling so tired and drained. I almost want to ask Mum if I can take a nap in her bed. What can I do to help her? I'll testify for her; she won't hold herself together in front of a judge. Someone will have to do the talking for her. I'm not sure what that vet is willing to do.

'When are you going to court?'

'I'm not sure. It could be six months. It could be a year.'

'Who told you that?'

'The police officer who was there when they stole my cats. I hope I can get them back.' Mum's index finger ruffles the pages at the top of the book. 'The ones they haven't euthanized.'

I get up from the bed. I just can't be here anymore.

'Are you going home?' she says.

'I am.'

Mum looks down but doesn't ask me to stay. I'm almost at the door when she says: 'Do you know who called them, Carys?'

I turn around, thinking of her neighbours. Maybe it was

them, but I don't want to tell her that in case she goes over there. God knows what she'd do.

'I really don't,' I reply.

I meet Mum's eyes and am startled by her cold stare.

'It wasn't me. I didn't call them.'

To my surprise she remains silent.

'You think it was me?'

She lowers her gaze. 'I didn't say that.'

'Yes, you did. You said it with that mean look you just gave me.'

Mum keeps her head down and doesn't speak.

I slam the door behind me.

Chapter 17

Maybe a quick tarot reading before Ryan picks me up? I know I promised Patrick to cut down on readings; it's just that I'd like a bit of an idea of how our trip to Brighton will pan out, which is only because of the way it came about. I sort of invited myself and then Ryan said, 'I guess I'll go with you then.' Hardly romantic. How does he really feel about me? And will he fall in love with me? That's all I want to know.

I take the cards from the shelf and sit down on a kitchen chair. Lulu immediately jumps up and nestles herself on my lap. Shrivelled petals drop from their browning stems, as I carefully push Annette's flowers to the wall to make room. A dusting of yellow pollen from the lilies, the only flowers still in bloom, covers my wrist and I wipe it on Lulu's coat.

Right. Centre. I begin to unknot the silk scarf that's wrapped around the tarot deck while I ponder how to phrase my question, when the sudden noise of a strident car horn in the street makes me start in my chair.

Annoyed, I glance at the front room window. It can't be Ryan. I'm sure he'd bother to come up to my door. Besides, he said twelve and it's only half eleven.

Another hideous beep pierces Sandycombe Road.

I get up and go to the window just to be sure. Lulu follows me and jumps on the radiator cover. My heart sinks.

It is Ryan. He's parked his blue Ford behind three other cars, a short distance from the house, and he's just sitting there, behind the wheel, staring into the middle distance, not looking too happy.

James and I travelled together. If I'd been going to Brighton with him today, he would have come up to my door, with a bunch of flowers. He would have sat down on the sofa, smiling, chatting, petting Lulu, while I was getting ready. James and I weren't just lovers, we were also friends. I should never have left him, but it is what it is.

Ryan sees me and I wave at him but all he does is stare, so I move away from the window and look for my shoes and bag.

James and I loved each other equally, I think, slipping on my shoes. Somehow it feels as if Ryan's making me work; like I need to prove to him that I'm special enough to be with him. He even put that on his dating profile—sort of. He said he was looking for someone who was very special and stood out from the crowd. He's not even taken his dating profile down yet. I deleted my account even before our first date because we clicked so well in our emails and on the phone. And last Friday, after we'd watched *Amélie*, I asked him if he wanted to see some pictures of me as a child. 'No,' he simply said. I've not forgotten about that. James would have said yes. It's like Ryan has decided to put a limit on how well he wants to get to know me. Emotionally that is. Physically we're fine. Anyway, for now we're off to Brighton and we'll take it from there. At least he's turned up. I'm looking forward to telling Flora she was wrong about that.

I put the tarot cards back on the shelf and write a quick note to Kieran, reminding him his microwave meal is in the fridge.

♪

Ryan gets out of the car when he sees me; his mouth curves into a half-smile. He kisses me on the lips, then glances at my new Dorothy Perkins ensemble: a flowy red skirt dotted with small blue flowers, a sea-blue spaghetti-strap top and yellow canvas peep-toes.

'You look nice.'

'Thank you,' I say. 'I got a new skirt.'

'It's pretty,' he says, but then his face clouds over and I have no idea why.

He turns back to the car and stoops to flip the driver's seat forward and puts my red leather tote bag and summer jacket on the back seat while I walk around the front of the car.

'You should take Leah out shopping sometime,' he says, straightening himself up.

We look at each other over the roof. Was that a joke? He's not smiling.

'I suppose I could do that.' I think of Leah's picture on his phone. But I wouldn't want to.

In the car, I settle myself in the passenger seat and Ryan puts the key in the ignition but he doesn't start the car. Instead, he tilts his head sideways, and when we have eye contact, he flattens his lips and says: 'I almost called you to cancel the trip, to tell you the truth.'

'Oh.' Confused, my gaze wanders from Ryan to the gear lever and back to Ryan. Was Flora right after all? Is he dumping me now? Right here in the car? If he is, I'll put my dating profile back up immediately. I will also raid the fridge and devour Kieran's creamy salmon tagliatelle microwave meal. I'll chuck shedloads of extra cheese on it.

I make an effort to straighten my shoulders and hope my chin won't start wobbling on me. 'Why?' I say in a defiant tone. 'Is it because you didn't really want to go to Brighton with me, but I put you on the spot?'

Ryan turns his face to the windscreen, seemingly mulling over what I just said, then one corner of his mouth curves up. 'You did put me on the spot,' he says. 'I'm glad we can agree on that, but no it's not that.' He puts his hand on my leg.

In a way he's like Mum, messing me around like that. Are we happy? Are we sad? I'd like to know where I stand.

Ryan pulls his hand away. 'It's my dog. I'm worried I may have made a mistake in selecting her from the kennel.'

♪

We arrive in sunny Brighton around one in the afternoon and pull up at a sports complex where parking is free. I'm looking forward to the two days we've got here, but I do hope his mood will improve soon. I wish he hadn't taken his dog to a shopping centre for practice just before our trip. Then maybe I could've got a word in edgewise on our way over here. He still doesn't know I'm sharing my flat with Kieran and they'll meet tomorrow. All Ryan talked about was Sally, although I'm glad he didn't mention Leah again.

Sally gets distracted when she walks on smooth floors. Too distracted to properly carry out her tasks. Unfortunately, Ryan only found out about this last night, when he'd asked a potential buyer to come and look at the training. The buyer lost interest and told him the problem may not be solvable. Canada is off the table, for this summer at least.

We start the thirty-minute walk to the greyhound stadium and turn into a road with an asphalt pavement and low red-brick garden walls.

'What did you tell your boss this morning?' Ryan asks, sipping from a small water bottle. 'Did you pull a sickie?'

'I didn't speak to my supervisor. I spoke to someone from Scheduling. I just told them I needed to extend my leave to sort out a few more things and that I'd be available again next week.'

Ryan twists the cap back on the bottle. 'They're not very difficult where you work.'

He's right. With thousands of colleagues to cover for me, I'm not exactly pushing the company to the brink of liquidation with my absence, but they do think my time off is still family-related. I hope Annette won't call me again.

'My next flight is on Thursday,' I say. 'I'm going to Tehran for four days. After that I'm going to Johannesburg, then to Chicago and then Osaka. Osaka will give me six days' leave and that's when I'm going to New York for my birthday. You're welcome to join me if you want.'

I glance at Ryan's profile. He's silent; keeps his gaze on the footway, but then he takes my hand. 'How long are you going for?' he says.

'Probably four days.'

He's silent again, and I listen to the dull sound our steps make on the pavement.

'Do you get a discount for Canada as well?' he asks.

'I do. I get discounts for any flight I want. You basically just pay taxes.'

'Can't we go to Canada?'

'No. We could go there some other time, but I want to be in New York for my thirtieth birthday.'

More silence.

'I want to get a second opinion from another dog handler.'

Ryan lets go of my hand. 'I know this guy who's got two decades of experience in training police dogs. Only it will cost money and I just haven't got it at the moment. I'm still waiting for three customers to pay me.'

'Pay you for your IT services?' I ask, but I'm disappointed he's changed the topic.

'Yes,' Ryan replies. He's got a deep furrow between his brows. 'They're supposed to pay me within eight working days. I've already chased one of them up, but... it's just a nightmare.'

My thoughts turn to Gareth. Freedom-shmeedom, as they would say in America. I'm sure there are benefits to being self-employed but having a bit of money to get by clearly isn't one of them. Ryan told me when we were driving over here that his dad had given him money for petrol. He turned down my offer to go halves and said that I could pay for dinner. I'm not doing so badly for myself, when I think about it. Maybe I should just be grateful to have a good job and see so much of the world, and not constantly think about leaving the company.

♪

Ryan and I are approaching a zebra crossing where a handful of protestors stand around holding up banners. One reads: *Your Bets, Their Blood* and another has a drawing of a black dog lying in a pool of red paint.

'Just walk on and ignore them,' Ryan says. 'They were here last time too.'

But ignoring them seems impossible. A guy is shouting through a megaphone that greyhound racing is animal abuse. I'm a little shocked. I remember James once went to the dog races in Walthamstow with his dad and his brother and sister.

'I never realised there was a darker side to dog racing,' I say.

Ryan glances at me. 'Greyhound racing is not animal abuse.'

'It's not?'

'Of course not. These dogs want to work. It's in their blood. They'd be totally bored if they didn't race each other. And you hear no one complaining about horse racing. It's the same thing.'

But when we pass the protestors, the man with the megaphone, who vaguely reminds me of John Lennon from up close, with his goatee and small round glasses, looks directly at me.

'Visiting the races today?' he says.

I stop and notice that Ryan's crossing the road without me.

'Did you know that during every race there are dogs that sustain such serious injuries they need to be euthanized?' the man says, and he thrusts a leaflet into my hands.

'Thank you,' I say and run after Ryan who's waiting for me on the other side of the road.

The entrance to the stadium is marked with a broad blue sign with white letters.

'Are you sure we should go in?' I say when we get to the door.

Ryan looks at me and frowns. 'Well, I'm definitely going. It's my sole purpose for coming here.'

I take another look at the leaflet.

'Did what that guy said bother you?' Ryan asks.

'No, this dog bothers me.' I shove the leaflet under Ryan's nose. 'Look at it. I think it's dead and it's lying on a track. Do you think the picture was taken in this stadium?'

Ryan glances at the leaflet. 'I don't know, maybe.'

'We shouldn't support this.'

'It's always the same with you bloody veg-heads,' Ryan suddenly says, although his tone is playful.

'What do you mean?'

'Leah didn't want to watch the races because she says it's animal abuse and she's a vegetarian too.'

'You asked her first?'

'I was at hers when Ian called me to cancel the trip.'

'Right, so… Leah didn't want to come with you because she felt sorry for the dogs?'

'No, she couldn't get the time off work. She's a nurse.'

Ryan takes his phone from his back pocket and glances at the screen. 'It starts in twenty-five minutes. It's the last race. Look, you don't have to come with me. If this is not for you, I'll understand. I'll call you when it's over and meet you somewhere later. Would you be alright with that?'

I stare into Ryan's eyes. He calmly looks back at me. I don't believe it. I wasn't expecting this. I thought he'd try and win me over, coax me into going with him. I would have let him win, but I can't back down now.

'Of course; that's alright,' I say, struggling to make my voice sound upbeat. 'I'll go and visit a museum or something.'

'See, this is what I like about you.' Ryan smiles; his eyes smile too. 'I could never have done this with Leah. She'd just insist that I don't go either and my plans would've been totally spoiled again. With you I can do my own thing for a few hours and there's no drama.'

I smile feebly as he talks. At least he approves of who he thinks I am, but really, I could just weep.

'It's only one race. I shouldn't be too long, alright?' Ryan leans in and plants a firm kiss on my lips, then walks through the doors, turning once to wave at me.

On the other side of the road, the man who gave me the leaflet is shouting through his megaphone that greyhound racing is animal abuse. A lady, who's pushing a pram across the zebra, turns her head towards him with an annoyed expression on her face. He lowers the megaphone, shifts his feet and looks at me and I'm suddenly feeling embarrassed. Does it look like Ryan and I just had an argument because of the leaflet? I slip it in my bag and start walking in a direction that will hopefully lead to the city centre. I'll go and have coffee somewhere, I suppose. And cake. I must have cake.

♫

After a fifty-minute walk, I do luckily end up in the city centre and plonk myself down on a wicker chair outside a café on the Lanes. A blackboard next to the entrance has a chalked-on message that advertises chai latte and homemade spiced cheesecake. That will do me. I put a copy of *Take a Break* on the table, take a pen from my bag and look around the busy, narrow street. So, here I am, in Brighton, not Toronto, but as usual—alone.

Flora would find it hilarious if I told her what happened. 'First you invite yourself,' she'd say, 'and then you ditch yourself.'

I'm feeling a stab of discontentment at the thought though, and Patrick's face begins to swim before my eyes. I had a session with him yesterday. Why oh why, did I tell him about my trip with Ryan? If only he won't ask me how it went when I see him next week. How embarrassing. Especially since I reminded him of something he'd said to me during one of our first sessions: that it was best for me not to date. I told him, yesterday— and in a rather cocky manner, to my shame—that I *was* dating and then I asked him why he'd said that to me.

Patrick didn't remember saying it. He had to flick back to the beginning of his notepad to jog his memory. 'What we talked about,' he said, 'is your lack of an environment in which you felt safe and wanted as a child, and how you look for these conditions in your relationships with men.' He looked up from his notes and to my horror, he added: 'You talked about your one-night stands, and how you often didn't realise you were having one because you believed the men you slept with were after a committed relationship.'

I cringed in my seat when he said that; I'd forgotten all about telling him that. And then he said: 'I asked whether you might consider putting your quest for the right man on hold for the time being and focus on your own life to avoid further disappointment. Especially as you have a tendency to get emotionally attached quickly.'

Ridiculous! I don't get emotionally attached quickly! Ryan and I have known each other since January this year. Did I even mention that to Patrick? Maybe I didn't tell it right. But I do agree with his comment about disappointment. I have been disappointed a lot with men and the relationships I've tried to get off the ground after James. Yes, disappointment is the word of the day, really. How did this even happen? I drive over here with a guy, but I end up alone on a café terrace and we didn't even have a fight. Why is it so difficult to find love? Real love, I mean. Other people find it all the time.

Carys, have you considered the possibility that you might be alone because you wanted Ryan to prove his loyalty to you? It backfired. Do you really believe he's the right man for you?

Patrick's voice sounds so clear in my head, it's almost as if I've channelled him. The chair opposite me is no longer empty.

'Is that the reason?' I reply, sarcastically, but Patrick just smiles at me. The skin around his eyes crinkles.

'Pardon?' a female voice says. The woman at the table next to me gives me a quizzical look.

'Oh, nothing.' I flash her a smile and quickly turn to my hot chai latte. Disappointment really is the word of the day. This tea is disgusting and it cost almost five pounds. Flora and the young, spotty waiter from Kew Gardens pop into my head. When he'd cleared her soup bowl last Saturday, he asked if everything was alright and she said, 'Not really. Your soup smells diviny but it tastes like hiny. Tell your chef that.'

He'd flushed bright red and told her he'd pass on the message.

A titter escapes my mouth. I can still see Flora's face when she said it— the drooping bottom lip and big eyes. Now a chortle gets out, and another one when I notice Patrick's laughing too.

The woman at the table next to me gives me an awkward smile. She also has a magazine spread out on the table before her, next to a muffin and a cup of coffee. Sad cow; all alone, like me, on a Friday afternoon in Brighton. She hasn't got a ring on her finger either.

I burst into a fit of laughter and tears start running down my face. She's just making it worse with those looks she's giving me! I shake in my chair and when I notice Patrick's belly wobble from laughing too, I picture him dressed up as Santa and almost double over the table. OMG—this is just what the doctor ordered. I sniff hard and wipe my face with the napkin that came with the cheesecake, then blow my nose in it, making sure to avoid eye contact with the woman next to me. Seeing her face will only set me off again.

It takes me a few moments to realise my phone is ringing and I quickly pull it from my bag.

'Where are you?' Ryan asks.

'I'm in an art gallery on the Lanes,' I reply.

The woman turns her head to me, and this time she boldly holds my gaze, as if she wants to figure me out. I smile at her and she quickly looks away. It's beginning to look like flirting now.

'Where are *you*?' I ask Ryan.

'I'm on a bus; just getting off now.'

'Yes, but where *are* you?'

'I'm on King's Road. Hang on.' I hear him talking to a man, then Ryan says: 'Yeah, the driver tells me it's a ten-minute walk to where you are. I'll see you in a bit.'

♪

The purple flowerpots attached to the white brick wall and the red and pink geraniums spilling from them on either side of the door are what made me notice this gallery earlier. The late afternoon sun is still strong and I enjoy being on my feet again and studying the gallery's eclectic art display in the window, while I wait for Ryan. I'm especially drawn to an impressive seascape in oil of a medieval ship with three tall masts cutting through white-crested waves, fighting for survival in stormy waters. Dad would have loved it. It was his dream to have work on sale in art galleries. I know he had ambitions way beyond that Sunday-market on Bayswater Road and the art fair in Wales where he exhibited his work a couple of times.

I turn away from the window and spot Ryan sauntering towards me; a phone glued to his ear. He looks boyish in his blue jeans, dark green shirt and black All-stars. His sunglasses are perched on his head and the strap of his black satchel is slung across his chest. He casually glances left and right at quirky shops. Right before he catches up with me, I hear him say: 'I'll speak to you tomorrow,' and then he ends the call.

'Was that Leah?' I ask.

He examines my face. 'Yes, that was Leah.'

'What did she want?'

'Nothing. She just called for a chat.'

'Did you tell her you're here with me?'

'No.'

'Why not?'

Ryan narrows his eyes. 'It didn't come up.'

An uncomfortable silence hangs between us. He's standing, rigid, one foot before the other, and it feels as if he's waiting for me to make the next move.

'Did you have fun at the races?' I ask, not knowing what else to say.

'I lost, but it was interesting,' is all he says, but at least the awkward moment has passed.

Ryan glances at the paintings in the gallery's window, and at one of a beach scene in acrylics in particular. 'It's my dad's birthday next month,' he says. 'I wonder how much it is.'

'It's probably very expensive,' I say.

'Yeah, probably. Would you mind taking another look?' A bell jangles when he opens the door.

The gallery is pleasantly cool; a large fan whirs from the ceiling. The space is narrow and long, but bright with lots of daylight streaming in through four large skylights.

I think of the dark little shop in Singapore I visited two weeks ago, and of the polka- dot girl who lied to me, saying I looked like a model. Her shop could have done with some skylights. In my head, I ask the Universe to give her love and prosperity. I say these little prayers often. They centre me and make me feel more connected to the other side.

The owner of the gallery, a bejewelled woman of maybe sixty with a smoker's face and clad in a ketchup-coloured suit, greets us with a curt 'Good afternoon.'

Ryan and I wander around, along with a half-dozen other visitors. More sea-themed paintings decorate the wall to our left. A number of marble sculptures, the smaller ones perched on pedestals, are dotted throughout the premises.

Ryan moves to the left and I don't follow him. In a corner, I notice a man and woman admiring a large bronze sculpture of two naked lovers in a horizontal embrace. The heads of the lovers are adorned with olive wreaths. It's a lovely sculpture but I'm more interested in the flutes of champagne the man and woman are sipping from and glance at the counter near the door. Is there a tray with drinks you can help yourself to? If there is, I don't see it.

'*Heel passioneel*,' the woman says. Her slim fingers rest against her throat. She's got a sophisticated style about her. The man says: '*ja*,' and starts to rattle on about something. I think they might be Dutch.

I look for Ryan and find him talking to the owner. When he sees me, he says: 'That painting in the window is only eight-hundred pounds, Carys,' before resuming his conversation. The look on his face suggests genuine interest and the ability to hand over the dough and leave with the painting under his arm. What an idiot.

'We have more of Cisz's work over there,' the owner says, indicating a wall deeper down the gallery. I follow behind them, careful not to knock over any of the sculptures.

'These are by the same artist.' She gestures at four paintings on the wall. Two of them are beach scenes, similar to the one in the window, and the other two are portraits of a blonde woman. The artist's muse? She's lying on a sofa reading a book in one of them, but of course, Ryan is more interested in the one that shows her standing before an open window in a barely-there nighty that shows off her curves.

The gallery owner moves away and Ryan leans forward to read the placard on the wall. 'The artist is Brazilian,' he says. 'That probably explains why she's got such an enormous backside.'

I'm about to tell Ryan we don't all have to fit into a size ten, when my phone's ringtone rudely cuts through the gallery's serene ambiance. The landline number looks vaguely familiar, but I don't know who's calling me.

'Hello?' I say.

'Carys! How could you!' my mother screeches. 'Going behind my back like that. How dare you?'

Ryan stares at me and I turn my back to him, feeling my cheeks burn. I know exactly what Mum is talking about and clearly see that I've made a big mistake…

'They think I'm crazy now,' she shouts, 'and I have you, my own daughter, to thank for that.'

'I'm sorry,' I stammer. 'I thought I was helping you… I just thought that if Dr Seymour had more information he could help you better, give you the best medication and—'

'Shame on you, Carys. You've gossiped about me. About your own mother.'

'I'm sorry,' I stammer again, but I'm starting to feel so angry that for a moment I'm seeing spots. I can't believe that Dr Seymour. What a bastard! He blabbed everything I told him back to Mum! I thought our conversation was confidential. And I really did think I was helping her because everything seemed such a mess when I left her.

'Could you take your call outside, please?' The gallery owner gives me a stern look. 'You're bothering my patrons.'

I nod apologetically and walk towards the door. I hear Ryan answering back behind me. 'My girlfriend's not being loud.'

'The person she's talking to is,' the owner retorts.

'Don't you come here again,' Mum rants on. 'Don't you ever set foot in here again. I don't want to see you anymore, do you hear me? And I know it was you. You called the RSPCA.'

This makes my chin wobble, because I honestly didn't and it's so unfair. Yes, I spoke with Doctor Seymour last Sunday before I left. I told him everything I know; how she hit us when we were children, how she sometimes speaks in a child's voice, especially when you call her out on something and she doesn't want to be responsible, how she's obsessed with the RSPCA, I said all that and I shouldn't have, but I did not call the RSPCA. I didn't.

'Don't you ever show your face here again, do you hear me?'

'Yes,' I say quietly. 'I heard you the first time.'

Ryan closes the door behind us. The bell jangles.

'Who was that?' he says, when he sees me ending the call.

'No one.'

'Your mother?'

'No.' I look through the glass panel in the door. The gallery owner is standing near the counter, firm, with folded arms, as if trying to guard her fort from the invader; the undesirable one. Me.

'Do you still want to see the paintings?' I ask. 'I won't answer my phone if she calls back.'

Ryan glances at the woman, who's glaring back at us. 'No, that's alright,' he says. 'They probably have a website. I'll look the artist up online.'

'Good idea', I say. 'We're here now, but let's look at it on the internet.'

Ryan smiles at me, links his arm through mine and steers me away from the door, down the cobbled shopping street. He makes me feel better; cared for, and he called me his girlfriend too. Maybe he's more into me than I thought.

'That *was* my mother actually,' I say. 'She isn't feeling very happy at the moment, unfortunately, but she's getting help for that.'

At least I have my window of opportunity now. I can tell him that Kieran is living with me and why, but I'll make sure to stick to the basics.

Chapter 18

It's the first Saturday of July. We've just pulled up before my home in Sandycombe Road and Ryan's fetching our bags from the car while I'm waiting on the pavement. The weather's been gorgeous all day and so was our second day in Brighton. Ryan kept holding my hand and putting his arm around my waist as we strolled around the Royal Pavilion Garden and the museum this morning. He still talked about Sally quite a bit but he didn't mention Leah at all, and when I explained the situation with Mum and Kieran to him yesterday, he seemed quite understanding. But, most important, he said he'd think about coming to New York with me! I've had that song, 'Things Can Only Get Better' on the brain all day.

I'm a tad nervous too, though, because if Kieran is in, they'll meet in a minute. Quite an official moment, brothers-in-law meeting for the first time. I hope he's home.

I peer up at my front window because I've become aware of something: music. Is that… Dad's piano? Kieran doesn't play, but I'm definitely hearing it. A gentle melody. A song.

I frown. Is that… Cadi's voice?

Ryan shuts the car door with a bang and moves to my side. He glances up at my window too although there's nothing to see apart from the pink curtains that are partially drawn. 'That's beautiful piano music,' he says, and adds a little surprised: 'It sounds like it's coming from your place.'

'It is coming from my place,' I reply. 'That's my sister Cadi. She didn't tell me she was coming over today.'

We walk around the house to the backyard and my heart sinks when I see Mrs Meads reading a newspaper with a magnifying glass on the bench. I want to find out why Cadi's here but now there will be introductions first, and pointless chit chat.

Trevor, is romping around at the end of the garden and rushes up to us, sniffing at our bags and at Ryan's legs. He glances down on Trevor but doesn't stoop to pet him.

I introduce Ryan to Mrs Meads and he asks her how old Trevor is.

For a moment I worry he'll have a go at her, like he had at me, about the overbreeding of Pugs, but he doesn't mention it, and I don't know why, but they strike up a conversation about dogs they had that died.

'I buried my Chloë over there,' Mrs Meads says, pointing to a spot under one of the poplar trees. 'In a box that used to contain our fake Christmas tree. I never wanted a fake tree.' She chuckles. 'A florist with a fake Christmas tree, everyone always said. I threw it out when Joseph died but I kept the box, and now Chloë's in it. We had a good life together, so a festive box was fitting, I thought.'

I smile at her, then look up at my kitchen window like Ryan because Cadi's started singing and playing again. It's the same brief, sad song. Her voice is a lot clearer here than at the front of the house.

'Lovely voice.' Mrs Meads smiles at me. 'You've got a

lovely sister. She came to my door a few hours ago because she didn't have your key. She was carrying lots of bags. She said she'd just come from Hammersmith on the tube. What a sweet girl, she is. She reminds me of myself, when I was her age.'

'Was she alright?'

'I don't know, dear. I'm not one to pry.'

'Don't you want to come in for a cuppa?' Mrs Meads calls after us when we start for the staircase. We turn around and she looks at Ryan. 'I can show you our stained glass. My husband made it.' Her gaze briefly moves to the coloured glass fruit bowl that decorates her kitchen window. 'I've got apple pie with lemon curd and clotted cream.'

'Some other time, Mrs Meads,' Ryan says.

I'm feeling a pang of guilt, because she looks so frail and lonely. I always assumed she was alright, but is she though? She must be eighty-six by now and she lives all by herself.

'Yes, definitely some other time, Mrs Meads,' I say. 'But I just want to check on my sister now.'

Trevor lies down before Mrs Meads' feet and she picks up the magnifying glass on her lap and holds it above the paper. 'You do that, dear, you do that,' she says. But when Ryan and I are half-way up the staircase, she calls me again:

'Carys. If your sister is moving in, you and I must talk finances.'

'She's not,' I reply, and I think of Kieran. 'I haven't even told her he's living with me. It hadn't occurred to me that she might want money for it. I can have guests, can't I?

I'm about to stick my key in the lock when the piano

playing and singing start again. Same tune. I use my body weight to push the door open and instantly my gaze falls on several Tesco carrier bags that are neatly lined up against the right side of the hallway. Cadi's voice— jazzy and pure— reverberates around my home.

'Stunning voice but this is the saddest song I've ever heard,' Ryan says. We put our bags on the floor beside my suitcases.

"Hang on to a Dream' by Tim Hardin is even sadder,' I say.

Cadi's doesn't hear us when we walk into the living room. She's behind the piano on the black leather-buttoned stool, almost in profile to us. Her long blonde dreadlocks are scraped back into a ponytail.

I move around the piano and stand before her. Green eyeliner runs neatly along her closed eyelids but there are some black mascara smudges on her cheeks and her nose is red.

'Cadi?'

She gives a start, then stares at me, as if she needs a few moments to centre herself. 'P'nawn da,' she says groggily. 'Can I live here?'

An awkward silence follows. I gape at my sister and then my gaze flits to Ryan who's watching us from the door. He must think our eye contact is a cue because he walks up to Cadi with an outstretched hand.

'Hiya,' she says, shaking it. 'I'm Cadi, Carys' sister. Sorry I'm still dressed in my pyjamas.'

'That's alright.' Ryan looks her over; his gaze lingers at

the boob gape between two buttons on her silky blue top.

I pull up a kitchen chair and find Lulu dozing on it, so I pull up the next chair and sit down. Annette's wilted flowers are still on the table near the wall. Heaps of petals and pollen lie scattered around the base of the vase.

'Kieran already lives here,' I say. 'I've got no more rooms left.'

'Yeah, I know,' Cadi says. 'But I thought that I could share your bed. You do have a double bed.' She glances at Ryan. 'And when he's here, I can sleep in the sofa.'

Ryan looks at the floor.

I don't really want to get into all this with him here; she's obviously not moving in with me, but I know she'll just start whining when I tell her that.

'Did you and Gareth have a fight?' I ask.

Cadi glances at Ryan again. In a reluctant tone, she says: 'Yes, we did.'

'Why?'

'I don't know. I think we're taking a break.' She gets up from the piano, scoops Lulu up in her arms and sits down on the sofa. 'I'll tell you what happened some other time, alright?'

'Hey, um,' Ryan says in a low voice, 'I should probably go.'

'Why?' I reply. 'You don't have to. You were going to stay until Sunday.'

'I'm having a déjà vu,' Ryan says with a slight grimace.

'So am I,' I say. 'You don't have to leave.'

'Don't change your plans because of me,' Cadi says from

the sofa. 'Just pretend I'm not here.'

'Well, I think the two of you probably have a lot to talk about,' Ryan says, after a short pause. He glances at the clock on the kitchen wall. 'If I leave now, I can still have dinner with my parents.'

I don't know what to say anymore and Ryan starts for the door. 'You're a great singer, by the way,' he says to Cadi.

'Thank you,' she replies.

'Carys told me you want to study art, but why don't you go to a conservatoire to study music?'

Cadi's face clouds over the moment Ryan mentions the word art, but I don't think he notices.

'You're sitting on a goldmine with that song,' he goes on.

'Nah,' she says. 'It's not that good. The last line needs a bit of work still.'

'I know a guy who's a manager.' Ryan looks at me. 'Leah's brother actually. He's also a record producer and he's got his own boy band. They had a huge hit in Japan last year and they've just released an album called Cheese Board. It's really cheesy Euro-Pop, but in Japan everybody goes wild over their music.'

He turns back to Cadi. 'Marcus knows a lot of people at record companies. I can give you his number if you want.'

'Nah, that's alright, thanks.' She smiles thinly.

'Alright,' Ryan says, 'well if you change your mind…' He puts his hand on the doorknob. 'I'll call you next week, okay?' he says to me.

I don't reply and follow him into the hall.

'You've got quite a bit of drama going on in your life, haven't you?' Ryan grabs his satchel from the floor.

'Have I? Why?'

'Your mother… you've taken on your brother, and now your sister.'

'That's their drama, not mine.'

'Right. Because your only drama is getting paid to fly all over the world but loathing your job.'

'Right,' I say weakly. I don't really get his comment. Was it a joke? Was it cynical?

Ryan shoves a hand in the pocket of his jeans and his car keys jingle and then he sighs. I've never heard him sigh before—outside of the bedroom. Is my family now draining my boyfriends too?

'Anyway,' Ryan says, turning to the front door, but I interrupt him. 'When will I see you again?'

'That's a—'

'Yes, that's a song.'

He gives me a wan smile. 'I'll call you next week. Probably Monday night.' He presses a kiss on my lips and opens the door.

I stay in the hallway until I can no longer hear his shoes clanging on the metal staircase.

♪

Cadi's in the kitchen putting cheddar cheese squares on a sandwich. 'So, that was Mr Dating Site,' she says, without looking up. 'He's got an arrogant face. Do you really like him?'

'Of course I like him. He doesn't have an arrogant face.'

Cadi glances out of the kitchen window. 'Alright, maybe arrogant isn't the right word, but he's got a stroppiness about him. Don't you think? Or is it just me?'

I step past her and open the fridge. 'I know what you mean, but he's alright. We had a great time in Brighton and he's probably coming to New York with me too, next month. I've known him since January.'

'Have you? Well, maybe I got him wrong, then.' Cadi points at her sandwich. 'Would you like one?'

'No, thank you.' I peer at my fridge contents. Plenty of vegetables and there's still goat's cheese. 'I'm cooking a veggie lasagne in an hour or so,' I say. 'Wouldn't you rather have that?'

'I might have some later, if that's alright,' Cadi says, 'but I'll have this for now; I'm starving.'

I close the fridge door and move to the piano because I've noticed a sheet of paper on the music rack. 'You wrote this song, didn't you?' I ask, picking it up.

'Yes, I did.'

'The music and the lyrics?'

'Yes, both.' Cadi takes her plate to the kitchen table and I study the song.

RAIN WAS COMING DOWN

'Is this song about you and Gareth?'

'Of course it's not. It's just a song.'

I sit down across from her and put the sheet of music on the table.

Cadi glances at it. 'It's a teeny tiny bit about me and Gareth,' she says.

'Is it? Have you been a fool?'

'No, I haven't.' She casts me a hurt look.

'What's going on with you two then?'

'I don't want to talk about it right now.'

'Why not?'

'Because I don't, alright? I told you I would tell you later.'

'You haven't split up, have you?'

'Carys.'

I drop it and we're silent. Cadi nibbles on her sandwich.

'Where's Kieran?' I ask.

'He went to Camden with Gareth. He said he'd be back around eight.' She picks at a bread crust. 'Gareth's like a father to Kieran.'

'Like a father?' I repeat, a little bemused. 'I wouldn't go that far. More like a brother.'

She takes another bite and stares at her song. 'Gareth's always there for him,' she says with her mouth full. 'He's always there for everybody. He's always driving around, helping his mates, doing things for our family. And now…'

Cadi's bottom lip forms a curl and she bends her head forward. A sticky lump of chewed-up food drops from her mouth onto the plate and she starts sobbing.

I walk around the table and put my hands on her heaving shoulders. Lulu's on the chair next to Cadi, squinting her eyes at me and purring.

'I miss him so much,' Cadi cries.

'I know, I know,' I say. An image of James floats through my mind. 'Has Gareth split up with you?'

'Yes.' The word shudders from her mouth.

'Poor thing.'

I stand beside her for a few minutes, but then she sits up straight and wipes an arm across her face. 'I'm fine.'

'No, you're not. It's alright to cry. Would you like a cup of tea?'

'I would,' she says, getting up from her chair.

'I meant I'd make you one.' I put my hands on her shoulders and push her back on the chair. 'You just sit. Do you still want this?'

Cadi shakes her head and pushes her plate away.

'I've got regular tea,' I say, walking over to the kettle, 'but I've also got laven—'

'Can I live here, please, Carys? Please? I've got nowhere to go.' She looks at me with big, watery eyes.

'Cadi… you can't live here.' My voice falters. 'Kieran's already living here. I haven't got the space.'

'Oh, please Carys, please. I've got nowhere else to go. I'll do all the cooking and all your cleaning. I'll make you tiffin every day.'

I fold my arms and lean my back against the worktop. 'Why are you the one who's moving out? When I left James, he kept the flat because I was the one who wanted to split up.'

'Because Gareth's got nowhere to go.'

'Well, neither have you.'

'I've got family here. Gareth's whole family lives in Wales. Well, and in Southport, but that's too far away. And we're going to give the landlord our notice anyway because neither of us can afford to live there alone. When you left James, one of his friends moved in with him a few months later, right?'

'Yes, that's right.'

'Because the flat was too expensive?'

'Yes.'

Cadi leans her chin on the palm of her hand. She's got a worried expression on her face.

'Mum's house is not an option?' I carefully suggest.

She opens her mouth in horror and I look at the floor and then I turn back to the kettle and make us both a mug of lavender tea with honey.

'You can stay here for a little while,' I say, a few minutes later, when we've moved to the sofa.

'How long's a little while?'

'Would a month help?'

Cadi doesn't make a reply. Lulu is sprawled on her lap, paws in the air, and Cadi scratches her belly.

'Can't I stay for three months?'

I mull this over for a moment. It's not like I'm here every day. I'm away from home a lot, so we wouldn't get in each other's hair all the time. And it would be better for Kieran to have someone here. But still, I'm not keen on the idea.

'I'm hoping that Ryan will come over more often,' I say. 'You'd have to sleep on the sofa every time he's here.'

Cadi shrugs her shoulders. 'I wouldn't mind that.'

'I'll think about it,' I say. 'But meanwhile do look out for something else, alright?'

We're silent again, until Cadi says: 'Oh, I wanted to ask

you. Who's Leah?'

'Leah?' I repeat, caught off guard. 'Um, Leah is Ryan's best friend.'

Cadi frowns. 'He told you that?'

'Yes, he did.'

'And you believe him?'

'Yes, I do.'

Cadi holds my gaze. 'I don't.'

Chapter 19

'Good to see you, Carys.' Gareth gets up from the wooden table outside The Cricketers pub in Richmond. It's Monday afternoon and they've just opened up for lunch. A few besuited men carrying briefcases hurry past us and go inside.

Gareth's unshaven and the buttons of his open jacket press through the thin fabric of my dress when he hugs me.

I don't hug him back. After all, he very unexpectedly split up with my sister, called her a slapper, and I'm not even sure what I'm here for. He sent me a text yesterday, asking if I could see him today. Alone.

'Thanks for taking the trouble,' he says, sitting down.

I take the seat across from him. 'It's no trouble.' I glance at Gareth's Boots carrier bag on the table. 'But I can't stay for too long. I'm going to Hackney this afternoon; my train leaves at 14:21.'

Gareth checks his phone. 'It's only a quarter past twelve, so we've got a while then. Are you visiting someone?'

'Yes, I am.'

'Your boyfriend?'

'No. A woman. Ryan lives in Godalming.'

Gareth picks up the bag. 'Here,' he says, handing me a sandwich pack. 'It's cheese and onion. Vegetarian.'

'Oh.' I cast the pub's lunch special that's scribbled on a chalkboard a wistful glance. 'Thank you. But we're not having lunch here?'

Gareth grimaces. 'Can't afford it. I'm having a bit of a crisis at the moment, as you can imagine.'

'Right,' I say. 'Well, we'd better not hog this table then.'

I get up and so does Gareth, and I face him squarely. 'So, what's going on with you and Cadi? Aren't you getting married anymore?'

'I don't know.' Gareth gazes at a stretch of The Green on the other side of the road. 'I don't know what to think anymore.'

'That's very sad,' I reply. 'And I'm so sorry for Cadi. She's gutted.'

Gareth looks at his feet.

'I must say though, Gareth, I did always think you were a bit young to get married.'

'I'm not too young. I'm twenty-six.'

'Cadi's only twenty-three. What's the rush?'

'See, this is why I wanted to talk to you.' Gareth's voice is tinged with despair. 'You're like the sister I've never had and I really want to hear your thoughts on it all. A lot has happened. But shall we look for somewhere to sit down first?' Gareth holds up the bag. 'I've got drinks and crisps too.'

We cross the road and walk past an old stone drinking fountain to a shady bench that's flanked by two huge, leafy trees. This may well be the prettiest spot on The Green, I think, settling myself down beside Gareth.

At the far end of the open area, behind a line of trees and parked cars, there's a white period townhouse which hosts the SGI centre where Flora goes to chant. I've been there a couple of times with her.

'Sparkling water or Coke?' Gareth holds up two plastic bottles.

'Water please, unless you want it.'

He hands me the bottle and puts his hand back in the bag. 'Prawns or vinegar?'

'Vinegar, please. Do you want me to give you the money?'

Gareth makes a dismissive hand gesture. 'That's alright. My treat.'

He twists the Coke bottle open and takes a gulp.

I think about what he said, the morning we picked up Kieran in his car. That nothing beats the freedom that comes with being your own boss. Two weeks ago that was, but it feels longer. Gareth had been in charge then, of our 'getting Kieran to Sandycombe Road project,' but today I find him rather dejected. I can't believe he sees me as the sister he's never had. I've resented him, so often, and I don't blame myself for it. He doesn't just smoke weed, he deals in it and even grew it in their bedsit. He bought an instruction manual and a lamp and seeds and everything. And his attempts at running a business...

First, he tried his hand at selling tie-dye batik T-shirts and when that didn't pan out he thought of beanie hats. Cadi's responsible for paying the lion's share of their bills. Patsy never had a sister; she was an only child. She keeps popping up in my head.

Gareth stretches his legs before him and takes a bite of his sandwich. 'I've just been to see a fabric designer in Strawberry

Hill.' He pauses. 'She's got her own studio. She's really a fabric *artist*. She makes lovely stuff, but she's too expensive. Thinks she can charge me fifty-five quid for a metre of bespoke design. I'd told her I was just starting up. My hats would become unaffordable if I went with her.'

'Cadi said you're thinking of moving back to Wales.'

Gareth glances at me. 'Not just thinking; doing it. Maybe as soon as next week.'

'So, you're giving up your bedsit?'

'Yes. Unless Cadi wants to hold on to it and live there with a friend.' Gareth puts his empty sandwich pack back in the bag. 'But I don't think that's what she wants. And most of her friends live with their boyfriends anyway.' He reaches inside his jacket and pulls out a cigarette. 'Do you mind if I smoke this?'

'Yes, I do.'

Gareth flattens his lips and puts the cigarette back and then we glance at a woman, a few feet away, who spreads a blanket out under a tree and lies her baby down on it.

'The worst thing about it,' Gareth says, 'is that she can't even tell me how many she's sold. I asked her: "Ten? Thirty?" But she says she doesn't know and I'm having a hard time believing that.'

'What did Cadi sell?'

Gareth turns his face to me. 'She hasn't told you?'

'Told me what?'

'I thought she'd told you. She told you I'm moving back to Wales.'

'She sold something? What was it?'

He grimaces. 'You should really ask her.'

'She doesn't want to talk about anything.'

'I'll bet she doesn't.'

'She hasn't helped you with selling weed, has she?' My stomach churns at the thought; I worry about Cadi.

'Carys, seriously. What the effin fuck do you take me for?' Gareth's shaking his head and takes the cigarette back from his pocket. 'What I do is no big deal. A mate of mine in Amsterdam sends me a bit of Ketama and Polm once in a while, which I sell on to a couple of my friends, but that's all. And I haven't smoked a spliff myself in six months.'

He puts the cigarette back in his pocket. 'Like I would wreck Cadi's life by dragging her into a Marihuana business… But you believe what you want to believe, Carys.'

I cast Gareth a sceptical look. 'You smoked a spliff in my mother's attic at Easter.'

His eyes widen. 'Kieran told you that? It was out of the window.'

'That was in April.'

'Alright, so I've not smoked them for four months.'

'Three.'

After a silence I say: 'Cadi told me to tell you she loves you.'

Gareth leans forward and puts his head between his hands.

'Do you still love her?'

He turns his face to me. 'Of course, I still love her. You don't suddenly stop loving someone. It's nothing to do with that.'

'What is it then?'

'I can't get past what she did. That's what it is; she's pushed me too far. I can't just forget about this and move on as if nothing's happened…'

He sits up straight and looks at me squarely. 'She sold her knickers, Carys, on eBay. She's sold her knickers to raise money for art school.'

Gareth's leaning forward again and massages his scalp with his fingers. 'Why couldn't she have been more patient with me? If I'd known she was that desperate to study art I wouldn't have started up my beanie hat business. I would've gone for a well-paid job, God knows where…'

Gareth jabbers on while I let the information sink in. I must say that I agree with Gareth. I don't know what to think either. I can't believe Cadi did that. But I also think it's brilliant. I wonder how much money she made.

Gareth runs his hands through his hair. 'Why couldn't she have been more patient with me?' he says again. 'We were going to move to Wales after the wedding. She could have studied there. I would have helped her. There was no need for this.'

I'm still not talking, just thinking. I can only help Cadi if I say the right thing at the right time, but I can't decide on the best approach.

'To think that men,' Gareth goes on, 'complete strangers, have stuck their noses in her snail trails and—'

'Excuse me?'

Gareth glances at me. 'I said, to think—'

'Yes, I heard what you said and it was very condescending of you, Gareth. You don't compare a woman's natural discharge to that. Show some respect.'

'Oh, sorry...' he stammers. 'I just—' But I cut him off.

'So, Cadi's sold her knickers. Is that all?'

He blinks his eyes. 'What... is that all?'

'Yes. She sold knickers, and I assume you mean knickers she's worn. That's the reason you're angry with her and why you've left her.'

'Is-that-all?' Gareth says again, incredulous. 'Well, I think it's quite a lot, don't you?'

'I completely understand you're a little disappointed in Cadi, but don't forget that only five months from now, you were going to promise her you'd have her for better or for worse.'

Gareth looks baffled.

'You thought you were mature enough to get married,' I say. 'Now you can show us how mature you really are by dealing with your problems like an adult without walking away. You could see this as practice really, for when you're really married.'

I smile at him but he averts his eyes and scratches the side of his head. 'For better or for worse,' he mumbles. 'Yes. But this?'

'This is nothing.'

'It's not?'

'Nah. Lots of women do this.'

'Lots of women sell their knickers?'

'That's right.'

'You know anyone who does that?'

'Yes, Cadi.'

'Besides her.'

'No, but I've heard about it. It's quite fashionable, apparently.'

After this, we're silent. I eat my sandwich and Gareth eats my vinegar crisps.

'I do love Cadi,' he says after a while. 'Maybe I could get past this. But whatever happens, I don't want to live in London anymore. I definitely want to move back to Wales.'

Chapter 20

Cadi's calling me again; her number flashes on my screen. I switched off the sound when I was on the train on my way over here. This is her third call. She wants to know what Gareth said of course, but I'm not answering. I only want to think about my Patsy plan right now. Besides, now she knows what it's like when you're desperate for answers but your sister's not picking up the phone.

I'm in Costa Coffee, sipping iced coffee from a black straw at a small window table, and watch red double-decker buses driving down Amhurst Road and people walking by. When I got off the train at Hackney Central, ten minutes ago, I asked a homeless guy for directions to the estate where I think Patsy lives. He asked me for a pound, which I gave him.

'Five minutes at the most,' he said, telling me how to get there. That took me aback though because, somehow, I'd imagined a good thirty-minute walk over to Patsy's place, and during that walk, I would've had time to think.

I suppose I'll hang around Costa Coffee for a while longer and do the thinking here. Should I just go home? Send Patsy a message on Facebook? No, it wouldn't be the same if I did that; I want to look her in the eye, even if I'm scared.

For months now, I've envisaged looking her up, and

imagined conversations with her in which I had the courage to speak my mind. But the physical reality of being here now, in Hackney, is so stark it almost feels surreal.

I'm not even sure if Patsy's home of course. She could be at work. Who knows, maybe she's a nurse, like Leah. But what if she is home? I'll be intruding on her life. She's happily getting on with things and suddenly there's me at the door, demanding answers. What would I even say to her? *I'd like to talk to you about what happened with my sister.*

It's been twenty-four years, get a life! She might throw back at me.

It's not about time, I'll tell her. *It doesn't feel like twenty-four years to me. It's about what happened and what you did. I'm having counselling for it. Your mother didn't even come to the funeral. It's not like Wales is at the other end of the world.'*

You leave my mother out of it, she might say.

But I'll tell her: *You didn't leave my mother out of it! If you had, I might have seen the hole. You angered me, with your lies, and I forgot to watch Bethan, for just one moment. It was all your fault, Patsy. And you bullied me all the time. Why?*

Because... she'll say, and I can just picture that mean smile on her ghastly lips, *I was just a child.*

Ugh. She'd have a point with that.

Frustrated, I spoon whipped cream into my mouth. Kids can get away with anything, just because they're kids. Kids can inflict damage, lifelong damage, and they won't be held accountable for any of it. It's just not fair.

Life isn't fair. That's a given. Patrick said that once. He's been quiet today. He usually turns up when I'm feeling like this—wobbly— but he's not here. It probably means I have to do this by myself. I know what I'll do… I'll go to the estate, look up her flat, and decide then whether to pursue this or not. I'll give myself permission to retreat if I want to.

♪

The housing estate, grey and run-down, consists of a tower block and several low-rise flats. I'm not sure in which one of the buildings Patsy lives, so walk across a patch of grass that's littered with discarded coke cans and sandwich packs to check the flat numbers on the tallest building first. Long columns of nameplates are fixed to the wall beside long columns of small, round bells. I spot Patsy on the sixth floor; V. and P. Manozzi it says. It's thanks to V. I'm even here. Nothing came up when I googled Patsy but when I googled her husband's name I found a phone number and then this address.

Right. What's the worst that could happen? I'm here now; let's do this. I press the bell and wait. The intercom crackles.

'Hullo?' a man says.

'Oh, hello,' I reply, my voice an octave higher than usual. 'I'm Carys Wynne. I'm an old friend of Patsy's. I was wondering if she's home?'

There's a buzzing sound and then a lock clicks, and I quickly pull the door open. The communal entrance looks clean but smells dank.

I decide to skip the elevator, but when I start to ascend

the grey concrete stairway, my legs feel wobbly and my stomach hurts. I'm supposed to be rehearsing what I'll say but my mind's gone blank. I don't think, now that I'm here, that I'll have the courage to be myself. I'll smile and make small talk; I'll play a role, like I do at work. But I'll accept that I am who I am. I don't have to be a flawless human being; it's all fine.

The door of their corner flat is already ajar. I must have sounded quite convincing when I said I'm an old friend of Patsy's.

'Hello?' I call, with my mouth near the opening.

Hurried footsteps come through the hall, and a guy, Vincenzo I assume, appears in the doorway. Italian Stallion not so much. He's barely taller than I am, his eyes squint a bit, tufts of wispy hair stick out on the sides of his head, while he's bald on top. I feel a pang of misplaced gratitude for having bagged myself a guy like Ryan.

'You Carys?' he says. He's got an East London accent so I don't really get why he speaks like a Mafioso, but I smile at him.

'Yes, I'm Carys.'

'Vincenzo,' he says. He steps back from the door and indicates I should come in, which I do, but then my heart skips a beat. On the floor, next to the grey doormat, there's a pair of clunky brown boots with thick black soles and three large Velcro straps. She wore those special shoes as a child too. I'm definitely in Patsy's house again. Back in the lion's den. The last time that happened Bethan was with me. I can almost feel her small hand in mine. We had her for only one more hour, and we didn't know it.

Hyper alert, I follow Vincenzo. A vague aroma of fenugreek and cumin lingers in the hallway, which only adds to my feeling of being a lamb that's brought to the slaughterhouse. I should have listened to Patrick. Is it too late to bolt for the door?

I recognise Patsy DeMelo instantly. She's lying on the sofa, clad in a gleaming purple sports jacket, but her lower body is covered with a small tartan blanket. The blanket is pulled taut where her toes form an elongated point. Already, it's not how I imagined it. I hadn't thought of her in a horizontal position. She always towered over me.

Vincenzo disappears through a door curtain of colourful plastic strips.

'You've not changed much,' Patsy grunts. Behind her, London's architecture and a dozen scattered trees stretch far and wide.

'Neither have you,' I say. God, she's big. Much bigger than when she was a child. Her eyes are sunken in her pudgy face. The ghastly finger rests on her hip above the blanket. I remember her lips as puffy but heart-shaped, but now they resemble the mouth of a horse.

Patsy stirs and closes her eyes. 'Did your mother tell you I live here?'

'Yes, she did,' I say, trying to hide my surprise. Does Mum know where Patsy lives? Not once had that occurred to me. If she does, how come?

Vincenzo reappears with three glasses and half a bottle of Coke which he puts on the coffee table. Patsy and I watch him crouch and twist the red cap open. The three of us are silent; there's just the sound of fizzy liquid whooshing into a glass. Vincenzo quickly sticks a finger in the bubbles to keep them from flowing over. 'Do you want some?' he says to me, pouring a second glass.

'I'm fine thank you,' I reply.

Patsy sits up. Her arm trembles when she reaches for the glass that Vincenzo passes her. Her thumb and two fused fingers fold around it. Vincenzo sits down on the floor, near her legs, and gulps from his drink. They don't offer me a seat.

'How are you?' I ask Patsy, in a deliberately upbeat tone.

Vincenzo takes the glass from her and she sinks back onto the sofa, rearranging the blanket over her legs.

'Exhausted,' she says, a little breathless. 'I was at the hospital for three days. We just got back.'

'Oh.' I shift my feet. 'Are you alright?'

Patsy closes her eyes; her heavy chest rises and falls. 'I had an abortion last night. I was twenty-three weeks pregnant.' She opens her eyes and they seek out Vincenzo. 'But she wasn't right. She was like me.'

Vincenzo crinkles his forehead; a pained expression moves over his face.

'I'm sorry,' I say, because that's what I'm supposed to say. I'm not sorry though. I'm sorry for the baby but not for Patsy. I'm not angry with Patsy either. I don't feel anything, apart from a little surprise. About what she just said. The baby was like her, meaning: not having a standard set of fingers and toes? And does that mean life wouldn't have been worth living? I don't really get it. Patsy's here. She's found love. I can tell from the way Vincenzo looks at her. I never realised the finger and toe thing was such a big deal to her. But maybe there was more going on with the baby.

Patsy presses the palm of her hand against her forehead and I stare at the finger.

'Patsy's very tired,' Vincenzo says in a low voice.

'Yes, I should get going,' I say, but I don't move and glance around the living room. Not a single plant have they got here, and judging from the damaged laminate flooring and chipped wooden furniture they must be pretty skint. This is not a homely home, which fits the image I had of Patsy. I can't even imagine a child growing up in this place, with these people for parents.

'I'm sorry for your loss,' I say, turning to the door.

Vincenzo catches my eye and nods at me. I do feel sorry for him.

I look at Patsy. A bit of eyeball is gleaming through half-open lashes.

'Bye,' she says.

Vincenzo glances up. 'Bye,' he says.

Is anyone even going to let me out? I guess not. This has been absolutely useless. Patrick was right.

'Wait. Carys?' Patsy lifts her head. 'I've got—Vince... I've got something for Carys. In the cabinet.'

I hover near the door. Patsy's got something for me? What on earth could that be? A bullet? This is Hackney and I know she can't stand me.

Vincenzo gets up and moves to the cabinet, his eyes on Patsy, as if waiting for further instructions.

'In the china cup... Have a look.'

He opens the door and takes out an old dainty cup. 'This one?' he says.

'Yes. There's a small ring...under the marbles.'

I hear clinking as Vincenzo's fingers scrabble around in the cup and I step a little closer.

He holds up a child's ring.

The moment I notice the ladybird on it, I gasp with utter surprise.

'That's it,' Patsy says. 'Give it to Carys.'

Vincenzo holds the ring between thumb and forefinger and places it in the palm of my hand.

'My ladybird ring,' I say quietly. 'I never thought I'd see this again. My Nain gave it to me... so I wouldn't be jealous. She gave Bethan a pearl bracelet.'

'I saved it for you, all these years.'

'Did Jason give you this?' I ask.

Patsy's eyes flit from me to Vincenzo. 'Who?' she says wearily. 'No, you gave it to me once, a long time ago. I thought that—'

'No. I didn't give this to you.'

Vincenzo casts me a surprised glance.

'Jason took this from me. I remember it very well.'

'Who?' Patsy says again.

'Jason, that boy you always played with.'

'I didn't play with boys.'

I stare at her. 'You did Patsy. There was a fire. Behind your house. And he took it from me.'

'We never had a fire behind our house. We had a ditch

behind our house. But I'm tired, Carys, I—'

'Of course you had a ditch behind your house.' I clench my fists and the ladybird pinches the palm of my hand. 'My sister Bethan drowned in it. But I suppose you don't remember that either, do you?'

Vincenzo stares at me, then at Patsy. 'Are you alright, babe?'

'Sweetheart, you gave me that ring.' Patsy draws up her knees and winces. 'You gave it to me once, when we were playing in my bedroom.'

'No.' I shake my head and a tear rolls down my cheek. 'That's just not true.'

I put the ring in my jeans pocket and wipe my face. 'I only played in your room twice. The first time without Bethan. She was downstairs with your mum and mine.'

Vincenzo watches Patsy. She's closed her eyes and presses her palm to her forehead.

'You put me on your rocking horse and you pushed it so wildly, I fell off, against the edge of your wardrobe, and I had a big graze on my back that was bleeding through my clothes, and you went downstairs and you didn't tell my mum. You came back with salt and pepper and you sprinkled it on my graze and you said it would help, but it really hurt Patsy.'

'Carys…' Patsy's voice sounds strained. 'I am sorry for what happened with Bethan. Of course, I remember her. But I think you have me confused with someone else. I didn't even have a rocking horse when I was a child.' She catches Vincenzo's gaze and gives him a tight smile. 'I wish I had.'

But Vincenzo doesn't speak. He just studies her face, with what looks like a glint of doubt in his eyes.

'You don't want to remember it!' A sob catches in my throat. 'That's what this is, Patsy. You—'

I pause. Something's just occurred to me and now there's a chill in my heart. Oh, God. Couldn't I say the same about myself? The reason we went to Patsy's house that day. I... *No, no, stop it!*

Somewhere at the back of my mind, a noose dangles from a stairwell; inviting me, coaxing me. *Use me. Come on. You should.*

'I didn't know there was a hole in the ice,' Patsy says flatly.

Another tear rolls down my cheek. I want to ask Patsy why she didn't try to pull Bethan out of the hole. I want to ask her why she held me back when I tried to help Bethan. There's so much more I want to say and ask, but I can't be here anymore; my energy's gone. Maybe, if she hadn't just lost her baby. Maybe, if Vincenzo hadn't been here, I could have shouted at her, broken down in front of her for denying everything. But it's two against one. Even though Vincenzo hasn't said much, he's on her side, of course. I wish Patsy would come with me to Patrick's office. If she played with his Playmobil figures, I'm sure she'd stop denying everything. But that will never happen.

I turn around and walk out of the room without saying goodbye.

'Was she talking about Sheppy?' I hear Vincenzo ask, when I'm in the hallway.

'Eh?' Patsy grunts.

'Jason Sheppard.' Vincenzo's voice sounds tense. 'Was she talking about him?'

For a moment, I'm tempted to eavesdrop, but don't. I want to move on. I close the door behind me and rush down the stairs. I just have to get away from her.

♫

Outside it's warm and sunny. Two black teenagers stroll by me holding hands; construction workers fill the distant air with clanging metal echoes; a dog barks nearby.

I walk across the patch of grass where three men with litter pickers are shoving rubbish into blue bin liners. One of them, an older guy with a weathered face, is singing Humperdinck's 'Release Me' to himself in a baritone voice.

What was I expecting? A cathartic heart-to-heart? How naïve. Patsy hasn't changed. But at least I cried at the right moment in front of the right person, and I needed that. Patsy saw me. She heard me. I am real. Bethan was a real child. Our family's pain is still very real. Patrick was wrong; this has helped me.

I see my reflection in a shop window, and above my reflection the endless blue sky. I stop, and close my eyes, and breathe. *I love you Bethan*, I tell her in my head. *I will see you again.* A warm glow flows through me and my heart lifts. I'm not alone.

♫

I'm home just after six. Cadi and Kieran set the table for the vegetarian curry I bought down the road. I suppose, subconsciously, the cumin and fenugreek smell at Patsy's home must have triggered something, but I only realised this after placing my order. Had it occurred to me earlier, I would have gone for fish and chips.

It's nice to come home to people you care about and to have dinner with them. Cadi's only been living with me for two days, and Kieran's been here a fortnight, but I can't even imagine them not being here now, and me living on my own again. How lonely. Although my loss of privacy still niggles.

After dinner, Kieran starts clearing the table and I go upstairs. I kept quiet about the ladybird ring during dinner, even though I felt it tingling in my pocket. My siblings don't share this part of my past; they only know Bethan from pictures. I regret that sometimes.

I tuck the ring away in the matchbox that also holds Dad's yellow feather, and stuff it back under some socks in my underwear drawer. Burglars probably wouldn't look there, I hope. I do want to get a pretty box for the ring though, and for the feather. A colourful one, with sequins and beads, like the polka-dot girl in Singapore used for her money.

When I come downstairs, I discover that Kieran has taken a Paulo Coelho book from my bookcase and has settled down on the sofa with it. He's also put a bottle of beer out for himself on the coffee table. I stare at it for a moment, then think, *never mind. Can't nag him about everything.*

Cadi's waiting for me at the kitchen table, ready for her

tarot reading. She's all hopeful again, after I told her what Gareth said this morning. I spread the cards out on the table; the minor as well as the major arcana, and she eagerly watches my moves.

'Maybe you can do a reading for Mum after mine,' she says. 'To see what will happen in the next couple of months, and if she'll come home soon?'

'No!' Kieran shouts. 'Don't do that, Carys.'

'I won't,' I say. 'You should only ask questions you're prepared to hear any answer to. What if we get negative cards? We'd be even more worried.'

'That's right,' Kieran says. 'Don't do it Carys.'

'She just said she wouldn't,' Cadi grumbles.

'Stop it you two,' I say.

Kieran mutters something back and takes a swig of beer.

'Right.' I turn to Cadi. 'Do you want to pick the cards yourself, or shall I do it?'

She frowns. 'Um…you do it, please.'

I take a few moments to centre myself, then slowly move my left hand over the cards. Cadi's face is tense. I just hope the cards will be good and not dash her hopes. I'm about to pick one when the landline rings.

'Argh,' Cadi says, but then she seems to have a thought because she claps her hands and says: 'Maybe it's Gareth!'

'I hope it's Ryan,' I reply.

Kieran picks up, says a few words, and walks over to us with the phone. He teasingly waves it in our faces a few times and grins when we both reach for it, but then he hands the phone to me.

'Ryan,' he says with a broad smile, before walking back to the sofa.

It crosses my mind to take the call upstairs for a bit of privacy, but I don't bother.

'Hi Ryan,' I say.

'Hello you,' he replies, but after that there's an awkward silence.

Cadi's watching me. I wish she wasn't.

'Did you train your dog today?' I ask, for want of anything better to say.

'No, I did that yesterday.'

'Okay. Did you practice walking on smooth floors again?'

'No, I'm leaving that for now. I'm waiting to speak to someone about that. Hey...um... I don't want a relationship.'

For a few seconds, I'm too stunned to react.

'Oh.'

'Um... yeah... I've thought about it all day, and this is what I've decided.'

'Oh.'

Cadi fixes me with a curious stare and Kieran's glancing at me too.

'Why not?' I ask feebly.

Cadi's eyes grow wider. God, I'm feeling invaded. Why did everyone have to move in with me?

'I'm just not in love with you,' Ryan coolly replies.

'I know,' I say. 'I'm not in love with you either.'

My retort is met with an uncomfortable silence on the other end of the line.

Cadi walks around the dining table and presses her ear against the back of the phone.

I try to push her away but she keeps coming back, so I leave it. I need to concentrate.

'You make it sound so serious,' I say. 'We were just having fun. I don't know if I want a relationship with you either. What's wrong with just meeting up and taking things as they come?'

Cadi gives me a pitying look. I quickly avert my gaze.

'Well... when you put it like that,' Ryan says, after another pause. 'It's not that I don't like you. I do. But every time I meet up with you, I think of all the other things I could be doing, you know, like seeing my friends and biking and training my dog and stuff.'

'Well, we have been meeting up a lot lately,' I say breezily. 'We don't have to do it like that anymore. We could just see each other once a month or so.'

'Really?' Ryan sounds doubtful.

'Of course. I have a life after all.'

'Yes, I know,' he quickly says. He's silent again for a few moments. 'If you're really okay with just meeting up once a month...'

'I am.'

'Alright,' Ryan says, 'I'll call you next month then.'

'Right. Because our date for this Wednesday is off?' I ask lamely.

'Um, yes. I'm going over to Ian's Wednesday. He rang me this morning, asked if I wanted to come round. So...'

'Right. Well, you have fun at Ian's.'

'Thanks, I will. I'll text you.'

'Yes,' I reply. 'That's fine.'

The phone clicks dead.

'Oh my God! I can't believe he dumped you!' Cadi's staring at me, her eyes drenched with pity. There's something condescending about it, although I know she doesn't mean it like that.

Kieran's quietly observing me from the sofa.

'He didn't dump me,' I say tightly. 'He said he still wants to see me. He just needs more time.'

'Time?' Cady repeats.

Kieran's shaking his head.

'You started seeing each other in January, didn't you?' Cadi says. 'It's been like, six, seven months.'

'No,' I correct her. 'We started emailing each other in January. We've been seeing each other since May, but not even that much. I'm away all the time.'

'But you just said that you'd been meeting up a lot,' Cadi says, looking confused.

'I just told him that to appease him, didn't I? I didn't mean it.'

'God, give me strength.' Kieran sighs dramatically.

I glare at him. Dad used to say that to Mum.

'I'll ask Ryan if he still wants to come to New York with me next month,' I say.

'And if he does, we'll see how that goes and take things from there.'

Cadi frowns. 'You still want to go to New York with him after this? He won't do it.'

'You don't know that,' I reply.

'Shall we ask your tarot cards?' Cadi says, excited.

I glance at the cards on the table. Am I prepared to hear any answer?

'No,' I tell Cadi. 'We'll just do your reading for now.'

Chapter 21

'How long are you planning to stay here?' The immigration officer at JFK Airport, a short, unsmiling man with spikey grey hair and spider veins decorating his nose and cheeks, leafs through the passport I've just handed him. He is seated in a booth behind a grey counter with a fingerprint scanner and camera perched on top.

'Probably until Tuesday,' I reply.

'Left finger, please.' The man glances at me. 'What do you mean by probably?'

I put my finger on the glass plate and hold it there for a moment. Behind his booth, droves of travellers are heading for the exits. Half an hour ago I watched my colleagues disappear through the crew lane. It felt weird to see them leave without me; as if I was left behind.

'I'm a flight attendant,' I reply. 'I'm travelling on a staff ticket.'

'So, they've put you on standby,' he says.

'That's right.'

He looks at my passport again. 'Have you been here before?'

'Yes. I come here all the time. For work.'

The immigration officer looks at me squarely. 'So you have a crew visa.'

'I have, but I didn't bring it.'

'Why not?'

'Because I'm not working.'

A female voice announces over the tannoy that passengers should keep their luggage with them at all times and I instinctively pull my carry-on closer.

'I came here as a passenger,' I add. 'To celebrate my thirtieth birthday.'

But something has shifted, and, shaking his head, the officer seems to be inspecting my passport even closer now. I know it's perfectly in order, and I don't need my crew visa, but I'm suddenly alert: I am meeting resistance, and I'd picked an angel card this morning. What did I get? That bloody Signs card again. Is this a sign?

The officer leans his elbows on the counter and shows me a page in my own passport. 'If you have a crew visa,' he says, 'it should be in here... and it's not.'

We stare at each other. His eyes are filled with suspicion but there's a hint of triumph too. Like he's sure he's caught me out. Exposed me as a big fat liar, a fraud trying to get into his country for unsavoury reasons. I hate moments like this, when total strangers who know nothing about you think they have you figured out.

'I know it's not,' I say tightly. 'It's in my other passport.'

He knits his brows together. 'What other passport?'

I glare at him and feel a warm flush creeping up my cheeks. What an arrogant bastard. But I have to compose myself, like I do at work. It's not a sign. I'm sure my birthday will be great.

'My old passport expired,' I say, 'but the crew visa that's in it is still valid, so when I come here for work, I always bring both of my passports. Look—' I grab my passport from his hands and point to some small print on a particular page. 'It says here, *this passport has been issued to replace passport number....*'

'Oh, okay.' The officer slumps his body a little and glances at me. He has noticed my irritation and I can still see his.

'Are you travelling by yourself?'

'No.' I turn and point at a sullen-faced Ryan who's in the booth next to mine, answering questions from his customs officer.

'I'm with him.'

Ryan hears me, and briefly catches my eye. I smile at him but he doesn't smile back.

'And who is he to you?' the officer asks.

I hesitate. I want to say boyfriend but that feels wrong.

'He's a friend of mine.'

'Just a friend?'

'Yes,' I reply, sharper than intended.

'A guy who's just a friend.' The officer sounds somewhat bemused and I have to repress the urge to spit it all out, right here, right now. *You want the dirt, you nosy prick? Well, here it is. That guy in the booth next to ours? He tried to dump me last month, but I managed to talk him out of it. Yes, I really did. My best friend Flora called him spineless but she's just jealous. Her boyfriend is married and mine is single. My angel cards keep telling me to look out for signs, but I am looking out for signs! I think it's a fantastic sign that despite everything, he still came with me on this four-day trip. We're going to spend some proper quality time together at last, without my crazy mother and my needy siblings breathing down my neck! That's the story, are you happy now? Idiot!*

Obviously, I bite my tongue. I've not been admitted into

the country yet and this guy has the power to put me back on the plane, so I warily echo, 'That's right, a guy who's just a friend.'

The officer shoots me a knowing glance and stamps my visa waiver. 'Welcome back to America ma'am.'

♪

'Summers in New York are more humid than our summers back home,' Ryan says wisely, as if he comes here all the time. He rips the luggage tag from his suitcase handle in one go, scrunches it up and stuffs it in his satchel. 'Must be the Atlantic Ocean air.'

I have no idea whether or not this is correct and don't make a reply. We've been waiting on this platform in the bright August sun with some fifty other travellers for the arrival of an AirTrain for ten minutes. I stifle a yawn. We've been up since five o'clock this morning.

Ryan takes a pair of sunglasses and puts them on his nose. 'Did you not bring yours?' he says. A tiny version of myself is reflected in his dark glasses. I always find him handsome, but with these Ray-bans on he's irresistible. I just hope that after this trip he'll realise he wants to be with me too. This trip with him is all I have now. If it doesn't happen here, I think we'll split up.

I shake my head. 'Cadi borrowed them and I forgot to ask for them back. Maybe I'll buy a new pair.'

Ryan ties his jacket around his waist and I follow his example to free my arm that has served as a coat hanger ever since we stepped off the airplane. A soft breeze feels warm on my skin.

When a jam-packed train pulls in, we squeeze our way onto it, like everybody else, and it's not until we switch to a different train at Jamaica that we can sit down and breathe.

Ryan offers me an orange from his suitcase and I take it. 'See? It pays off to be a bad boy sometimes,' he says, reminding me of our quarrel last night, when I told him he wasn't supposed to bring fruit into the USA and he told me to shut up.

'I guess,' I say, and plant a kiss on his shoulder. I put the orange in my lap and take my phone from my bag. 'I got a message from Flora,' I say, tapping keys. 'I'm sending her a quick message back.'

'Flora?' Ryan says, munching on an orange segment, while stuffing peel into the vomit bag he took from the plane.

'My best friend. She's the one who's having an affair with a married colleague. Actually, Edward's not really married, and Flora told me she's glad he never married his girlfriend, but I told her that after sixteen years and three kids, she's his wife, even if they never made it official.'

Ryan's looking around the carriage.

'When you've been with someone for sixteen years and you've got kids… that's married, don't you think?'

Ryan nods. 'I'd say so, yes.'

I scan Flora's text message. She wants my advice. Should she extend the ultimatum she's given Ed? Again? She shares a few details about his personal problems. I feel sorry for his kids so I reply, *yes, extend it. Maybe by a few more months? Ryan and I are here!*

♪

We get off the train at 103rd Street and weave our way through a sea of people towards the exit. Ryan grabs my suitcase and we bounce up the metal-capped stairs to street level, where we halt, in the middle of the sunlit sidewalk, and take in the spirit of Manhattan. Yellow taxis roll by, revving and tooting; Z-shaped fire escapes are mounted on the facades of apartment buildings, and skyscrapers stand tall in the background wherever we turn. The air smells of hot concrete, car fumes and fried onions and now and again I catch a whiff of the suntan lotion we slathered on somewhere between Jamaica and Penn.

Ryan puts our suitcases down and rolls his shoulders back. 'Amazing,' he says, tilting his head in every direction, and even though I've seen it all before, I agree. I've often wondered, hypothetically, if I ever moved to the US, would I go for New York or San Francisco? It's just as well I'm not doing it because I wouldn't be able to decide. And there's Chicago too, of course.

'Grub,' Ryan says, nodding at a hotdog stand some 10 feet away. We trundle our suitcase over to the vendor who's starting to look younger the closer we get. His head and face are abundantly covered with jet black hair, but there's a youthful glint in his pale brown eyes. Ryan strikes up a conversation with him while I survey the goods on his cart. It's a small stainless-steel cart, with a blue and yellow umbrella. Images of hotdogs with sauerkraut adorn the side, and bottles and canned drinks are stacked on top.

The vendor tells us his name is Nazin. 'American dream, you know,' he says, with a thick Arabic accent.

'Really?' Ryan casts a doubtful glance over his cart, and even I study Nazin's face for signs of cynicism, but he flashes us a pure smile and when he hands me a bun with just onions, he's got a cheerful energy about him.

'Of course, of course. I am a writer.' Nazin hands Ryan his bun too and indicates his goods with an upturned hand. 'Please, take some mustard or ketchup.'

'Screenplays?' Ryan asks. He reaches for a large plastic bottle of mustard and slathers it liberally across his bun.

'Poetry and essays,' Nazin says.

Ryan squirts a line of ketchup on top of the mustard. 'My girlfriend is a writer,' he says and Nazin suddenly regards me with interest.

'I'm not,' I huff, aware of where this is going.

'You're not his girlfriend?' Nazin asks.

Ryan and I exchange an uncomfortable look. 'She is,' he says. 'I meant someone else. My best friend writes, and she's a girl… She's published a couple of short stories.'

'I thought Leah was a nurse,' I say through gritted teeth. I'm sick and tired of hearing about Leah everywhere we go.

'Of course she's a nurse,' Ryan snaps. 'She writes in her spare time. Not that she's got much of that.'

Nazin awkwardly looks from Ryan back to me. 'That's good, very good,' he says with a thin smile.

I watch Ryan biting into his hotdog. *You believe him?* Cadi had asked me, and I told her that I did, because I want to believe him and I want to trust him. But am I a hundred per cent convinced he's not lying to me? No, I'm not, and if things don't change—if I'm still not getting a sense of commitment from him by the time we go home on Tuesday— then I think I'm going to have to call it a day. It's not what I want, but I don't want this either. It's been eight months, and I'm thirty on Monday. I want to be with someone who loves me. Someone who wants me for his wife. Not someone who constantly brings up a nurse named Leah.

When we've finished our buns, we ask Nazin for two pretzels to go and wish him a good day, but as soon as we're out of earshot Ryan says: 'Can you believe that? He came to America to get rich with poetry. How stupid can you get?'

I glance behind me and see Nazin's taking money from a man. 'He didn't say he wanted to get rich.'

'He said *American Dream*, so that's obvious,' Ryan says. 'But the closest he'll probably ever get to the American Dream is getting a second cart.'

'Flora had a food stall at the Ealing Jazz Festival once and she made loads of money that weekend.'

Ryan glances at me. 'Oh, shut up.'

♫

The hostel I booked online is housed in a five-storey, grey limestone building. Seven stone steps lead to an old wooden double door.

Ryan pulls one of the doors open. The moment we step inside a stale smell wafts towards me and I remember some of the atrocious reviews I read about this place, something I chose to keep from Ryan as this hostel was the only thing I could afford in Manhattan, and besides, I assumed he wanted something cheap too. I did call the hotel where I stay for work but even with a crew discount it was far too expensive.

Seven or eight young-looking people hang around in a small lounge area to our right, slouched on sofas draped with plaids. They're watching a rugby game that blares from a TV set that's mounted on a wall. The guy closest to us is perched on the armrest of one of the sofas. He's got an amazing mop of tiny shoulder-length curls. A few feet away from the sofa, four guys are playing table football. Behind them is a small kitchen area with a huge refrigerator in a corner, a kitchen top with a flip-over Belgian waffle maker and three round tables with six chairs each.

Nobody seems to notice our arrival. We could have been flies on the walls. Before we reach the reception desk, a cheer goes up from the lounge. The people on the sofas jump up and give each other hi-fives and slaps on the back.

Ryan looks at them with furrowed brows. 'This place is a bit shoddy, don't you think?'

'They only charge forty-two dollars per person a night, and we're in Manhattan,' I say. 'What were you expecting?'

The receptionist, a tall and skinny, fair-haired guy, who's standing behind the desk greets us politely and apologizes for the noise with a lame smile. He's wearing a white shirt and a smart black waistcoat with swirling silver lines. A name tag pinned to the left side of his waistcoat says *Kevin*. A larger tag under it reads *How may I serve you?* I notice that the lashes of his left eye are rapidly twitching.

I give Kevin my booking number while Ryan glances at some notices on the wall behind the desk. One of them is an A4-sized print of a young girl with a caption that says: DO NOT GIVE THIS GIRL A BED. I can tell by the girl's face that she's had a hard life, so I say a quick prayer in my head, asking the Universe to help her and make sure she is loved.

After I pay Kevin a fifty-dollar deposit, he hands me a key that dangles from a rectangular, metal hanger. 'You're on the fourth floor,' he says.

Ryan asks him where the elevator is but Kevin shakes his head. 'No elevator.' He nods towards a staircase on his left.

Ryan shoots me a stern glance, but I ignore it.

Next to the stairs, a cardholder is fixed to the wall. It's stuffed with leaflets about museums, bus and boat tours, and shopping arcades.

'Oh look,' I say, pulling one out. 'The Sex and the City Tour. Shall we go on it?'

'No thank you,' Ryan says, taking one of the Staten Island Ferry. 'That's not exactly my idea of culture.'

I glance at my leaflet and stuff it in my bag.

♫

A few minutes later, a little out of breath from the stairs we climbed, I turn the key in the lock, but the moment I open the door, I realise Mum's room at the hospital isn't that cold and poky after all. Ryan pushes past me, then stops in his tracks. 'Okay, I'm not staying here.' He glares at me accusingly. 'This is the skankiest hotel I've ever seen. How on earth could you pick this?'

'It's not a hotel, is it?' I spring to my own defence. 'It's a hostel.' But I feel embarrassed. I knew our room was going to be nothing like the rooms in the crew hotel near Times Square but I hadn't expected it to be this shabby. The walls near the ceiling show brown damp stains and the smell in the room is far from the fresh linen kind—more like eggs hatching into grubs underneath a damp carpet.

I glance at the two single beds. Each one is covered with a white sheet and has a thin duvet, a duvet cover, and a white towel neatly folded on top. One bed is against the wall, the other under a window with no curtains, and there's a bedside table in between them. Opposite the beds, three clothes hangers dangle from a rail in a wardrobe that has no door. Still, one of my strengths has always been my adaptability.

'It doesn't really matter that it looks like this because we'll be out all day. We only need a place to sleep and shower. And it's only for three nights.'

'I don't care,' Ryan snaps. 'I'll stay here for tonight because I'm knackered, but tomorrow we're looking for something else.' He sits down on one of the beds and opens his suitcase.

I sit down on the other bed and watch him unpack. He's different, more distant, I suddenly realise. He's been different ever since he arrived at my place last night, the first time I saw him again after our Brighton trip, but I didn't think much of it. He told me he'd worked all day and when he came home, he'd had an argument with his parents when he asked them to look after Sally while he was in New York. I thought he was a bit standoffish to me because of that. He'd been fine on the phone. He still called me a few times a week for a chat and he texted me every day after he said he wanted to split up with me.

Ryan walks over to the wardrobe and puts two shirts on two clothes hangers.

'We already paid for three nights,' I say, following him with my gaze. 'We won't get our money back.'

'I don't care if we don't get our money back.' He sits down on the bed again.

'Well I do, we paid over two hundred dollars.'

Ryan doesn't reply. He's emptied his wallet on the bed and is busy separating his dollars from his pounds.

I'm worried now. I can't afford anything else besides this shit hole. I'd done alright for myself, before Cadi and Kieran moved in. But Mrs Meads charges me an extra one hundred and sixty quid in rent, which is only twenty pounds a head a week, she's being lenient in a way, only Cadi and Kieran aren't paying for themselves—I am. Cadi and Gareth have given up their bedsit in Hammersmith but they still have to pay rent for it until the end of this month. Gareth still lives there and Cadi helps him with the bills. He's moving back to Wales on the first of September, but Cadi's still hoping that he'll change his mind and they'll get back together. At least the tarot cards were positive and she's stopped selling her knickers. Kieran hasn't got any money at all. He actually asked me for pocket money. I told him to take a hike and then confronted him with his abuse of my landline. I almost had a heart attack when I saw the bill. When I called the phone company for an itemisation, I discovered that Kieran had been making dozens of calls to 07-numbers. He became a bit weepy when I shouted at him. He said he was only trying to save credit on his pay–as-you-go-phone, but I told him I would have to get rid of my landline if he didn't stop using it.

♪

Ryan's coins clink on the bed and I get up to find out if the window opens. It does, but only a few inches. I pull at the safety latch but it's stuck, so I give up and take in the view. Grey tower blocks wherever I look. From my angle I can just make out people walking down the street below me. On the other side of the road, more New Yorkers amble in different directions. Traffic whizzes by and emergency sirens blare, some in the distance, some nearby. There are probably people staring death in the face at this very moment. Dad tried to help those people. He always feels near when I think of him.

I turn away from the window and take another look at the room. It's starting to grow on me. 'I'm fine with this, really,' I mutter, mainly to myself.

'Well I'm not fine with this,' Ryan snarls. 'Really!'

I watch him fold a pair of his trousers over the third

clothes hanger. He really is different, but maybe he'll change back—when we have fun together here.

'We could get some flowers and candles to make it look nicer,' I try.

'Can you help me put the beds together?' he asks, ignoring my comment. We push his bed against mine, next to the wall, and put the bedside table on his side, under the window.

Ryan has— what I take to be— a contented expression on his face, and wanting to hold on to his improved state of mind, I say, 'At least the hostel is close to Central Park.'

'Depending on where in the park you want to be,' Ryan sneers.

'And it's not too far from Fifth Avenue.'

'It's a forty-minute walk!'

'So what? You told me in Brighton that you liked walking. And there is a metro service.'

'This is a crap hotel, Carys,' Ryan says, sitting down on his bed with an orange in his lap. 'You can say what you want, but I'm not going to change my mind about it.'

I take some toiletries from my suitcase. This could go on forever, I think, and suddenly feel how tired I am. 'All right,' I say. 'We'll look for something else tomorrow.'

Chapter 22

With a start I wake up, fixing my eyes on the thin, creased pillow that looks grey in the morning twilight. A low noise, outside… I remember it from last night. This is not my own bed. Have I flown somewhere for work?

The sound of turning pages makes me glance to the right. Ryan. Of course… we're in New York. I thought he'd fall in love with me here.

'Morning,' Ryan says, without looking up. 'Did you sleep well?' He's lying on his front, reading his Lonely Planet Guide in the soft light that seeps in through the window. There's no warmth in his voice. I could always tell James loved me, from the tone of his voice when he spoke to me. Why did I think Ryan would fall in love with me here? We're still the same people.

'I had a nightmare, I think.'

'Did you? About what?'

I turn on my back. The thin duvet feels light on my body. Bits of scenes float through my mind like jigsaw puzzles. *Over here blank, I'm a tab, connect with me.* I was in Patrick's office, sad, telling him that Ryan had left me. The dull ache I felt in my sleep is still with me. Next, Patrick and I were in my bedroom, having frantic sex, but Patrick's body froze and his eyes turned cold and hateful. 'Why did you bring Bethan over to the RSPCA?' he snarled at me. 'She's a child.

It's your fault she's dead. Snitch.'

I stare at the rectangular shadow on the ceiling that seems to sprout from a spot above the window. 'I don't remember,' I say.

Ryan flicks pages.

'Weren't you bothered by that machine last night?' I ask. 'Do you hear it?' I raise a finger.

'Yes,' he says. 'You mean that generator?'

'Yes! It's so loud and monotonous. Doesn't it bother you?'

'No. I was bothered by the sirens at first, but other than that, I slept like a dog.'

'I hope dogs sleep well.'

'They do.'

'What's the time?' I sit up and pull the covers to one side.

'Almost five-thirty.' Ryan closes his guide. 'Ten thirty for us. I'm starving. Do you think anything's open this early on a Sunday?'

'Definitely in an hour or so,' I say, crawling over the duvet to the foot of the bed.

The threadbare carpet feels scratchy under my bare feet. It's all so unromantic. And we only have three days left here. It doesn't seem likely that he'll be madly in love with me by Tuesday.

'I'm going to the bathroom,' I say.

But the bathroom that's just outside our room on the corridor is locked. I wait a few moments, but then hear water clattering on tiles and I quickly go down a floor to see if I can find one that's free. I'm pretty desperate. There is one, and I plonk myself down on the toilet seat. The bathroom is cramped, just like the one on our floor. It has an open shower to the left, and I can fill up my water bottle in the sink while seated on the loo. My colleagues who flew us here have gorgeous bathrooms, with spacious bathtubs, salts, fluffy towels and everything. Good for them. They'd been really lovely yesterday. The purser upgraded us to first class when she heard I was going to New York for my birthday. It feels weird to be in America and not part of a crew, even when I always choose to go out by myself. I feel lonely at work, and yet I'm not a group person. I want to discuss this some more with Patrick. The other day, when I mentioned to him how nervous my job makes me, he told me he could refer me to another psychologist, one who specialises in career orientation and switches. But I don't want to talk to someone else. I just want Patrick. Besides, I've been thinking. Maybe I could become a ground hostess. That way, I'd still be with the company. I'm going to look into that; I don't need to discuss everything with a psychologist.

When I return to our room Ryan's already dressed, apart from his trainers, and he's perched on the foot of his bed, eating an orange.

'My last one,' he says, holding up a cluster of segments. 'Do you want some?'

I shake my head and rummage through my bag for mascara and the mirror inside my powder compact.

'I thought that we could go to Little Italy first,' Ryan says. 'Have some breakfast there and then walk around Chinatown and SoHo for a bit. And in the afternoon we could pay the

Museum of Natural History a visit.'

'Sounds great,' I say, 'but checkout is at 10 a.m.'

'Eh?' Ryan looks up and I nod at a placard on the door. 'It says here that checkout is at 10 a.m., so if we want to leave here, we have to take our stuff with us. So, I suppose we'd better look for a different hostel first before going out on the town. Otherwise, we'll have to carry our luggage around all day.'

'Not really,' Ryan replies. 'We won't get our money back, so that means that even if we leave this place, this room is still ours.'

'Yes, but then we'd have to come back here to collect our stuff when we've found another hostel and that might be miles away from here.'

Ryan wipes his chin with the palm of his hand and chucks the bits of orange peel in the bin next to the door. A few pieces miss their target and land on the floor. 'You know what?' he says. 'Let's do it tomorrow. We'll stay here for one more night, we may as well, we paid for it, and we'll look for something else tomorrow morning. A hotel that is, not a hostel.' He shoots me a stern look.

♫

Sunlight captures Canal Street, despite the early hour, and Ryan and I hover near the steps of the subway station we just emerged from.

'Little Italy is near Mulberry Street,' Ryan says, studying his map. 'It's this way.'

I follow him, eyeing my surroundings. I never noticed it before, but the wrought-iron fire escapes they've got everywhere don't just come in black. There's one in brown just over there, two in red and on the other side of the street I spot a green one. And the stairs are part of beautifully designed balconies; also wrought-iron. San Francisco or New York. Both so wonderful and so different. I can't choose.

Ryan stops again. His finger traces a line on the map.

'Why don't we ask someone for directions,' I say. My gaze follows a girl who looks like she's just finished her night shift at a brothel. 'It's probably quicker.'

But Ryan tells me to hang on, and after a couple of minutes, he folds his map away.

'We could even walk back to the hotel from here,' he says. 'It would take about two hours.'

'Were you looking at that?'

'Yes, and at Little Italy. We need to find Howard Street first.'

I prod Ryan with my elbow. 'How about that Starbucks?' I point to a large Chinese pagoda-looking building with rows of red columns. 'Shall we have breakfast in there?'

Ryan's silent so I glance at him. His face has suddenly turned all serious, and he locks his dark eyes with mine. 'I fancy a shag,' he blurts.

I hold his stare. This is an important moment, only, couldn't he have thought of this when we were still in our room? I was looking forward to coffee and a sandwich. But I want him to want me, and we only have three days left here; maybe it will serve the purpose.

'Me too,' I say.

'Do you want to do it in that Starbucks?' Ryan already takes a few presumptuous steps in the café's direction.

'Are you mad?' I reply. 'If we get caught, I'll be extradited and never allowed to come here again.'

'So?'

'I'll get the sack if I'm banned from this country.'

'Can't you just fly to other destinations?'

'No, it doesn't work like that. I'm required to take any flight they've got for me. And what if I'm on standby?' I pause for a few seconds, letting the hypothetical disaster sink in. Cadi, Kieran and I, we'd all have to move back in with Mum. 'Besides,' I say, 'I really love coming here. I don't want to be barred from this country.'

'All right,' Ryan says, 'no public places, I get it. Shame,' he adds with a grin. 'So, do you want to go back to the hotel?'

'It's not a hotel, it's a hostel.'

A dark expression crosses his face.

'I do,' I quickly reply. 'Do you?'

We stare at each other, as if we're both having a little reality check. We've only just arrived at Canal Street after sitting on a train for nearly half an hour. It's a bit drastic.

'I do,' he says.

♪

'Back so soon?' Kevin smiles at us on our way to the stairs. My cheeks flush.

'Um, yeah, we forgot something,' Ryan mutters.

I just hope he sounds convincing. For some reason, I feel like everyone knows what we're going to do.

'I wish you'd brought your uniform with you,' Ryan says, while I trudge up the carpeted steps behind him. I ignore his comment. I wish he wasn't always banging on about my flight attendant uniform.

'This is good exercise, I suppose,' I say, when we've almost reached the third floor.

Ryan glances at me over his shoulder. 'Can I shag you up the bum?'

My eyes blink. 'Shhh,' I whisper. 'No, you can't.'

'Why not?'

'Because, I don't want you to.'

'But why not?'

Taking a firmer grip of the banister, I stare at his buttocks, tightening and slacking in his blue jeans. Where is this coming from? He's never asked me this before.

'I-just-don't-want-that,' I huff.

We trudge on in silence, and it occurs to me that maybe he worries about me falling pregnant and being stuck with me for life.

Back in our room, we sit down on the bed, kick off our shoes and start kissing. I'm not bothered by the low noise of the generator, or the blaring police sirens and the angry honking of cars in the background, but I hate the daylight. Ryan kisses me hard and his hands caress my bare back.

'I'm really horny,' he breathes, after a few minutes of what he thinks is foreplay. He fumbles with my bra and I unhook it for him.

He gets up and drops his trousers and shorts, then gives me a lopsided smile. 'I have a boner.' He almost sounds proud.

'Yes, I can see that,' I dryly remark. My gaze moves to his face, his narrow nose, his dark eyes. *You tried to dump me. You didn't care if you ever saw me again. You're indifferent to me.*

Ryan unbuttons his shirt, and I undress too—we're here now— and he grabs me by the hips, swivels me around and firmly positions me on the bed on all fours. He takes a condom from his toiletry bag that's on the bedside table and comes up behind me. The bedsprings creak, and I lean on my elbows and wait. I can't be bothered to look behind me, as I'm quite uncomfortable in this position, but what's taking him so long?

'Are you still taking the pill?'

I frown. 'Yes. Why?'

'I broke the condom.'

'Haven't you got another one?'

'No, I haven't.'

'But there are three in a packet.'

'It's not new. Do you still wanna do it?'

Is this a sign? I wonder, but my thoughts flit to Canal Street, our thirty-minute metro journey to get there, hopping back on a train just ten minutes later, followed by another thirty-minutes of traveling, for the sole purpose of having sex.

'Yes, go on, then,' I reply.

Ryan's fingers tickle the bits between my legs, but he seems to hesitate. 'You do take that pill every day, don't you?'

'Yes. Every morning before I brush my teeth.'

He moves into me and moans, but I'm fretting now. He was taking really long before he told me about the condom. God. I hope he didn't reach for his phone and secretly film my backside. His jeans are on the foot of the bed. His phone's in one of the pockets. We filmed ourselves at it in Brighton—Ryan's idea of course—but it had been at night time, with flattering candlelight and, more importantly, my consent. I was horrified though, when we'd looked at the recording together and he suddenly blurted that he wanted to send it to his mates. I hadn't expected such a childish comment from him; it had freaked me out a bit. Ryan promised me he would delete the recording and I did see him tapping at some keys, but I would've felt better about it, if I'd had the chance to check it was really gone. I didn't have the heart to ask him for his phone though, in case he thought I didn't trust him.

Ryan grabs my hair and moans loudly and a few fast shudders later his body becomes still. When we did it at my place, he was never this self-centred. We only have three days left here for him to love me. This, whatever it was, doesn't count.

He pulls out of me and fluid drips down my thighs.

'Can you get me some loo roll, please?' I'm still on all fours, and feel like I'm a cum disposal unit.

Ryan's already on his feet, picking up his clothes and getting dressed. For a moment, he observes me, through narrowed eyes and with an expression I can't really place. He nevertheless disappears through the door into the hallway and returns with a wad of harsh grey toilet paper, which he shoves into my hands. I stick it between my legs and get dressed too.

♪

Just over an hour later, we saunter into the pagoda Starbucks on Canal Street where Ryan wanted to have sex. It's a few minutes before nine-thirty, but what with all the travelling we've been doing this morning, it feels much later. And the time difference between London and New York is still a factor too, of course.

'You get the food and I'll hog that table over there, alright?' Ryan says. 'I'll have a large cappuccino and a sandwich. See if they've got anything with bacon. Oh, and some fruit.'

He crosses the café to a sunny window table and I join the queue, rather miffed that I'm the one who's paying for everything now, and besides, it wouldn't hurt him to say *please*, once in a while.

I scan the selection of refrigerated cakes and sandwiches and the drink menus on the wall behind the counter, then take a couple of items and wait my turn. There are five people in front of me. The woman who's being served wants a flavoured coffee and she's drawing out her words: sugar *freee*, *naaan*-fat, *naaan*-dairy. The barista takes the order stone-faced. When I order, I'll say: coffee, with all the sugar and fat, please.

As often happens, when I'm in a Starbucks or other coffee place, the African-American couple I once encountered on the 71 bus from San Francisco city centre to Haight-Ashbury, drifts into my thoughts. It had been a scorcher that day. The bus's air-conditioning system was actually circulating hot air.

They'd sat down in front of me, on a broad, aisle-facing front seat. Both corpulent, with close-cropped hair and clad in dark tracksuits. The woman carried a Burberry-style bag.

The man casually took the woman's hand and she lovingly squeezed his, but strangely enough, from that moment on, he became fixated on her hand; holding it up to eye-level, examining it, and twisting it sideways. Then his focus shifted to one of her fingers. He put her hand in his lap and started picking at the finger with dogged determination, while the woman silently watched him work.

I wondered what he was picking at and leaned forward in my seat. Ah, a bit of loose cuticle. He was trying to prise it off. Just as I thought how special it was that as a flight attendant you got to see so many snippets of people's everyday lives, all around the world, she said: 'Iced coffee from Starbucks.'

The man looked up from his labour, but his fingers kept picking, and he brought his head closer to hers. 'What?' he said.

'Iced coffee from Starbucks,' she repeated.

'I don't care,' he shot. 'We ain't got no money.' But I heard a hint of regret in his voice.

'Who wants hot coffee on a day like this, anyway,' he added.

'No. Iced coffee,' she replied. But he dropped the subject, still picking at the finger.

By the time I got off the bus, I was parched and looked

around for a place where I could buy a cool drink before hitting the vintage shops. I felt really awful when I ordered that iced coffee in Starbucks. And now I'm feeling it again.

Staring at the food in my hands, I say a quick prayer. I don't know where they are, or what they're up to right now, but I wish them love, happiness and money for iced coffee. And I wish all these things for the polka-dot girl in Singapore too.

♪

I put Ryan's coffee, his BLT sandwich and a plastic cup with fruit in front of him on the table.

'Do you hear that?' I say, pointing a finger in the air. "Summertime.' By Billie Holiday.'

Ryan listens for a moment. 'Yeah. Not a bad song.'

'Not a bad song? It's brilliant!'

I walk back to the counter to fetch my own food, then sit down across from Ryan. He's already chomping away on some melon pieces and scans the café with a contented look on his face.

I sip coffee and take a bite from my grilled cheese ciabatta.

'I'm glad I've come here with you,' Ryan says, removing the plastic film from his sandwich pack. He smiles at me and leans in a little closer.

I smile back and lean towards him too. 'So am I. I wish we'd booked a whole week.'

'Being here sharpens my focus, you know.'

'What do you mean?'

Ryan bites into his sandwich and chews for a few moments. 'Well, I realise now that I really do want to move to Canada. I'm just not sure how to go about it. That's the problem, you know. I already lived there for a while of course, but it's— '

'You never lived in Canada,' I cut in. 'You told me you were there for ten days. That's a holiday.'

A flash of embarrassment crosses Ryan's face. Clearly, he forgot about telling me this.

'Well, I was there for a while,' he says, annoyed, 'and I want to go back, but permanently.'

'I thought you wanted to set up a dog training school.'

'Yes, I want to do that too. That's always been my dream, but it's not my ultimate dream. My ultimate dream is setting up a dog training centre in Canada.'

'I see...'

Ryan takes a slurp of coffee. 'I already discussed it with my friend in Quebec, and he'd like to help me with it. We might even do it together. He's handled police dogs too.'

I watch him talk and think of Leah. I believe him now; they are just friends. This is a singleton talking, about the dreams he's got for himself, without factoring in any other half. I don't think he sees me as his girlfriend. I don't think that, right now, he's got settling down with someone on his mind, but he does like me. He came to New York with me, after all, and we've known each other since January. I still think that this could be the start of something special, but I should probably be more relaxed about it, if I want this to work out. Take a step back; look at it with a bit of detachment, and who knows how our relationship will develop over time? It wouldn't be hard for me to visit him in Canada anyway, if he really is moving there. I'd miss him, but I'll be supportive.

'I meant to ask you,' Ryan says, regarding me with interest. 'When you moved to Sweden, how did you manage to find accommodation and a job?'

'I went there with my ex, James,' I say, after a pause. 'We moved there for his studies at Uppsala University. He arranged our accommodation, but I did find a waitressing job by myself, and I taught English as well. I had my own income.

'Were you teaching at a college?'

'No, private tuition. I stuck a note on a board in a supermarket, saying I was a native speaker. I got loads of calls.'

Ryan nods. 'Interesting. So, this was before you became a flight attendant?'

'Yes. I started flying after I came back from Sweden.'

I break off a chunk of ciabatta—the cheese is greasy and still hot.

Ryan pops another piece of melon into his mouth. He chews on it with a far-away look in his eyes.

'What did your ex study?' he asks.

'Philosophy. He wrote papers on Transhumanism. He believes that humans will one day become walking computers. Or something like that.'

Ryan smiles. He takes a tissue and wipes at a dollop of mayonnaise that's on his chin but he doesn't catch it all. 'They already speak English in Canada,' he says, 'so teaching wouldn't be an option for me, as a backup plan.'

'There's a large Chinese community in Vancouver, I believe.'

'No. I want to go to Quebec.'

Ryan glances around the café and I follow his gaze. A barista shouts: 'Latte for Melvin!' while Doris Day is singing 'Love Somebody'—another marvel.

'You look nice today.' Ryan smiles at me.

'Do I?'

'Yes, you do. I like what you did with your hair, and that skirt you're wearing looks really nice. *Très distingué.*'

'*Merci,*' I say.

We finish our food and Ryan gets up. 'Shall we make a move?'

'Yes.' I drain my coffee. 'Let's go.'

♪

Outside, we take a moment to find our bearings and look around the noisy street for the direction of Little Italy.

'Maybe we can ask someone.' I glance at Ryan, surprised he hasn't taken out his map yet. He seems preoccupied; a stern frown has set on his face.

'Hey, um…' he says, locking eyes with me. 'I think I'm just going out by myself today.'

Bewildered, I stare at him. 'What do you mean?'

'I just feel like being by myself today, you know. Do my own thing.'

'But…' My voice falters. 'We were going to Little Italy, and China Town, and the Museum of Natural History together.'

'Yeah, I know, but we can do that some other time. We'll do something together tomorrow, alright? For your birthday.'

I look at him in disbelief. 'Really?' My bottom lip is quivering. I wish it wasn't but it's beyond my control. Ryan's looking at it, and I hang my head so he can't see it.

'But I don't want to be here by myself all day,' I say, staring at his feet and trying to fight back the tears that prick behind my eyes.

'Well,' he huffs. 'This is just what I want. I'll see you tonight.'

I look up and watch him walking away from me. I watch him, for as long as I can, until the crowd has completely swallowed him up.

I'm discarded, like a bin bag you put out by the road. My tears take over. I don't even cover my face to hide them. Rooted to the spot where Ryan left me, I weep and wait, in case he comes back.

Why can't he see what I could be to him? I thought he'd come here with an open mind, but nothing's changed for him. New York. My thirtieth birthday. It hasn't made the slightest bit of difference.

I fetch a tissue from my bag and blow my nose. Feelings are susceptible to change, aren't they? Over time, anything could happen. There are people who couldn't stand the sight of each other when they first met. And yet, over time, they fell madly in love. That's what made me remain hopeful all these months. I just thought I needed to give it more time.

After ten minutes of waiting, I give up. Ryan's not coming back to say he's sorry, or to tell me he wants to spend the day with me after all. More tears flow as I start walking back in the direction Ryan and I'd come from.

'Hey,' someone says.

I've got a feeling this is directed at me and instinctively look up. Through my haze of tears, I see two guys curiously eyeing me up.

'Would you like to go out with us,' one of them says.

I move on without responding.

'Take care,' one of them calls after me.

I cross the road when I spot the entrance to Canal Street Station, and descend the steps to the subway platforms. Fresh tears flow when I join the queue for the ticket machine, because being here only reminds me of everything Ryan and I were going to do today. People are looking at me but I don't care. I'm a tourist anyway. Nobody knows me here. I can cry for as long as I want and wherever I please. It actually feels good, this wallowing in self-pity.

I fumble in my bag for my wallet and pull out the crumpled SATC leaflet. Staring at it, my heart lifts. This is brilliant! Just what I need. If I hurry, I may still catch the eleven o'clock tour.

♪

Near the Pulitzer Fountain, I spot the SATC tour bus and make a dash for it in case it takes off without me. But when I inquire about the tour, the African-American woman who's in charge, asks me if I've got a ticket. My heart sinks. I haven't. Thank God, she tells me there will be another bus within the next couple of minutes, that I can probably go with that one, and that I can buy a ticket from her.

I loiter near the fountain for a few minutes, but when the extra bus and more people arrive, we are lined up: people with tickets in one queue, people without tickets in another. All the while I'm thinking of Ryan. What's he doing right now? Is he having a good time? Does he think of me at all? Does he regret ditching me like that? Why did he even come to New York with me? Why does he always bring up my flight attendant uniform when we have sex? I'm alone again. Even though I came here with a bloke, and share a room with him, I'm really here alone.

I wonder what Flora will say. When I told her I was still seeing Ryan after he tried to dump me over the phone, she said: 'Why didn't you tell him: I appreciate your honesty and I wish you the best?'

'Because I've been there and done that!' I replied, indignant. 'So many times. This time I want to fight. I want to win!'

'Carys,' she said calmly, suddenly sounding like the mother I never had. 'I think you should know that there's a fine line between optimism and delusion, and if you think you can win him over after everything he's already done, you're definitely deluded.'

Of course, I had to bring up Edward then. I told Flora I thought he was a toad, cheating on his wife like that.

'For the millionth time,' Flora retaliated, 'he was leaving her anyway. He's just doing it sooner now. And at least Ed has told me he loves me. Has Ryan told you that? Have you told him?'

'I hope we'll get on.' A male voice behind me. Is he talking to me? I turn my head and look straight into the faces of a man and a woman. The man's got a red moustache, piercing blue eyes, and black discs in his earlobes with holes in the middle. The woman has managed to pull off the floral goth look: long black hair, thick black make-up around the eyes, while wearing a frilly dress embellished with artificial leaves and white and purple flowers.

'I hope so too,' I reply, then realise he must've been talking to his wife.

The people in front of me are slowly filing into the bus. The first bus is already gone, and the group that wants to do this tour is quite big, but it looks like there'll be room for all of us.

Once inside, I peer towards the seats at the back. All taken. I hope I can sit alone, and preferably in a window seat. Gosh, it smells as if the driver's emptied a ton of air fresheners in here. Just as well, I suppose, it's sweaty bodies galore. Everyone seems just as impatient to find a seat that's perfect as I am: I'm prodded by limbs left, right and centre.

Two Japanese girls in front of me turn their heads and glance at some people behind me. I realise I've broken up their group.

'*Konnichiwa*,' I say to the girls.

They cast me tiny smiles and move forward.

Once we're all seated—I found a spot next to a window and only my bag occupies the seat beside me—the atmosphere is lively. As the bus slowly pulls away and the driver manoeuvers us through a bustling Fifth Avenue, a blonde, smartly dressed tour guide, standing at the front of the bus, introduces herself as Gillian. She tells us the tour will last up to three and a half hours, and as we drive through Manhattan, she will point out sites to us where scenes were shot for the series and movie.

'But first I have a question,' Gillian smiles. 'Who here owns a vibrator?' With a twinkle in her eyes, she encouragingly raises her own hand. She needn't have bothered though, because six or seven rowdy girls at the back of the bus immediately shout: 'We do, we do!'

Everyone turns their heads to look at them. I saw them earlier. They're all clad in tight blue jeans with rips in them and crop tops that expose pierced bellies. Must be a hen weekend, I think. One of the girls is wearing a willy hat.

Gillian smiles at them. 'Which one have you got?'

'Roger Rabbit,' one of the girls shouts. The group shrieks with laughter. I'm not sure if they've had a drink, but I admire their candidness. My lips are sealed; I still have to share a bus with these people for the next three hours. They don't need to know squat about me.

Through the space between the headrests of my seats, I suddenly catch the earlobe man staring at me. Oddly intense. He's a few rows behind me, in the opposite aisle.

A chill runs through me. I quickly shift my gaze back to Gillian.

♪

Gillian's question was clearly a prelude to the first stop of the tour, because shortly afterwards we're all browsing a sex shop called The Pleasure Chest, where Charlotte once bought a pink vibrator.

A few whimsical, erotic figurines in the middle of the shop catch my attention. I pick up a bare-breasted mermaid salt and pepper set. Maybe I should get Mum one of these; what with her being into boobs and all that.

'How are you?'

I put the figurine down on the glass shelf and turn around. Earlobe Man.

'Fine, thank you.' I glance at Flower Goth. She's standing a few feet away from us, holding up a strap-on and admiring it from all angles.

'Having a good time?' he asks. His face is not unfriendly, it's just that there's something about him I find weird.

'I am,' I reply, coolly. It's the way he looks at me. I'm not interested in his attention. With my luck, he and his woman are looking for a third person to spice things up in the bedroom.

I nod at him and move to a different glass display with fluffy handcuffs and fruit-flavoured lubrication gels.

Gillian walks around the shop, clapping her hands. She wants us back on the bus.

At the next stop, we are treated to cupcakes from the Magnolia Bakery and have another opportunity for stretching our legs. Most of the women want to have their pictures taken on Carrie Bradshaw's iconic doorstep, so Gillian, the hen girls, the Japanese girls, Flower Goth and I, all head over to Perry Street.

After this, the entire tour group ends up in a jam-packed bar named Onieal's, which was called Scout on the series and had been owned by Steve and Aiden.

I join the hen girls at the bar and we indulge ourselves in pink Cosmopolitan cocktails served in elegant Martini glasses. I ask the girl who's wearing the willy hat if she's getting married.

'I am,' she beams, with an American drawl. 'Not until Christmas but I'm having my bachelorette party now because one of my friends has incurable cancer.'

A little blind-sided by this matter-of-fact bit of information —they'd seemed such a cheerful bunch, but there you go— I congratulate her first, then tell her I'm sorry about her friend. She smiles at me and I move away because I've just noticed some people freeing up a tiny corner table.

I sit down and sip from my Cosmo. Over at the bar, Flower Goth and Earlobe Man are chatting to each other, but now he scans the premises and something tells me he's looking for a seat. I sink into my chair—I'm not even sure why—and watch him cross the floor and come my way.

'Mind if me and my wife join ya?' He says.

'That's alright.'

He sits down and nods towards the bar. 'She's getting us a couple of Red Bulls.'

I smile at him, but don't really know where to look, so I take a few more sips of Cosmo.

'How are you enjoying the tour so far?' he asks.

He does sound friendly. It's just that talking to strangers tends to drain me. It's a huge problem at work.

'Oh, a lot,' I say, making an effort to sound cheerful. 'I'm a big fan of the series.'

'So's my wife. It's her birthday today. That's why we're in New York. We're from Trenton, New Jersey. Ever been there?'

I shake my head, and Flower Go—his wife, joins us. She puts two cans of Red Bull, covered with upside-down glasses, on the table. Hopefully, her presence will end the need for small talk with me.

'This is my wife Ellen, and I'm Freddy.'

'Carys,' I reply, watching them take the glasses off the cans.

'Do we need glasses?' Freddy says.

'I'm using mine,' Ellen replies.

Freddy carefully pours his drink into a glass. 'So, what brings you here?' he asks.

Ellen smiles at me. 'Are you here by yourself?'

I glance at her. She almost sounds concerned about me; as if she regards me as someone who's just shed her teenage skin. They are much older than I am. Freddy must be fifty-five at least, but with her it's harder to tell.

'Well, yeah, I am,' I reply, hesitant. I glance at the group of rowdy hen girls further down the bar. They're drinking cocktails with the Japanese lot. I should have stayed with them. I could've stood quietly to the side, or chatted a bit more with the willy-hat girl. I could've told her about Cadi and Gareth's December wedding. Pretend it was still going ahead.

'I came to New York for my birthday, too,' I say. 'Mine's tomorrow.'

'Oh, it's her birthday too!' Ellen squeezes Freddy's arm.

'Tomorrow,' I repeat, glancing at Freddy's hand. I've just noticed he's got *hate* tattooed on his knuckles.

Freddy looks at me. That intense gaze again.

'Are you from Great Britain?' Ellen asks.

'Yes, I live in England.'

'She came all the way down here from England!' Ellen beams at Freddy. 'Don't you love her accent?'

'Did you come here by yourself?' Ellen asks.

'Um, no. I did come here with someone. But the Sex and the City Tour is not his thing.'

Ellen gives me a pitying look. 'He wouldn't do that for you?'

I smile at her and sip my cocktail.

'Someone's here for you,' Freddy says.

Ellen's gazing at his face.

'Thank you. That's nice,' I say, a little awkwardly. They're here for me? I barely know these people, and it's not like we'll see each other again after today.

'I don't mind doing this by myself,' I say. 'I'm a flight attendant. I'm used to being on my own when I travel.'

'No. Someone's here for you,' Freddy says. He frowns and seems to be thinking hard. 'Bethal?'

I freeze.

'Something with Beth?'

Freddy looks into the middle-distance, concentrated, as

if he's thinking. Or listening?

But I don't speak. I can't believe this, and yet I do. He can't know this.

Freddy fixes his gaze on me. 'I have someone here for you. This person wants to tell you something. I'm trying to get her name though. Beth? I don't think she said Betty. Is it Bethan? Sometimes it's difficult to hear.'

I stare at him. Cold goosebumps dot my skin. What is this? He could never have known her name.

'Okay,' Freddy says. He sounds a bit exasperated. 'Bethan?'

'Yes,' I say quietly. 'Bethan.'

'She's here because she wants to tell you something. She says she's always been with you. She wants to let you know she's been looking after you.'

'I always think about my sister,' I say, but my tone is stoic because this doesn't feel real, even though I think it is. He could never have known this.

'I always wondered if she was thinking about me too. I know she's still alive…still aware, without her body.'

'She definitely thinks of you.' Freddy smiles, but then his smile freezes. 'But she wants you to change.'

'Change?'

'Yes. She says she loves you, but she would also like to grab you by your shoulders and shake you hard, because you're not getting it.'

'What is it that I'm not getting,' I ask, puzzled.

'Your obsessions. You're doing it for the wrong people. And if you don't change, something will happen. Sorry,' Freddy adds sheepishly, 'but that's what she says.'

He turns to Ellen. 'Have you got a pen and something to write on?'

She looks in her bag and pulls the items out.

Freddy puts the pen to paper and I look at what he's writing: *Nam*—just three letters, but I already know the rest. I look inside my bag for my Laura Ashley diary— very fittingly, a Christmas present from Flora—and open it. 'Look, I say. *Nam-myoho-renge- kyo*.'

This time Freddy looks puzzled. He stares at the words on the first blank page of my diary, which I wrote in bold block letters, then at the identical words he jotted down himself.

A bemused smile appears around his lips.

'Chanting is really my best friend Flora's thing,' I say. 'But I've been to a few meetings with her. She saw a leaflet in a health food shop, a few months ago, and she asked if I wanted to come along in case they were an evil sect. They were lovely people of course. My friend goes there almost every day.'

'You should go with her more often,' Freddy says. 'If you can't because you're a flight attendant, you can just chant at home, or in your hotel rooms, it doesn't really matter.'

He glances at Ellen and she nods at me. 'You raise energy vibrations with chanting,' she says. 'Including your own.'

I think of Flora. She'll be happy to hear this. Quite surprised too, I imagine.

'Is Bethan still here?'

A thoughtful expression sets on Freddy's face. 'She's with a man. I think it's your father?'

'I hoped they were together,' I mutter.

'They are.' Freddy squints his eyes. I don't know him very well, but it seems to me he's getting tired.

'She's showing me pond… or… frozen water. And a hole.'

Freddy looks at me. 'She says this was the outcome. There couldn't have been another.' He cups his chin in the palm of his hand.

Ellen reaches out to him and rubs his wrist with her thumb.

Under the table, my legs tremble, as Freddy's words sink in. There couldn't have been another outcome? I disagree. If Mum wasn't a lesbian. If Patsy hadn't suggested going out. If Patsy hadn't stopped me. And then… there's me. If I hadn't… No. I can't bear it. My eyes well up. I see the noose again, dangling from a stairwell. Every fibre in my body tells me to use it.

'Are you alright, Carys?' Ellen asks. There's concern in her voice. She looks in her bag and hands me a tissue.

I cry into it, then dab my eyes.

Ellen hands me another one. 'You gotta stop this Fred. It's too much for her.'

I sniff and try to compose myself. I hadn't expected to do this much crying on my birthday trip. I want to talk with Patrick. I wish he was here.

'How can you be this spiritual and have the word hate tattooed on your knuckles?' I ask Freddy, after a few minutes.

Ellen laughs. Freddy looks down at the table and smiles. 'Let's just say that for a very long time, I'd lost the connection. I didn't know who I was. My past is part of me. I don't want to deny parts of me. But I've been forgiven.' He narrows his eyes. 'You must forgive too. This place is where we learn about forgiveness, and we only have limited time, although most people go through life thinking they'll be here forever. But before you know it, you're holding Bethan's hand again. And your Dad's.'

A coldness grips my heart when Freddy says that. Am I going to die soon? Is that what he means? I'm still not sure what I should change about myself.

'Back to the bus, please!' Gillian's standing next to the table, smiling at us. She claps her hands and walks over to the bar. 'The Sex and the City Tour people, finish your drinks and go back to the bus, please!'

♫

I return to the hostel around nine p.m. but Ryan isn't there yet. For a moment I'm worried; this is a big city and he's a tourist. But then I remember what a knob he'd been and I shrug my worries off. So what if he gets mugged and murdered? Would suit him right.

I push Ryan's bed to the other side of the wall and I put the bedside table back in its original position. I have to see it for what it is now. If I don't change, something might happen to me. Ryan doesn't want me as his life partner. Not now, not ever, and nothing I could ever do will change that, because the truth is: you can't make someone love you when they're really not interested. Amen.

Once in bed, I can't sleep. I should've asked Freddy for

his phone number. I didn't even have a chance to speak to him and Ellen anymore after we boarded the bus and drove back to the Pulitzer Fountain. I sat next to a Canadian woman who kept banging on about what a doormat Carrie was. Her breath stank of anchovies; God knows what she had in that bar. I offered her a tic-tac, but she didn't get the hint and politely declined. I'd kept glancing over at Ellen and Freddy, but they were all the way at the front of the bus. When the tour was finished, I looked around for them; asked Gillian if she'd seen which way they'd gone, but she couldn't help me.

If you don't change, something is going to happen. Sorry. What did Freddy mean by that? Am I going to have another accident? And has Bethan grown up in heaven? Freddy said she wanted to shake me, but I always thought of her as a child.

Everything unfolds as it should. Someone told me that thirty years ago. I'd stopped believing it. But if Ryan hadn't ditched me today, I wouldn't have gone on the bus tour and I wouldn't have heard from Bethan. A rush of joy suddenly floods through me, like warm sunlight. Even if I do die, I'll be fine. I'll still be alive, and with Dad and Bethan again. Ultimately, we'll all reunite.

Hours later, still tossing and turning, I hear Ryan coming through the door. He stumbles around in the semi-dark, presumably not wanting to switch on the light for me. He does have a few decent bones in his body. Two or three or so.

'Oh.'

He's just found out about the beds.

'Carys,' he whispers. 'Carys? Carys! Are you asleep?'

I pretend I am. Sod you.

Chapter 23

'Have you seen my shirt?' Ryan's scanning the open closet, bare-chested, a white towel wrapped around his waist. His shoulder blades glisten with moisture.

'Which one?' I ask.

It's around ten a.m. and I'm still in bed, with my phone, scrolling through the happy birthday messages Kieran and Flora sent me. Cadi sent me one too, but it came with a PS: *Do you want to hear the latest? Mum's furious with Dr Seymour. She demanded to read his evaluation report of her and discovered that he'd classified her level of intelligence as low/average. It's funny but also sad, don't you think?*

'My Abercrombie shirt.' Ryan glances around the room.

'I think I saw you put it back in your suitcase yesterday morning.'

'Oh, right.' He crosses the room to his suitcase that's near the foot of my bed and crouches down in front of it.

Poor Mum. It's not funny. This hit her where it hurts. Is low/average really such a bad score though? I'll ask Patrick about it.

'What are you up to today?' Ryan asks, donning his shirt.

'Nothing much,' I reply. 'I'm just going to stroll around for a bit. You?'

Ryan drops the towel on his bed and reaches for the shorts and jeans he laid out for himself. 'Probably the Empire

State Building and the Rockefeller Center.' He sits down and puts his socks and shoes on. 'Well,' he says, getting up. 'Have fun, and I'll see you tonight. I've got my own key now, by the way.'

At the door he puts one hand on the knob, pats his pockets with a quick gesture and adjusts the strap of his satchel across his shoulder. 'Bye,' he says, and a few seconds later the door clicks shut.

I glance around the shabby room. So, this is how I'm spending my thirtieth birthday. Can't say it's not memorable. One day, I'll tell Amélie about it. How I went to New York with a guy I'd met on a dating site, who'd tried to split up with me over the phone but let me talk him out of it, and who then proceeded to dump me on the streets of Manhattan after all, and ignore my birthday. I can't help thinking of Flora's thirtieth birthday. We'd gone to a fancy restaurant in Ealing. All her friends were there, and a few colleagues; celebrating her, saying kind things and making her feel special. I would have preferred that to my funny anecdote.

I get up with a sigh and head for the bathroom.

A little while later, I'm sauntering along 106th Street, on my way to Central Park, taking in the hustle and bustle that's Manhattan. I am glad to be here. I'd thought of celebrating my thirtieth birthday in New York for years. I'd just envisaged it differently; assumed I'd be here with someone who cared about me—Flora, Cadi maybe, or a boyfriend. I thought I'd be having fun. But it's alright; it's fine as it is. And Cadi was right. Ryan does have an arrogant face. His arrogant face perfectly reflects his arrogant personality.

He's hardly marriage material. James's knob was much bigger, too.

I sit down on a park bench, enjoying my surroundings and the sunshine on my arms. New Yorkers and visitors are everywhere, jogging, cycling; mothers push prams, dogs sniff at each other's bums, and two brown horses languidly step by me. Sunlight glints on their coats.

'Come on, Bay,' one of the riders says. He clicks his tongue and the horse listens, moving it ears.

I close my eyes and breathe in the summer air. I love it here. I want to move here. I want a change. Apparently, British people can't get a green card though. Canada? I could have moved there with Ryan. I would have done it. I could fly for Air Canada. I would have loved to set up home with him there…

Yup, it's back— the familiar pang of loss. I know that I won't share my life with Ryan, and that I'll get over him, but losing the dream still hurts. I built my hopes up for eight months after all. But Flora was right. I was delusional; putting my life on hold because I wanted to win. How stupid. I must detox now, and never do this to myself again.

I take my phone from my bag and send Flora a message. *Thank you for your birthday wishes. Having a horrid time with Ryan, but can still see the beauty that's New York. I wish I could move here. I want a change. When I turn forty, I'm coming here with you!*

I switch my phone off to save batteries and watch a group of eight people doing Tai Chi on the grass, barefoot. I wonder if they do this every Monday morning. An appealing idea. Regularity, routine. Seeing the same people on the same day, every week; getting to know them. I don't want to be a flight attendant anymore. I'm going to sort my life out and thirty is a great place to start from. Everything that came before today, including Ryan, well, I'll chalk it up to experience.

I have a thought. The arrogant knob didn't even get me anything for my birthday. I'll go and get something for myself. One of those glorious Magnolia cupcakes. No, two at least! And I saw a small second-hand bookshop on Bleecker yesterday. It was shut, but maybe it's open for browsing today. And I want to go back to Union Square too. I loved it there when I was here in May.

I get up from the bench and start for Grand Central Terminal. A lovely walk. I'll take a train from there.

♪

When I get off the train near Bleecker, I feel disorientated for a moment. It's a very long street, but I remember the bakery and the bookshop I saw are near Bleecker Playground. I look around for a friendly-looking woman I could ask for directions—I've stopped asking men for directions in New York after I was yelled at twice on previous visits.

I spot a lady who's walking a long-haired poodle, and continue in the direction she tells me to go. It's not as hot as it was yesterday and I'm traipsing along, feeling quite contented. Now and again, I pop into a boutique that seems interesting and snoop around for a bit.

After a while I come to a busy junction where several

people are waiting for the Walk sign to flash up. Joining them, my gaze falls on a shop on the other side of the road. It has a purple façade and flowers in pots lined up against it. Red, lacy curtains are draped on both sides of the large window. The shop oozes an oriental, mystical atmosphere.

I cross the road and move to the big sign in the window, which says:

Have your fortune told here. Palm Reading $10.00, Crystal Ball $15.00, Tarot Cards $25, I-Ching $35.00. No appointment needed.

I peer through the window and see a woman sitting at a square table with a thick red cloth and a crystal ball on it. She's a bit plumb, clad in a long dress. Her white hair is tied into a knot on top of her head. I'd say she's in her sixties. I'm not sure if I want to go in though. I do have a couple of burning questions, like when will I meet the love of my life, and when can I expect Amélie to come along, but Patrick told me to cut down on this sort of thing. I think he's right, I should. Besides, it's embarrassing if people see me going in here. They'll probably assume I'm a desperate nut, looking for answers, which I am, in a way, but no one needs to know that.

Oh, she's looking up! Through the window, the woman and I hold each other's gaze, and she gestures with her hand for me to come in. I could just ask for information, I suppose. Is anyone watching me? No.

I open the door and step inside.

'Hello,' I say.

'Hi,' the woman grunts. 'Do you want a reading?' She's got a deep, husky voice.

I tentatively walk over to her table. 'Um, I was thinking about it.'

'Take a seat', she says. It sounds like an order. I sit down on a gold-painted chair with a purple velvet cushion on it. The place smells like old dust, incense sticks and candles. I glance at the red tablecloth and the crystal ball. It feels strange to be near to everything I'd just observed through the window.

The woman barely looks at me. I'm surprised at how standoffish she comes across. She did wave me in.

'I'm thirty today,' I blurt, trying to break the ice.

Congratulations,' she grumbles.

'Thank you.'

'Do you want me to consult my crystal ball, the tarot cards, the I-Ching, or do you want a palm reading?'

'Um, tarot cards please.'

'Why?'

'I've got tarot cards myself. I'm familiar with them, so that's why I prefer them. Do I have to tell you why I'm here?'

'No. You don't have to tell me anything. Shuffle this deck and divide them into three different piles.'

I do as I'm told, but I'm feeling a bit uneasy. She's so unfriendly. Maybe it's all part of some kind of mystical image she's created for herself?

'Okay,' she says. 'I will tell you everything. The good stuff and the bad.' She takes several cards from the piles

I've formed, lays them down on the table, and frowns while she examines them.

I'm not interested in hearing doom-and-gloom scenarios about my life and I'm feeling even more nervous now. I try to see which of the cards she's selected, but it's hard because they're upside down and different from the deck I've got at home. I recognise a few cards though. There's Temperance, The Magician and a few aces. Not particularly bad omens, I think.

'You are a friendly, outgoing person,' she begins. 'Giving, but too much at times and you're not getting anything back. This is disappointing to you and has caused problems with you and certain members of your family. You are there for them, but they aren't there for you. You work in the public sector. You are also creative.'

'I'm a flight attendant,' I reply, wondering if that's the public sector. I'll google it. And am I creative? I did make bumblebees once, by wrapping black and yellow yarn around some brown catkins I found in Mrs Meads' garden. Does that count?

'Also,' she slowly continues, 'the cards show me that your childhood was traumatic. You endured several traumas... I can see two, I think. Yes.' She frowns. 'Definitely in your childhood.'

I don't reply.

'I definitely see marriage for you,' she says brusquely, 'and you will have two children.' She smiles mysteriously. 'But not yet.'

The woman takes two more cards from the left pile and

studies them for a moment. 'You will live a long life, mid-eighties.'

I shift uncomfortably in my seat. I didn't really want to know about that.

'You have to pay attention to your stomach and find a way to deal with stressful situations. Otherwise you can get problems in that area later on in life.'

I glance at her with a start. What the bloody hell is that supposed to mean? Cancer? She's hardly the picture of health herself, with those puffy bags under her eyes.

'You have everything in your life in order, you're doing very well, but not in love.'

I perk up in my chair. There we are. Now we're getting to the gist of the matter.

'You've been going around in circles for a long time. Every time someone tries to come close to you, you're not interested, and when you like someone they are not interested in you.'

'Sounds about right,' I say. 'I'm actually here with a guy I've known since January of this year, but he's sort of dumped me. Twice. I hoped he would change his mind once he got to know me… but he hasn't.'

The woman stares at me in silence and I feel myself shrinking in my chair. She thinks I'm a sad dunce. I know she does.

'You thought he would change his mind if you kept seeing him,' she says, matter-of-factly. 'It's not gonna happen. There's an obstacle.'

'An obstacle?' I instantly think of Leah.

'Yes, an obstacle. And that's the reason it's not going to work out. There's also something with five years ago....' Her voice trails off and she studies the cards, while I pick at a cuticle.

'Five years ago,' she says, 'you lost someone... This was a person who meant a lot to you. It's also linked to an overseas journey.'

I stare at her cards, thinking of Dad and James, and of James and I moving to Sweden.

'I'm just wondering...' I say. 'Which tarot cards are you using, exactly? I've been doing tarot readings for myself since the age of eighteen and I've never been able to see things that are this specific. Certainly not past events.'

'I'm using my own.'

'You mean, cards you devised yourself?'

'That's right. If you're interested: a deck costs seventy-five dollars.'

'Oh, no. That's alright, thanks. My psychologist wants me to cut down on tarot readings.'

I laugh but she ignores me, and an awkward moment of silence hangs between us.

'Could you tell me more about the obstacle at all?' I ask.

The woman gives me a pensive stare, then says: 'I see what the problem is and why you've been going round in circles for so long.'

'You do?' I move to the edge of my seat and hold her gaze.

'You did something wrong in a past life and you are now being punished for that. That's the obstacle. It's like a curse, but I can solve this for you for three hundred dollars.'

'A curse?'

'Yes.'

I sink back in my chair. 'And you're charging me three hundred dollars for it?'

'Yes. You will need to come in for several sessions.'

'I'm not paying you three hundred dollars. I haven't even got that, and I also don't believe I'm being punished.'

A flicker of resentment crosses her face. I didn't mean to insult her.

'I do believe that, maybe, we have to learn lessons about things that went wrong in a previous lifetime,' I say, calmer, 'but I don't believe we are punished. Besides, I live in London. I'm going home tomorrow.'

The woman says nothing. Neither do I. We both stare at the cards on the table.

'I'll give you my phone number,' she suddenly says. She turns in her chair and starts rummaging through a drawer beside her. 'I also do readings over the phone. I have customers all over the world who do it like that.' She closes the drawer, then picks up a handbag from the floor and goes through that. 'I don't have any more business cards here.' She glances at me. 'I'll have a look downstairs, just a moment please.'

She hoists herself up from her chair— the blue and yellow dress she's wearing reaches to her ankles— and trots down a narrow staircase behind me that seems to be leading to a basement.

I ponder the reading. It hasn't really helped me with anything, apart from learning that I'll probably live to an average age for a woman, and that I may as well give up the last shreds of hope for a relationship with Ryan.

After several minutes the woman comes back up the stairs. 'I'm sorry', she pants, 'but I don't have any cards left.' She sits down at the table again and scribbles a few digits on a piece of paper. 'Here's my phone number. If you want a reading over the phone you can pay by credit card. My name is Crystal. My email address is on there as well.'

I glance at the note and feel torn between giving any value at all to what I've been told, and finding this woman, who's come across as rather unfriendly and money orientated, a complete and utter shambles. I take the note nevertheless and pay her twenty-five dollars.

'Have you got any more questions?' she says, tucking the money away in a drawer.

I hesitate. 'Well... yes actually. When will I finally meet someone who will reciprocate my feelings?'

Without looking at the cards, she says: 'I can see this person coming into your life very soon.'

♫

Out on Bleecker again, I remember I'd come here for cupcakes and a bookshop. The Magnolia Bakery is only a few minutes further down the street, and when I arrive there's no queue. Yesterday, the queue wrapped around the side of the building.

I buy two cupcakes, one chocolate, one vanilla, and a coffee, then head for Bleecker Playground and sit down on a bench. There are a few women with kids who play together.

I put the coffee down beside me and start on the chocolate cupcake, watching the mothers and the kids, while thinking about the clairvoyant. Did she say that I was outgoing? I can be, when I'm with Flora, or other people I feel comfortable with, but I can also be quite the contrary. James once told me he didn't think I was the bubbly type. Don't remember how it came up, but that's what he said. She has made me doubt my own beliefs though. What if she's right? I don't know everything, and some of the things she said were spot on. What if I really am cursed?

I have a thought. I once read a book about a man who was a hypnotherapist for a living, and for some reason, some of his patients had accidentally ended up in past lifetimes. I won't look for that small bookshop now—I can go there when I'm here next time—but I'll go straight to Barnes & Noble on Union Square. They're bound to stock a couple of books on hypnosis. If I can help myself with an instruction manual, I'll probably save myself around two-hundred and eighty dollars, and if all else fails, it's good to know that Crystal's there.

I glance at the Magnolia Bakery box on my lap. I've finished my chocolate cupcake, but barely tasted it. I'll save the vanilla one for later, when I have less thinking to do.

My phone bleeps when I switch it on to check the time. I have five new messages and a new voice mail. One of them is a birthday message from my friend Mette in Sweden! She says she misses me and when am I in Stockholm again? I think of James. For the first three years after we split up, we'd sent each other happy birthday and merry Christmas messages.

But then he met his new girlfriend and it stopped. Has he thought of me at all today? Probably not. He looks very happy in the pictures he posts on Facebook, of him and Sheila. I look at those pictures sometimes, to make myself feel more miserable when I'm feeling miserable already. God knows why I do that.

A new message from Flora. No, two.

Sorry to hear it's not going well in New York. Same here. Ed just told me to shove my ultimatums up my arse. I will have to for now. I'm feeling really low. You're back tomorrow, aren't you? Do you want to have dinner at mine on Friday? Or are you working? Miss you. Be safe.

How long will it take Flora to see she's delusional too?

I open her second message. It says: *'Loneliness is the way by which destiny endeavours to lead man to himself.' Herman Hesse.*

I ponder the words for a few moments. The man was absolutely right. I'd love to see Flora on Friday, but I can't. I'll be in Dar es Salaam. God, I hate my job.

The other messages alert me to a missed call that came in an hour ago, and the voicemail message. I glance at the number listed for the missed call. Looks like the number that rang me in Brighton. It must be Mum. My stomach tightens. Troubles again? I press the phone to my ear and listen to the voicemail message. 'This button here, Kathy,' someone says. Was that Maeve? After this, there's a ten-second silence, but then I hear her voice.

'Hi Carys.... it's Mum... could you give us a ring please, love?' There's the voice in the background again, and then the phone clicks dead. What was that about? Mum didn't wish me a happy birthday. She sounded quite serious. Is everything alright? I briefly consider the time difference—it's nine a.m. in England—then call the number back.

A woman I don't know picks up and I tell her my name, then ask if it's possible to speak with Kathy Wynne.

'Bear with me,' she replies, and a minute or two later, Mum's voice is in my ear.

'Carys?'

'Hi Mum.'

'Hi Carys. It's Mum.'

'Yes, I know it's you. You asked me to call you?'

'Yes, I did... I wanted to wish you a happy birthday.'

'Thank you. But I thought there might be a problem?'

'A problem? No, everything's fine. Why would there be a problem?'

Just a few sentences into a conversation, and my mood's already dropping towards arctic temperatures.

'Well, first of all,' I huff, 'because it's you. Second of all, you could have wished me a happy birthday when you left me a message, but you didn't. And third of all, you sounded rather serious, so… I thought that maybe you weren't alright.'

'Oh, but I *am* alright. Everything's fine Carys.'

There's silence on both ends of the line.

'Are you having a good day?' Mum asks.

'Yes. It's alright. I just saw a fortune teller.'

'You did?' She sounds hesitant. 'How's Ryan?'

'He's fine.'

'Is he with you?'

'Yes, he is. He's sitting next to me. We're eating cupcakes

from a famous bakery.'

'Oh.' Mum pauses. 'Well, that's lovely… Does he know I'm in here?'

'He does.'

'Okay.' Another pause. 'And when are you flying home?'

'Tomorrow evening. We're back at Heathrow on Wednesday, around eight in the morning. It was just a four-day trip.'

'Maybe I could come with you to New York sometime,' Mum says, wistfully. 'I'd love to see America.'

'Yeah, who knows. But I've got to go now, Mum. We're going to Barnes & Noble.'

'You're going to a bookshop?'

'Yes. But I want to hang up now.'

'Will you come and visit me again?'

'I'll see.'

'I miss you.'

'Yeah.'

'You are always welcome here, Carys. I'm sorry for what I said to you. I shouldn't have done that. I believe you. You didn't call the RSPCA.'

'That's right. I didn't.'

'But you did speak to Dr Seymour behind my back. And I wasn't very happy about that, Carys. But I'm not angry anymore. I know you thought you were doing the right thing.'

'Yeah, alright. But I'm going now.'

'Alright darling. You have a great day. Thirty years ago, I carried you inside me.'

'I know. Bye Mum.'

'Give my love to Ryan.'

'I will do.'

'I love you.'

'Yeah, okay. Bye Mum.'

I put my phone back in my bag. Another one of our great talks. Not.

Chapter 24

The square white ceiling looms over me, like a giant blanket, or a big fluffy cloud. On the green curtains, Mr Owl's holding a book between his wings. At least twelve times. Miss Stork has a long orange beak. Eight times.

Downstairs, I hear Mum's voice and I curl my toes, clench them. Bethan squeals. Dad's laughing. The lights that are wrapped around the tree? Dad played with them last night. He switched them on and off for her, and Bethan squealed then, like she's squealing now.

I had that dream again last night. I have it all the time. It frightens me.

I'm in my bed, but then my bed starts to sink, slowly, through the floor; I'm surrounded by white concrete, and come out in the living room, near the ceiling. I peer down over the edge of my bed. Mum and Dad are sitting on the sofa, each on one side of it, far apart from each other. They look up and see me on the bed. I keep sinking, slowly. Dad smiles at me; a bit silly, but kind. Mum glares at me. Her beady eyes move. She doesn't like what she sees. I'm getting nearer to them, but I'm scared of Mum. I want the bed to stop sinking. I've almost reached them, and the bed hovers before them. Dad's still smiling; Mum's still glaring. Then the bed starts to move back up, slowly, through the ceiling. I'm back in my bedroom. The bed's back in its spot.

Every night I dream this. Every morning, I wake up and look at the figures on the curtains, but I still see Mum's eyes in my mind. I'm angry with Mum, for always being angry. For always saying sorry, but then smacking me again, and shouting at Bethan. The sorries are no good.

I step out of bed. I've had enough. I'm going to tell Mum about my dream. It will make her fume. I want to see her fume. I used to have a wet towel in my tummy. Now there's just a brick.

♫

Downstairs, the lights in the Christmas tree are on, but Dad's not playing with them. He's sitting at the table near the window. Looks like he's writing cheques to pay the bills.

'Morning Carys,' he says. 'Did you sleep well?'

Bethan's on the sofa, watching TV.

She beams when she sees me and I wrap my arms around her and kiss her cheek.

Then I go to the kitchen, where Mum is doing the dishes in the sink.

'I had that dream again,' I wail, moving to her side.

'What dream?'

'A horrible dream,' I sniff. 'I have it all the time.'

Mum dries her hands on her apron. 'Did you have a nightmare?'

'Yes. About you. I dream about you every night.'

That's how I begin. I tell her the dream, while Bethan's on the sofa, watching telly; innocent, unaware she will end up paying for my words.

Mum's cheeks have turned red and she glares at me. Already, I'm sorry for what I said. She's acting exactly as I thought she would, but I don't want it anymore. I want her to behave like a mother, instead, she's like a child.

'How dare you dream such things about me,' she bellows.

I look at her, tearful. Doesn't she know that I didn't dream it on purpose? Can she not realise that?

Dad marches into the kitchen. 'What's going on here?' he says, his eyes on me. 'Are you alright?'

I shake my head. 'Mummy is upset because I had a dream.'

Dad's mouth drops open. 'You're angry with Carys for having a dream?'

'I don't deserve to be dreamt about like that,' Mum says, her voice raised. 'You were the good guy again. I'm always the bad one. Everyone thinks so, but they don't know you, Jac. They don't know you like I do.'

'If you and I don't get on,' Dad says, raising his voice too, 'you should leave the kids out of it. It's not their fault.' He looks at Mum with a deep frown between his eyes, but she turns her back to him and her hands disappear under soap bubbles.

'Carys dreams about me every night,' Mum says, her voice trembling. 'E-v-e-r-y night.'

'No Mummy,' I plead. 'I don't dream about you every night. I was confused. I thought I had a dream, but I didn't.'

'I don't believe you, Carys,' she snaps. 'You think I'm an angry person. Well, I'm not.' She throws her head back and laughs. 'I'm a cheerful person. See?' She laughs harder. 'I'm cheerful.'

Suddenly she pulls a breadknife from under the suds and points it at me. Her amber eyes are wide and water drips from her wrists onto the floor. 'From now on, you'll have nice dreams about me. And you will tell everyone about it.'

Dad lunges forward and grabs my arm. 'I can't believe I ever took you out of that ward,' he shouts at Mum. 'I shouldn't have. You belong there!'

Now there's silence. Dad watches Mum. She's leaning her hands on the edge of the sink. It sounds as if she can hardly breathe.

I hear the cartoon Bethan's watching in the living room. 'The Care Bears,' I say.

Dad glances down at me. 'You go watch that,' he says, but I don't move. I need to know if Mum will be alright.'

'You need to take your medication, Kath,' Dad says. 'From now on—'

Mum holds up her hand, her fingers spread out. 'Don't talk to me.' She unties her apron and throws it on the worktop.

'Where are you going?' Dad says, but she moves past us without giving a reply.

Dad still has a deep frown between his eyes. 'Are you alright?' His gaze moves over my face. 'She didn't hit you, did she?'

But I can't speak. I did this.

The front door slams shut and I run into the hall. Through the glass panel, I see Mum carrying Bethan down the garden path. I grab my coat, open the door and run after them.

'Mum,' I shout.

She doesn't wait for me. She's walking on the pavement and going so fast. Bethan's bobbing up and down in her arms, watching me over Mum's shoulder.

I catch up with them before Patsy's garden fence, but it's like Mum doesn't see me.

I follow behind them, and Rose opens the door before Mum's even rung the bell.

'It's all wrong again,' Mum says, and Rose steps aside and lets us in.

♫

Upstairs, Bethan's playing with Patsy's rocking horse, Daisy. Patsy doesn't allow her to sit on it, but she's given Bethan two pencils and told her to pretend they were carrots for the horse.

Patsy's in her rocking chair, moving back and forth. Her socks smell of cheese.

'I have a secret to tell you,' she says, smiling at me.

Her smile frightens me, and I think she knows that because now her smile is even meaner and her eyes are too, so I try to look as if I don't care what the secret is.

'Your mum's going to leave your dad and she's going to live with us. I'll have two mummies and you'll have none.' Patsy slides off the chair and lowers herself in front of Bethan, who's jabbing the pencils at the horse's mouth. She wraps her long finger around Bethan's wrist. 'Your mummy is leaving Bethan because she is going to be my mum.'

Bethan glances at me and puts a finger in her mouth, then she lets out a wail.

'Oh, don't cry little girl,' Patsy coos. It reminds me of when she wanted to throw me in the fire.

'You'll be fine, Bethan,' Patsy says. 'You can come and visit. We'll be sisters.'

It's like Mum's just slapped me across the face with a wet, rolled-up towel, and I'm biting back my tears.

Patsy notices. 'Oh my God,' she snarls. 'You two are such babies.'

Bethan cries harder now and I wonder if she understood what Patsy just said, or if she's crying because of her mean voice.

Patsy lifts her up. 'Don't cry Bethan, we'll be sisters. You know what? Do you want to see ice?'

Bethan stops crying. 'Ice cream?' she asks. Her lips quiver.

'No, not ice you can eat,' Patsy says, putting her down. 'Ice you can walk on. Would you like to see it?'

Bethan nods and wipes her nose on the back of her hand. She takes the two fingers of Patsy's left hand and they walk to the door.

'Where are you going?' I ask.

'To the ditch,' Patsy says. 'There's ice on it. I go on it every day. It's strong enough.'

'Can I come too?'

'Alright,' Patsy says.

Downstairs, Patsy helps us put our coats and shoes on. Silently, we slip out of the backdoor.

♪

Patsy is the first to lower herself down the edge of the ditch and onto the black ice. She turns around to help us.

'Walk slowly Bethan,' I say, holding her hand. 'It's slippery.'

She smiles at me. Tufts of brown hair stick out from under the sides of her pink hat. Looking at her, shuffling her little shoes over the ice, I feel a warm glow. I love it when she's happy. Like with the lights in the Christmas tree. I have been over the next moment, and what followed, a billion times. I've never really understood how Bethan came to walk off by herself. Patsy started talking about our mothers again and she angered me, but for the first time since I'd met her, I stood up to her, because I'd realised when we were in her bedroom that my fear made her feel stronger, and I wanted that to end.

I didn't understand the hole in the ice that I had failed to spot, until much later, when I learnt that people sometimes make them so that ducks have water to swim in.

A hollow splash. A feeble shriek.

I turned around and was changed forever. We all were. Bethan was lying up to her armpits in the freezing water. She pressed her small bare hands down on the ice and fought to stay above water. Her face was contorted in shock and fear, and she let out soft, high-pitched cries.

I lost all feeling in my body. I tried to rush over to Bethan, but it felt as if my feet were paralysed.

Patsy grabbed my arm.

'No,' I screamed. 'No, let me go. We have to save her.'

'It's dangerous,' Patsy yelled back. 'I'll get my mum.'

'No!' I pulled myself free and ran up to the hole, but Patsy was stronger. She tackled me to the ground and sat down on my back.

Lying on the ice, facing my little sister, I knew that everything was lost. Bethan was limp and pale, but she held my gaze, and from that gaze, I could tell that she knew I wasn't going to save her.

'Let me go!' I shouted at the top of my lungs and fought to wriggle myself free. 'Help her! Patsy, help her! Help Bethan!'

'Mum, Mummy!' Patsy yelled.

Bethan's eyes glazed over, with cold, with acceptance. She started to lose her grip on the ice. When I saw it, I wet myself, and for just a few seconds I had a sense of comfort, because the feeling was warm and familiar.

Bethan's hands slid away. Slowly she sank into the water and disappeared underneath the ice.

'Bethan, I'm sorry, I love you,' I yelled after her. It was the last thing I could do.

♪

I've talked to Patrick about Mum's harrowing screams that cut through the air when she and Rose came running towards us. I still hear them. They still slice through me. Was it my fault? In the moments where I'm convinced it was, I see a noose. And I want to stick my head through it and die because it's too much to bear.

Mum's face, her eyes, her hoarse moans. She lay flat on the ice, before the hole, and groped around in the black water. Rose helped her drag up Bethan's lifeless body.

Bethan died on Saturday, December 20, 1986. Three weeks before her third birthday. She was buried in Brecon, four days later.

Chapter 25

The children are laughing. There are even more of them now, running around Bleecker Playground. They hang from climbing frames and go down the slide. They throw sand at each other for fun and squeal with joy, like Bethan once did.

Mum was so young when it all happened. Dad too. I believe they were just twenty-six when Bethan died. My parents were emotionally immature. Too green behind the ears to raise children. Both of them.

Mum just made an effort on the phone. Calling to congratulate me, telling me she misses me, asking me to visit. And I put my wall up again. After all these years, I don't know how to take it down anymore. Freddy mentioned forgiveness. I'm sure that's important but I'm still angry with Mum, about so many things. I suppose that means I haven't forgiven her. Maybe that's why I can't get rid of the wall.

Suddenly, I have a thought. A brilliant idea! I quickly take my phone and scroll to the last number I dialled, then dial it again. A young-sounding woman answers. I think it's the brunette with glasses and the annoying cackle. I recognise her voice.

'This is Carys Wynne,' I say. 'I just spoke with my mother, but can I get her on the phone again, please? I forgot to tell her something.'

'Bear with me,' she replies. They must have been trained to say that.

I wait and bite my nails. They have to hurry. I can do this now, but I don't know about five minutes from now.

'Hello?'

I take a breath. 'Hi Mum, it's me.'

'Carys? Are you alright?'

'Yes, I'm fine. But I was thinking about what you said. About New York. You can come with me.'

'I can?' She sounds astonished.

'Yes, you can. You can join me when I'm working. I'll bid for a New York trip in October. I'll pay for your ticket.'

'Gosh.' She pauses, and it suddenly occurs to me that she might not even want to do this with me. Maybe she just wanted the fantasy, not the real thing.

'It would be lovely,' Mum says, 'but are you sure?'

'I am. But can you come though? Will they let you go?'

'Yes, I can come. I'm here on a voluntary basis. But, I don't think I can afford a hotel.'

'My company pays for my room. There's only a small charge for an extra person. I'll pay for that too. See it as an early birthday gift.'

'Oh,' Mum says. 'I didn't get you anything.'

'That's alright. No worries.'

After we hang up, I sit quietly on the park bench, letting the prospect of coming here with my mother sink in. New York's been a disaster for me and Ryan; maybe it will be balm for me and Mum.

A few feet away from me, a bearded homeless man parks

a shopping cart piled high with cans, bottles and a grimy blue sleeping bag. He starts going through a bin, pulling out cartons and paper cups and dropping them on the ground. When he finds something edible, he eagerly bites into it.

I get up from the bench and walk up to him. 'Excuse me,' I say. 'Would you like this?'

With a perturbed look on his face, he glances at the vanilla cupcake in the Magnolia Bakery box I'm offering him.

'Fuck off,' he says, turning back to the bin.

I lean forward and he watches me discard my empty coffee cup. 'It's much nicer to say Foxtrot Oscar,' I reply. 'Thought for the day.'

♪

That evening, I'm back at the hostel around eight and find Ryan lying on his front on the bed, reading a book.

'Hi,' he says, without looking up.

'Hi,' I reply, stonily, and sit down on my bed. It's warm in the room, and we've attracted a couple of flies. Ryan should have kept the window shut. Street noise filters in through the gap and the generator hums its usual monotonous tone. It seems Ryan's already been packing because the three clothes hangers in the wardrobe are empty.

'What are you reading?' I ask.

'*Atlas Shrugged.*'

The familiar pang of loss is back instantly. I love that Ryan loves reading. Where will I ever find another guy who thinks nothing of tackling a tome like that? We could have read books together, in our elder years, when Amélie and her brother or sister had flown the nest.

'Did you get it today,' I ask.

Ryan glances at me. 'Yes, I got it this morning.'

'Where?'

'Does it matter?'

'I went to Barnes & Noble.'

'I didn't get it there.'

'It's my birthday today.'

'Yes, I know. Did you have a good day?'

'I did. I had a lovely day actually.'

Ryan closes his book and sits up. 'What did you do?'

'I revisited a few places from the Sex and the City Tour I went on yesterday. And I went to Union Square and to the lower-level concourse at Grand Central Station.'

'I was thinking of having a look there,' Ryan says. He puts his book on the bedside table and takes a bottle of water. 'Do you want to do something together tomorrow?'

'We're going home tomorrow.'

'Yes. I know we're going home tomorrow, but we'll have most of the day here, so I thought that maybe we could do something together.'

'We haven't got most of the day here, tomorrow,' I reply. 'Our plane leaves at seven. That means we should be at the airport around four, which means we should start making our way over there at three.'

'We don't have to be at the airport three hours before departure.'

'Yes, we do. There's always an enormous queue for check-in, it takes ages to get through security there, and besides, we're on standby.'

Ryan takes a swig of water. 'That's crazy. An hour and a half would be more than enough.'

'No, it wouldn't.'

'Alright then,' he says. 'We'll leave at three. But we could still go to MOMA before that.'

I shrug my shoulders and open my wallet to check how many dollars I have left. 'I'm not sure what I'm doing yet. I'll see.'

'Alright,' Ryan says again, but he sounds as if I've taken him by surprise.

♪

Hours later, I'm tossing and turning in my bed.

'Can you switch that light off now,' I ask Ryan, annoyed. 'I can't sleep like this.'

'Only one more page,' he replies. 'Why don't you read something too?'

'Because it's the middle of the night and I'm tired.'

I close my eyes again, and after what feels like a few minutes, I hear the thump of *Atlas Shrugged* being put away on the bedside table, followed by the rustle of Ryan's duvet.

He walks to the door where the light switch is, and it clicks, but instead of going back to his own bed, he lifts a corner of my duvet and slides in beside me, draping an arm and a leg over me.

'Are you asleep?' he asks.

'No, I'm not. You kept the light on. And that hideous generator and the sirens aren't helping either.'

'Are you glad we're going home tomorrow?'

'Well… I wouldn't have minded staying a bit longer, and I'm not looking forward to flying to Dar es Salaam on Thursday, but I do miss my own bed.'

We're silent for a few minutes, and I'm beginning to doze off, when Ryan clears his throat and says: 'You know, Sunday, when I left you by yourself, I regretted it almost immediately.'

He pauses.

Am I supposed to say something now? I deliberately don't.

'But, um, I felt I'd made my decision, you know, so I didn't turn back, or call you.'

I shift my body. 'Turn back?' I say crabbily. 'I left after you did. Did you actually think I was going to stand there and wait for you?'

'No, of course not…' Ryan hesitates. 'I just wanted to say that… I made a mistake. And I'm sorry.'

In the semi-darkness, we glance at each other.

'And then in the evening,' Ryan goes on, 'I wanted to make it up to you. But you'd separated the beds, and I thought you were really pissed off with me, so…'

'I am not pissed off with anyone.'

'Alright, well, I just didn't know what to say. I did get you a present.'

'For my birthday?'

'Yes, I got it today. Do you want it now or in the morning?'

'It can wait till the morning. I want to sleep.'

'Alright.' He wraps his arm more firmly around me. It feels nice to be held; his skin smells of spiced body wash. I nestle my head against his chest.

'But I want to give you the present now.'

'I'm sleeping.'

'Alright.' He kisses my head, and then his lips search my mouth and he kisses me softly. Why can't he have been like this from our first day here? It's too late now.

♪

Ryan's arm is still around me when we wake up early in the morning. The room is light; the generator hums. It's our last day in New York.

'Ryan?'

'Hmm?'

'Your cock's prodding me in the back.'

'Oh, sorry.' He moves his hip and kisses my shoulder. 'That just happens in the mornings.'

Softly, he begins to tickle my back with his fingertips. He strokes my backside and the inside of my thighs. We kiss each other on the lips, and Ryan moves his hand between my legs and rubs my knickers.

I dig my fingers into his back and he moves half on top of me, lifting up my shirt, kissing my breasts, and my mouth again, and then he slides his hand into my knickers.

'I've got the painters in.'

Ryan stops; a look of surprise and disappointment in his eyes. 'You didn't on Sunday.'

'I know. But today it's Tuesday, and now I do.'

Without a word, he slips off my knickers—I instinctively lift my bum to help him— and then he tugs at the string of my tampon.

'What are you doing?'

'I wanna get in.'

'Didn't you hear what I just said?'

'I did, but I don't care.' He pulls the tampon out of me and puts it on the bedside table next to a bottle of water.

Another thing I like about him. He's not the squeamish type.

Afterwards, Ryan gets up and leaves the room, and returns with a loo roll. 'The bathroom's free,' he says, handing me a wad of paper. 'If you want to use it… Or shall I give you your present first?'

'No, I'm going to take a shower now.'

'Alright.' Ryan's gaze lingers on my bare breasts. 'Would you like to shower together?'

'Can't say that I do.'

He glances at the floor, then sits down on his bed with the loo roll in his lap. 'Alright.'

♪

When I come back Ryan's dressed and holding a flat, rectangular parcel, wrapped in red and brown paper. 'Here,' he says, holding it out to me.

'What have you done with the tampon?'

'I binned it.'

I peer at the bin. He's wrapped it in grey toilet paper and chucked it between the bits of orange peel.

'Here you are,' Ryan says again, and virtually shoves the present into my hands.

'Hang on, I'm not even dressed yet.' I grab a pair of knickers and a clean bra from my suitcase and drop my towel to the floor, then slip into my jeans and don a shirt.

'Thank you,' I say, sitting down on the bed.

Ryan sits down beside me and watches me unwrap.

I tear away the paper, and out comes a framed picture of a rainbow. I stare at it.

'See? Sharp colours,' Ryan says. 'I saw this and thought of you. Do you like it?'

I bring the picture closer to my face.

'It's better than that picture on your mantelpiece, isn't it? That was a little grainy and taken from a greater distance. You could replace it with this one.'

'I won't do that though.'

An uncomfortable silence hangs between us, and Ryan awkwardly gazes at the rainbow in my hands.

'Do you remember you asked me about the rainbow picture on my mantelpiece, and I told you a journalist had given it to me?'

Ryan tilts his head back a little. 'Yes, I remember that.'

'If *you* had told *me* a journalist had given you that picture, which you then chose to frame, I would've asked you about it. But you didn't ask me anything.'

'I didn't?'

'No, you didn't. Anyway, this is why I framed that rainbow.

My dad played me one of his favourite songs once, when I was fifteen or sixteen. It was called: 'Look for Me in Rainbows.' Dad said that if he ever died, he'd send us a rainbow to show he was alright. I thought he was joking at the time, but then, he did die. And the day after his funeral, when we were at my nan's in Wales, I noticed a picture in a newspaper. It was a picture of a rainbow over Brecon Cemetery, taken the day before, the day of my Dad's funeral. A journalist had taken it and written about it, because he thought it was so unusual there was a rainbow that morning. I contacted the paper and they put me in touch with the journalist and he sent me the picture. I framed it because I believe Dad sent us that rainbow to show he was alright. And I think, when he realised we hadn't noticed it, he put a thought in the head of that journalist, so that in the end we did see it.'

We're silent for several moments. Ryan's frowning and staring at a spot on the floor. I know he doesn't believe in what I've just told him. He doesn't have to. This is my story.

'I did ask you about the rainbow,' Ryan suddenly says. He looks at me accusingly. 'But you didn't want to talk about it. I'm sure that's what you said.'

I meet his gaze in silence; his eyes soften. Is he right? It was a Friday evening, I believe. We were standing in front of the picture on my mantelpiece. What did we talk about again? He kissed me, and then Leah called. I remember that.

'Anyway, you don't want this rainbow then?' Ryan shifts his legs and glances at the picture in my hands.

'I do,' I say, getting up. 'It's alright. You didn't know. Thank you.'

I take the picture and I'm about to stuff it in my suitcase, when I hesitate. The idea of taking it home with me, of holding onto it, fills me with resentment.

'Actually, no, I won't take it.' I face Ryan. 'I don't think we'll see each other again when we get home. I think it's best if we move on. So, here.'

I press the picture back in his hands.

'Oh.' He takes it, then stares at me, with an awkward expression. 'Well, can't we remain friends? Meet up once in a while?'

'For what?'

He shrugs. 'For a bit of fun? Dinner together. A shag.'

'A shag? As long as I'm wearing my flight attendant uniform, right?'

Ryan lowers his gaze.

'Is Leah really your best friend or is she your girlfriend?'

'She not my girlfriend. She's just my best friend! God, I wish I'd never brought her up.'

I think about what the clairvoyant said. About there being an obstacle. I thought that Leah was the obstacle. What else could it be?

'Are you sure you don't love Leah?' I ask.

My question seems to confuse him and his gaze darts to the wall. 'I never said I didn't love her. I'm just not attracted to her.'

'Are looks so important?'

A baffled expression sets on his face.

'Anyway,' I say. 'If you really are just friends, then I do have some advice for you: next time you date a woman, don't talk about her all the time. It's not nice.'

Ryan watches me put my shoes on without making a reply.

'So, are we doing something together, today? He says.

'Nah, that's alright. I'd rather go out by myself to be honest. Do my own thing. I'll meet you at the check-in desk at four. Make sure you're on time. I'm going downstairs now, and get my deposit back. Can I have your key?'

I take my suitcase and tote bag and our two keys. Ryan's still sitting on the bed with his rainbow picture when I close the door. Next time I meet a guy I like, I'll remember to stay true to myself.

Chapter 26

I'm at JFK five minutes to four p.m. and make my way towards the check-in desks. It's hot in the terminal, and a long queue snakes around retractable belt barriers. I join it, glancing around and craning my neck for Ryan, but he's nowhere to be seen. I check my phone. No sign from him there either, just a text from Flora: after careful consideration, she's decided to go ahead with her chin surgery. I quickly text her back that I can't see her on Friday and ask if we can have dinner together on Sunday instead.

By the time it's my turn to check-in, Ryan's still not there. I go up to the ground attendant, a woman with hazel skin and braided, ruby hair, and explain what's going on. She tells me I can wait for Ryan near the desk, and for the next twenty minutes, I watch her struggling to remain polite with customers who pick arguments when confronted with our company's luggage policy.

'Only one piece of hand luggage, ma'am.'

'That suitcase is too big for the cabin, sir.'

Now and again she flinches and a moist sheen covers her forehead.

The passengers don't cave just like that. They do eventually, but not before they've been rude, difficult and unreasonable.

Do I really want to do this? I wonder, observing my American colleague. I don't think I do. It wouldn't make me happy. I want peace and quiet, and fulfilment. That's all I'm after, which means that work-wise, I'm back at square one. Should I discuss this with Annette? I haven't got a plan B yet. Maybe it's wiser to wait.

I check my phone. Ryan's still not called or texted. I'm done waiting for him. I hand the attendant my ticket, passport and cabin crew ID and she takes my suitcase.

It's not my fault Ryan's not here. But I'll have my phone on standby. He can call me when he does turn up, and then I'll go back and fetch him.

Post-security, I wander around the main concourse for a bit, past duty-free shops and ATM machines, amidst hundreds of other passengers. I remember there's a coffee place near gates six and seven, and languidly start making my way over there, looking at some fridge magnets here, and some key hangers and chocolate bars there.

I pop into a Hudson News outlet for a copy of *O Magazine*, but when I queue at the tills, my attention is caught by a few curious headlines, splashed across the front pages of at least three newspapers on a stand near the counter.

Stepping closer, I take out a *New York Post*. A flight attendant named Steven Slater yelled something over the tannoy of a JetBlue cabin yesterday, after he was abused by a passenger. He then grabbed a beer and left the airplane via the slide that he inflated himself. Hallelujah! This guy is my hero! I wish I had the balls for this; I should have done this last week. An Irishman with a purple nose had asked me for another bottle of red wine. I'd kindly asked him which one he wanted, and the next thing I knew, he erupted in fury, yelling at me that it was my job to remember which wine he'd been drinking. I was stunned. And embarrassed. Everyone was looking at me. I told him he was wrong; it was my job to rescue him in an emergency situation, but then he asked the purser for a letter of complaint. He filled it in and gave it to her. I'm still waiting to hear back from that. My stomach twists at the thought. It can take a couple of weeks for a complaint to be registered, but it's not pleasant, having this hanging over my head. Rotten passengers. I hate my job. I'm definitely getting this paper so I can revel some more in this story on the flight home.

At the counter I pay for my items and stuff them in my bag behind two Mattie Stepanek poetry collections. I didn't look for an instruction manual on hypnoses when I went to Barnes & Noble yesterday. Thank God, I came to my senses on my way over there. I'm glad I got these uplifting books instead.

Flight departures are announced over the P.A. system, and I stroll over to the coffee place between gates six and seven. I buy a large cappuccino and a Danish pastry for on the plane, and sit down at a small round table that overlooks a hub for charging phones and laptops. Just when I take my phone out to check if it needs charging, it rings.

'Hello?' I say.

'Yes, hi,' Ryan huffs. 'Where are you?'

'I am where I said I would be, from four in the afternoon. I'm at the airport.'

'I'm at the airport too, but now the lady at the check-in

counter is telling me that my plane ticket isn't valid.'

'Of course, it isn't. You're on standby. Your ticket is only valid when I'm there with my cabin crew ID. Didn't you know that? It actually says so on the back.'

Ryan's silent.

'Hello?' I say.

'Yes. Well. Are you coming to get me?'

'Of course I am. But this isn't my fault. I told you to be here at four. It's five-thirty now. I told you an hour and a half was tight.'

More silence. A dark-haired guy pulls up a chair at the table next to me and opens a laptop. A female voice urges passengers over the tannoy to go to their gates.

'So, you're at the check-in desk?' I ask Ryan. 'I'll have to walk back past security, but I'll be there soon.'

I hang up and sip coffee. I didn't get a take-away cup and I still have more than half of it left. He'll have to wait a few minutes.

Suddenly, it occurs to me that I could leave Ryan stranded here. Flora would wet herself from laughing if I told her I'd done that, especially when I tell her about everything that happened here. But no, it wouldn't be very nice. And there's no point in it. I'm still not a hundred per cent convinced he's speaking the truth when it comes to Leah, but it's alright. Maybe she is the obstacle that stood between the two of us, maybe it's the fact that he just doesn't love me; maybe it's both—it doesn't matter anymore. I don't love him either.

Something he told me on Sunday drifts into my thoughts. He was glad to be away, he said, because seeing his life from a distance sharpened his focus. I can actually relate to that, and without feeling a pang of loss for all the deep conversations we could've had together. I feel different too. Stronger, and more balanced. I'm ready for the next phase in my life, and I can do this standing on my own two feet. I want to plant a rose in honour of Bethan, and tend to it and take care of it, and express my love for her that way. I first thought of this a while ago, when Patrick and I discussed rituals, although I didn't really see how it could help me then. But now I do see it. I'll bring it up again when I have my session with Patrick next week. Also, even though I'll miss my chats with him, I feel like I'm ready to wrap them up soon. I'd like to hear his thoughts on that.

My phone rings and I pick it up from the table. 'Hello?'

'Where the fuck are you? They're closing the gate in forty minutes. They told me to get back in line. There's a mile-long queue, and I still have to go through security. It's manic out here!'

'Of course it's manic,' I reply. 'We're at JFK. But I'll come now, Ryan, no worries. Oh, and look for a female ground attendant with brown skin and red braids. She knows I was waiting for you. Maybe it will save time.'

I end the call, take one last swig of coffee, then grab my bag and get up.

'Ah, crap!'

I glance at the dark-haired guy at the table next to me. He's dropped his take-away coffee on the floor and it's splashed everywhere. He pushes his chair back and awkwardly bends forward to pick up the paper cup from under the table.

I open my bag and quickly take out a handful of paper tissues. 'Here you are.'

I leave a few tissues on his table, then squat and put the rest on the coffee spill.

The guy looks a bit flustered. 'Thank you,' he says, with a British accent.

He takes the tissues I put on the table, lowers himself by bending a knee, and together we mop up the spill.

When we're done, we sling our lumps of soaked paper into the cup in his hand and glance at each other. He has pecan skin, and gorgeous eyes: grey with green specks.

He's quite tall too, I notice when we get up. I just can't shake the feeling I've met this man before.

'Thank you for that,' the guy says. His eyes search my face, as if he's trying to place me too.

And then my breath catches in my throat. I remember!

'This is probably a strange question,' I say, 'but did you fly to Singapore in June of this year?'

For a moment, a mistrusting glint moves through his eyes. 'Yes, I did.'

'Were you asked to change seats with an elderly couple by a female flight attendant?'

'I was...' His jaw drops. 'That was you?'

'I'm afraid so.'

We stare at each other.

'Don't be afraid,' he says, smiling. 'I figured you were just doing your job. And you were very apologetic.'

My gaze darts to his laptop on the table, while I try to

remember what I told him exactly.

'Are you flying back to Heathrow too?' he asks. 'I'm on the seven o'clock flight.'

'So am I,' I reply. 'I'm a passenger today.'

'We've got a little time left before the gate closes,' he says. 'I'm getting another coffee. Can I get you anything?'

'Coffee's always good,' I quip.

He flashes me a relaxed grin. 'Totally agree.'

He grabs his laptop and bag, and side by side, we walk towards the queue at the counter.

'I'm Fern by the way.'

'Carys,' I reply.

'Were you here for work, then?'

I'm distracted for a moment, and don't answer because my phone's ringing. I take it from my bag and peer at Ryan's number that's flashing on the screen.

'No,' I say, pressing the off-button firmly down with my thumb. 'I was here for my birthday.'

Fern smiles at me. 'Did you have a good time?'

'Yes, it's been interesting,' I reply. 'I love New York.'

I slip the phone back in my bag. Sometimes in life, you just have to go with the flow.

Epilogue

November's here again. The days are getting shorter fast. And colder, stormier. But I feel balanced, light and at peace. With myself. With my family.

I'm in my mother's kitchen, leaning my back against the worktop, waiting for the kettle to boil. Mum's coming home permanently at the end of this month. Kieran and Lulu will move back in with her. We're doing up her house this weekend and clubbed together to buy paint and laminate flooring. Everything on the cheap, but that doesn't matter. The cat cage is gone, and so is the putrid smell. Mum will return to a fresh, sparkling home for her new start. I even bought her a new oak dining table with four matching chairs, which will be delivered later this week.

My gaze falls on the seven I Love New York magnets she's stuck on her fridge, and a smile moves across my lips. I can still picture her in the souvenir shop.

'Oh, I don't know which one to get, Carys' she'd said with a worried look on her face, as if her life depended on them. 'I like them all.'

I thought of Leah and Ryan then, for a fleeting moment, because I was in New York, and because he'd once mentioned Leah's inability to make a choice.

I didn't think I'd hear from Ryan again, after I left him stranded at JFK Airport three months ago. So, I was surprised to see his name pop up in my inbox, the other day. Unpleasantly surprised, actually. I've moved on. And I'm with Fern now.

Hi everyone, Ryan's email started.

That's when I discovered he'd put me on a mailing list that gave updates on his dog-training practice.

Sally has successfully completed all of her tests and will soon find a home as a police dog with the Ministry of Defence. I've started training my new dog. He's a 12-month-old Belgian Malinois called Boaz. Check out the video below to watch us work together.

I scrolled down to the video and clicked on it. There was Ryan, the guy who didn't give a toss about me and whom I'd wasted eight months of my life on. He was training a big, fawn-coloured dog with a dark head, on a grass field. The dog bit into a protective sleeve on Ryan's arm. I peered closer at the screen; zoomed in on the bystanders who were watching Ryan because a female caught my attention. She was clad in dark tracksuit bottoms and a thick coat that almost reached to her knees. Her mousy hair was cut into a bob around the ears. She appeared to be egging Ryan on. I stopped watching after half a minute.

At the bottom of the email it said: *if you no longer wish to receive updates from me, then reply to this email, write UNSUBSCRIBE in the subject line, and I will remove you from my mailing list.*

I did so at once.

♪

The water boils and the kettle switches itself off. I walk to the cupboard near the window and take out four mugs.

Gareth and I are having instant coffee. Cadi asked for green tea and Kieran wants Tetley: one sugar and a dash of regular milk.

In the living room, Kieran and Gareth are on their knees laying down the last of the floor parts. Gareth's gone back to his old job of painting and decorating. Still self-employed of course. He hasn't given up his beanie hat business, but he's doing that on the side now, so he and Cadi have a steady income.

'You know what you should do, mate?' he tells Kieran. 'Get a trade behind you. You're good with your hands. I think you'd enjoy it.'

Kieran straightens his back and his fringe flops before his eyes. 'I've been thinking about that, actually' he replies. 'I quite like the idea of carpenting.'

'Carpentry,' Cadi corrects him. She's running a roller up and down the wall behind the sofa, daubing a pale yellow tone over the old, grimy white. She holds one hand on her tummy while she works. I asked her why pregnant women do that. She said she didn't know, but that it felt right.

I'm so pleased for her and Gareth. They've put the knickers-drama behind them and are looking to the future again. I am a bit gutted she's moved to Cardiff with Gareth though. I won't see much of the baby. They're expecting a girl in March. Cadi promised me they won't call her Amélie.

But first there's their wedding. We're all travelling to Brecon for it next month. Fern and I will drive over there with Kieran and Mum, plus Mum's girlfriend. They met when Mum was transferred to a different mental health unit in

August. We're staying at Nain and Taid's. I can't wait to see them again.

'Ah, you're a star,' Gareth says, when I put the tray with drinks on the coffee table.

He gets up from the floor and stretches his back.

Kieran sits down on the sofa and Cadi puts the roller in a tray and sits down beside him.

I hold up two packs of biscuits. 'Which one do you fancy?'

'I wouldn't mind a couple of chocolate digestives,' Gareth says.

'Are those ginger biscuits?' Cadi rests her hands on her bump. 'I'll have one, please.'

Kieran watches me with a contented look on his face. 'Mum always asks us that.'

I smile at him. 'I know.'

Acknowledgements

Thank you —

To the members of my reading group and everyone at the Manchester Writing School who offered encouraging criticism while my novel was still a work in progress.

To Sue Manning: I am so grateful to you. Your thoughtful comments and observations have been indispensable for the completion of this book.

To The Society of Authors: for your time and advice.

Also, a huge thank you and much love to Hans, Rowena and Anaïs. Thank you for your love and support, and your patience whenever I need to go out there and follow my dreams.

And to my readers: for picking up this book and sitting down to read it, while there are so many books to choose from.

Author's note: the song 'Rain Was Coming Down' was written by my dear friend Jo Amanda Lee. She's given me permission to use it for my novel. Thank you Jo. Much love, Bee.

Coffee Spills & Songs: A Reading Group Guide

1. There are two main plot lines running through the novel: Carys's guilt about what happened to Bethan, and her determination to win over Ryan. How do these plot lines come together, and do you prefer one plot strand over the other?

2. How does the novel's title reflect the story? If you had to rename this novel, what title would you give it?

3. What are the main themes in this novel and how do they drive the plot?

4. Are there characters in the novel you can relate to? And are there any characters you detest, or do you think there may be mitigating factors that compensate for someone's behaviour?

5. Do you sympathise with Carys? Can you understand her stubbornness with regard to Ryan, and does your opinion of her change

throughout the novel? What would you like to say to Carys?

6. Carys says that her mother betrayed her. Is that how you see it too?

7. Were there scenes that really moved you or stood out to you in any other way?

8. The story is quite dark at times, but is there any comic relief? If so, can you name an example?

9. There are a few psychic passages in the novel, such as Carys's out-of-body experience as a child and the moment Bethan 'comes' to her in New York. What do you make of these incidents?

10. Would you be interested in reading the sequel? It's the author's current work in progress and bears the (working) title: *A Rose for Bethan*.

About the author

Berendsje Westra lives in the Netherlands, in a small village near the sea. At home, she speaks Frisian and Dutch but she writes her stories in English. Her love of all things literature, led her to study Creative Writing at the Manchester Writing School and English Literature at Groningen University. Berendsje is particularly interested in writing about places, minority languages & culture, spirituality and identity. She's also a keen gardener and loves taking her dogs on long walks through the Frisian countryside.

Lightning Source UK Ltd.
Milton Keynes UK
UKHW041014190522
403171UK00012B/640